Unworthy

Susie Tate

For my wonderful husband.
To the moon and back, my love.

Contents

Unworthy

/ʌnˈwəːði/ *adjective*
Not deserving of respect or attention.

Chapter 1

Ridiculous

YAZ

"Please tell me this is not happening," I whispered as I pulled my mop of crazy, beyond tangled, pink-streaked hair back from my face to get a clearer view of the approaching car. Not my brother's tiny, sensible, electric car. No. It was the gas-guzzling monstrosity his best friend swanned around in – the big, global-warming-causing poser. I *told* Max I needed *him* to come and get me. If I'd known he'd send Heath, I would never have asked him.

Fervently wishing that I'd phoned my sister-in-law Mia instead of my useless brother, I stood up from the log I was sitting on with shaky legs. Every part of me felt stiff and my brain was fogged with exhaustion. That's what a five-hour trek through a forest in the middle of the night would do to you. Even my yoga-strengthened limbs weren't up to that particular challenge without consequence.

The Land Rover pulled up next to me and the window slid down.

"Alright, Midge?" Heath's smug tone which he so often seemed to use with me, combining an undercurrent of humour with exasperation, just made my humiliation worse. "Interesting outfit." His gaze travelled down from the mass of dirt-streaked tangles to the neon-green silent-disco headphones around my neck, and on to my now ripped Billabong t-shirt and sarong trousers. When he reached my bare feet, he frowned. "For fuck's sake, Midge. Where are your goddamn shoes?"

I shrugged miserably as he pushed open his car door and jumped out of the monstrosity to come and stand in front of me. As always, at the first sight of Heath my heart seemed to skip a beat and my breath caught in my throat. He was just *that* beautiful. Tall, muscular, with perfectly styled dark hair, a square clean-shaven jawline, and eyes so blue they almost looked unnatural. I'd always felt like a scruffy little urchin next to him. As if I was still only a skinny kid with that ten-year age gap yawning between us. It was only six in the morning and the man was in a tailored suit for God's sake. He crossed his arms over his broad chest and raised one eyebrow – an expression he'd been using with me since I was five years old. Movement from the car caught my attention, and I peered around Heath to see an equally immaculate woman sitting in his passenger seat. My heart sank even further. Perfect Penny – Heath's latest girlfriend. Another doctor like Heath. I gave her a low wave and a weak smile before focusing back on the man in front of me who was glowering now.

"I took them off." My voice was hoarse from all the shouting I'd done into the dark forest last night after I'd got lost.

"You took your shoes off? Why on earth would you–?"

"Heath, I'm sorry that Max woke you both up to come out here to get me, really I am." My words were trembling slightly now. I couldn't deal with an angry Heath's disapproval after being in a terrifying Blair Witch scenario for the last five hours. "But I just need to go home now." I blinked rapidly to stop any tears forming and ducked my head as I made my way around Heath to get to his car. Unfortunately, I'd forgotten how ripped to shreds my feet actually were, and how stiff my muscles had become – after a couple of limping steps my legs nearly gave out on me. Strong fingers enclosed my upper arms, stopping me from sinking to the ground.

"You're limping," he said, his voice harsh and accusing.

"I'm fine I just– Heath!" Both his large hands went to my hips, gripped me firmly, and simply lifted me off the ground. He marched forward then dumped me down onto the driver's seat facing him with my feet hanging over the side. I glanced over my shoulder at Perfect Penny and gave her an apologetic smile.

"So sorry about this. I rang my *brother*. I didn't expect him to send Heath."

She was taking in my appearance with a shocked expression, but managed to return my smile. "It's quite alright. I'm always up by five anyway."

Of course she was. On an average day she'd probably have shaved her legs, applied her perfect make-up and saved numerous lives in the intensive care unit she worked at before normal humans had even had their first cup of tea.

"How far have you walked without shoes, you lunatic?" Heath's sharp tone made me jerk my head back round, and I flinched as he lifted up one foot then the other to inspect the shredded undersides, his mouth fixed in a disapproving line. "You can't just traipse around a forest in bare feet, Midge. What were you doing in there, anyway?"

"It was a midnight silent disco."

"In the middle of a forest?"

3

I shrugged. "We were star gazing too. There's too much light pollution in the town. I thought... Look, one of my mates organised it and I thought it was more a *communing in the starlight* type deal than... well, it turned out to be a rave. An illegal one." I didn't mention the drugs – Heath's head might have exploded. When Bodhi had suggested last night, he definitely hadn't mentioned the drugs. "There were some blokes there I didn't gel with." The handsy bastards wanted me to take an E and weren't too happy with my *I-only-ever consume-natural-products* answer. I decided to leave that out as well. "I thought I could walk back on my own, but it was so dark and..."

"None of that pesky night pollution then," Heath said in a dry tone, still examining my feet.

"Well, no. I couldn't find my bike. And then I couldn't find my way out. Eventually I had to phone Max – he can track my phone. He talked me out onto the road and told me to wait. I didn't think..." I trailed off.

"Midnight raves and star gazing? When are you going to grow up, Midge? You're not sixteen anymore. You can't just keep getting into scrapes and calling out your big brother to save you at the drop of a hat."

I pressed my lips together and cast my eyes down into my lap, not wanting Heath to see the tears that were forming. I heard him sigh as he let go of my feet and stood up from his crouching position in front of me.

"There are a couple of lacerations that need gluing. You'd better come into the department."

My head shot back up and my eyes flew wide. "I'm *not* going to the emergency department. I need to go home. My feet are fine." No way was I going to the hospital in this state – to face all of Heath's fancy colleagues and friends so they could take the piss.

"Don't be ridiculous," he snapped. I tightened my grip on the seat beneath me and felt my face heat up with embarrassment and anger. *Ridiculous* was one of Heath's favourite words when it came to me:

You look ridiculous, Midge.

All this alternative therapy crap is a ridiculous waste of time.

Your obsession with windsurfing is getting ridiculous.

That ridiculous bike of yours is a bloody health hazard – when are you going to grow up and get a car?

Grow up, that was another firm favourite. The annoying thing was that the Heath I'd known when I *was* growing up hadn't been a hypercritical tosspot. When I was a kid, he was my champion. He'd defended my quirky ways to my brother and my parents back then saying I was one of a kind, unique. He'd smile whenever he saw me like I brightened his day, like he enjoyed being around me.

It all seemed to change after he graduated from medical school. I didn't see him much while he worked in London, but when he moved down here to Dorset a couple of years ago – following in the footsteps of his sister Verity and Max, who had moved their architecture firm here – his whole attitude towards me was different. Yes, to everyone else he was still the same posh, charming, smooth-talking Heath, but with me he was the complete opposite of what I remembered. He'd sooner scowl at me than smile. And my quirks, now that I was an adult, seemed to annoy him – these days he was even more critical of me than my parents were. And that was saying something.

It wouldn't be so hurtful if I could just write him off as one of Max's idiot friends and ignore him, but Heath's opinion mattered to me. I'd spent most my teenage years fantasising about the time when Heath would stop seeing me as a little girl and finally realise that *I* was the woman for him. It was a desperate, almost physically painful yearning, an obsession. I didn't care about celebrities or boy bands – I only wanted Heath. So, although I tried to relegate him to idiot status in my mind, it was difficult to shake that sense of longing, that admiration. Especially when in real life he was an actual hero. As an emergency department consultant Heath was saving lives every day. It was tricky to dismiss a person who was so widely admired for such solid reasons. That's why his low opinion of me was so upsetting and maybe another reason to consider leaving the country for a while. Maybe Bodhi was right?

"I'm not being ridiculous," I said through my teeth. "I want to go home. If you won't take me, then I'll phone Mia." I started levering myself up off the seat so I could drop to the ground below (I was not looking forward to my feet making contact with the road again, but this was a desperate situation). Before even one of my toes could touch the tarmac, Heath lifted me up into his arms against his chest.

"What the hell are you–?"

"Shut up, Midge." His voice was tight with anger. What did he have to be so cross about? Okay, so it was an inconvenience for him to come out and get me from the middle of nowhere, but he should have just told Max to bugger off if he hadn't wanted to do it. "You are not putting your bloody feet on the ground again. Have you no sense of self-preservation? You're a total liability."

I pretty much always managed to hide my hurt feelings from Heath when he was dismissive or critical. My go-to reaction was more often than not a one-finger salute or a swift elbow into his rock-hard abs. But after being harassed by a bunch of druggie ne'er do wells followed by a good five-hour trek through a terrifyingly spooky forest, I found that I wasn't able to muster the same response. My feet were aching, I hadn't eaten in over sixteen hours, I was covered in dirt, I was pretty sure a bird had crapped in my hair, and I was so tired I felt like I was swimming through custard. Heath deposited me on the backseat, and I took in a stuttered breath as my nose started stinging. My humiliation was complete when I felt a single tear spill over my eyelashes onto my dirty cheek. Heath froze as his eyes shot to mine. His face went out of focus as more tears filled my vision.

"I just want to go home," I said in a small voice. To my shock, one of his big hands came up to frame my jaw and his thumb swept away another tear as it fell. I blinked to clear my vision and his face swam into view. He looked almost like he was in pain as he watched me. It didn't make any sense.

"Alright, Midge," he said, his voice now so soft that I couldn't quite believe he was the same man from a moment ago. "I'll take you home." He pulled the seatbelt out over me, leaning across to plug it in like I was still a child. His clean male scent laced with expensive aftershave filled my nostrils as his body reached across mine and I took in a sharp breath. When he pulled back, I glanced down at his previously pristine shirt, now streaked with dirt.

"Oh no," I said in horror, my hand covering my mouth. "Your shirt."

He opened his mouth, closed it again, and then let out a loud exhale. "I don't care about the fucking shirt, Midge. I wear pyjamas all day anyway, remember?"

"But don't you have that meeting with the Chief Exec this morning?" Perfect Penny put in helpfully from the back. "Isn't that why you're wearing a–"

"Right," Heath said, shooting Penny a warning look and finally moving back from me so he could slam the door closed. "If you won't come in, I'll drop you at home now and we can sort the feet later."

I didn't question him at that stage. To be honest, I didn't have the energy. Heath and Perfect Penny started talking in low voices to each other, no doubt about Very Important Things. I let my forehead rest on the window. My shivering subsided as warm air blasted from the console in the back. Exhaustion swamped me like an immense wave, and within a minute, I'd fallen asleep.

The next thing I knew, I was being jostled and then hit by a cooler blast of air. One large arm was under my knees, the other around my back, and as I was being lifted.

"W–what?" I muttered as that familiar scent filled my senses again and I felt my body press against crisp cotton over a muscular chest. I blinked my eyes open and focused on Heath's tanned throat as he turned from the car and started striding towards my building with me in his arms. I glanced back at the Land Rover over Heath's shoulder to see Perfect Penny still sitting in the front passenger seat. She was watching Heath carrying me with her head tipped to the side – her expression was not angry as you would expect, if anything she looked curious.

"I can walk," I told Heath, wriggling as if to get down. He simply tightened his grip on me and held me more firmly against his chest.

"No, you cannot." His jaw was clenched so tight now that there was a muscle ticking in his cheek. "Will you stop squirming? Keys?"

I gave up my struggle to get down and pulled my keys off the chain I kept around my neck. Heath dipped down so I could open the door and then shouldered it wide before walking into the corridor like he owned the place and to the staircase leading to my flat.

"Oh, hello ,dear," Bryn's voice came from his door. I glanced over to see him standing in his doorway, eyebrows raised in his wrinkled face as he watched Heath and me making our way up the stairs. "I say, young man! What do you think you're doing with my Yaz?" He waved his stick after Heath. "Yazmin, are you okay?" His voice was a little panicked. Bryn worried about me as much as he relied on me.

"I'm fine, Bryn," I called back to him. "Just hurt my feet. Heath's going to dump me in my flat."

"Dump you?" Bryn's eyebrows were in his hairline now. He took a few wobbly steps into the corridor. "Now see here. *I'll* look after Yaz, young man. I don't want some fly-by-night gadabout taking advantage of her."

"Gadabout?" Heath whispered, his voice trembling with amusement.

"Just humour him, please," I whispered back. Bryn didn't need to get excited with his heart condition. Heath turned halfway up the stairs, still holding me in his arms.

"I assure you, sir," he said with grave sincerity. "I wouldn't dream of engaging in any gadabout activities around Yazmin. I'm merely helping her to her accommodation. Then I shall take my leave. You have my assurance that I am a complete gentleman."

Bryn huffed, and his eyes narrowed on Heath. "I could've carried her up," he called out. Then he wobbled slightly and clutched his stick harder, which rather went against that statement but Heath, to his credit, gave him a sombre nod of agreement, not letting out the laugh I knew he was holding in. "Fine, fine, on you go." Bryn waved his stick at us again, causing another slight stumble, then started back to his flat at his slow pace. Heath then jogged up the remaining stairs.

"You can put me down now," I told him in a strained voice when we reached my door. Being held against his chest in my weakened state was all a little too much. I was worried that I'd either burst into tears again or, worse, snuggle into his already ruined shirt. He lowered me to the floor and, without looking back at him, I made quick work of the lock and pushed my way painfully inside. Before Heath could follow me in, which I could see he had every intention of doing, I turned back and pulled the door to, with only space enough for my face to peer out.

His hand was resting on the wood, but he didn't push it open.

"Thanks," I muttered. More words seemed beyond me at that stage. He scanned my dishevelled appearance from the top of my bird's nest hair to my bare feet again and frowned.

"Listen, Midge. I've got to get to work now, but I can–"

"Just go!" I snapped, surprising him and myself. "I mean, you've done enough. I'm fine. You can go. Penny's waiting."

He glanced towards the stairs, then back at me, indecision clouding his expression. Why couldn't he just bugger off? I needed to nurse this latest humiliation on my own. Finally, he took his hand off the door and shoved both hands into his pockets.

"Okay, I'll–"

"Bye, Heath." I didn't slam the door in his face, but I did close it. Turning around to take in my small space, my safe haven, I leaned back against the door and let out a long breath before sliding down the smooth wood to sit on the floor with my knees tucked up to my chest. My head fell forward onto my knees, and I allowed myself to let out a small sob.

"Soak your feet." Heath's loud command from the other side of the door made me jump, my head flying up. I thought he'd left and I'd forgotten how thin those doors were. I bit my lip to stop myself from sobbing again and held my breath until I heard a loud sigh from the other side of the door, followed by his retreating footsteps.

When I scrubbed my face to wipe away the wetness, my

hands came away covered in dirt. This was the last time I embarrassed myself in front of the misguided crush of my life.

Grow up, Midge.

You're ridiculous.

Maybe it was time I stopped obsessing about him and started *listening* to him.

Chapter 2

Sting a Bit

YAZ

Bang! Bang! Bang! A loud impatient knocking startled me awake.

"What the hell?" I murmured as I levered myself up off the sofa, wincing when my feet hit the floor. It was late evening now, and I felt a hundred times better than earlier. After taking a shower to wash the bird crap from my hair and the caked-on mud from my body, I'd soaked in my bath with my aromatherapy oils for over an hour. On inspection, my feet did seem to have taken a bit of a battering. Two of the deeper cuts were still seeping blood after my bath, so before falling into bed I'd wrapped them up as best I could with supplies from the first aid box. By the time I'd woken up it was late afternoon, and I decided not to bother getting dressed. It wasn't like I could make it out anywhere with my feet the way they were anyway. Luckily I had booked no classes or clients in for today, as this was one of my first weeks off in months. But I wouldn't be able to afford to take any more time off than that. My feet had better hurry up and heal. I'd hobbled around and found some leftover lentil curry in the fridge, settled on the sofa and hadn't moved the entire evening. I was not best pleased to be having to get up now, truth be told.

"Alright, alright. Keep your knickers on," I called out as the banging on my door ratcheted up a level. Max was an impatient bastard. I swore as I limped over to the door and yanked it open, preparing to blast Max for disturbing me. When I saw who was actually filling my doorway, I exhaled in a whoosh and took a faltering step back.

"Don't you have the door locked when you're alone in the flat?"

I blinked up at a visibly annoyed Heath, wondering why he had decided to come over to my flat and lecture me at this time of night.

"I–"

"And where's your key chain?" He stepped into the flat, and started inspecting my doorframe. "You don't have one." He moved further inside and I shuffled backwards, too confused to object. "You don't even have a decent bloody lock on this door. Does Max know about this?"

"I'm not a child, Heath." I said through gritted teeth, feeling my face flood with heat. I was a pacifist, all about peace, love, harmony, non-conflict – it took a lot to rile me up. But Heath seemed to manage it within seconds every time I saw him. He was kryptonite to my chilled-out vibe.

"Could have fooled me," he muttered, still poking around at my door. He was inspecting the other side now. "Ridiculous."

I narrowed my eyes. Not this again.

"Did you just come here to tell me how shit my security is and call me a ridiculous child, or was there another point to your visit?"

"I'll have to get Max to help me sort this at the weekend,"

he went on, almost to himself. "He's got that drill. We could use it to put a peephole in as well."

"Heath! Will you stop fondling my door and tell me why you're here, you high-handed prick?"

He shut the door behind him, giving it one last filthy look before turning back to me. His eyes dropped down for a second and his eyebrows shot up.

"Christ, Midge. Do you make a habit of answering the door like that?"

Resigned to the fact that Heath was not leaving any time soon, I rolled my eyes and limped back to the sofa. "I thought you were Max. And I'm wearing my pyjamas *in my home*. It's not my problem if you barge in late at night and the sight of my bare ankles offends your delicate maiden-aunt sensibilities."

I'd collapsed onto the sofa by the time I'd finished my little speech and lifted my sore feet back up onto the cushions. There was nothing wrong with what I was wearing, but when it came to my clothes Heath had always been the biggest prude I'd ever encountered. When I ran my yoga sessions at Max's office, you'd think I was parading around in a G-string and nipple tassels from the way Heath went on about my attire – and I'd be covered from my neck to my ankles. Granted it was with skin-tight lycra, but half the office turned up in full lycra every morning when they cycled in, and he never eyed any of them like they were indecent. And now I was wearing a perfectly respectable vest top and sleep shorts. Okay so maybe I didn't have a bra on, maybe my cleavage was on display (there was really no hiding my cleavage – it was fairly abundant), and maybe there was more than a sliver of my stomach showing (I'd lost some weight recently and the shorts hung off my hips lower than usual). But I could wear what I wanted in my own damn flat!

Heath walked around the sofa to stand in front of me with

his hands on his hips and a scowl on his face. I sighed. My chest rose and fell with the movement and if I hadn't been so focused on his unhappy expression, I would have missed his gaze flicking away from my eyes to my body for a moment, and the two slashes of colour that appeared high on his cheekbones after that stolen glance. He cleared his throat and when he spoke again, his voice was tight.

"I told you I'd come back and see to your feet." He pulled his bag off his shoulder and chucked it on the coffee table so he could open it up and pull out some medical looking kit. "And I went and found your bike. It's got a puncture but otherwise the rusty piece of crap seems to have survived."

I blinked. "You went to get my bike for me?"

He shifted uncomfortably for a moment, flashing me a quick, irritated look.

"I know how much you love that thing."

"Thanks, Heath," I said softly and the colour in his cheeks deepened before he shook his head as if to clear it.

"Well, now that I'm here I'd better see what a mess you've made of those lacerations. You should have come into the department with me."

I looked at the ceiling, seeking patience. He may have rescued my bike but he was as high-handed and patronising as ever.

"My feet are fine."

In response to that blatant lie Heath moved to the end of the sofa where my feet were resting, chucked a whole load of my best crystals off the coffee table onto the adjacent chair and sat down in front of my feet.

"Hey! Watch it, some of those are delicate. And they were arranged precisely to align the energies in the room."

He ignored me and, to my shock, grabbed my ankles, swivelling me around so that my feet were resting across his lap.

15

"Your feet are not fine."

"What are you–?"

"Midge, I am a doctor. An emergency department doctor."

I rolled my eyes as he unpacked various dressings and a large bottle of pink cleaning solution. Typical Heath, banging on about how bloody clever he is: I *know* you're a doctor, mate – give it a rest for once.

"I know you believe in all your witchy hippie medicine," he went on, "but as a qualified medical professional, I can say your feet are not fine. They're very fucking far from fine. Blood is still soaking through your shit bandaging. You're still limping. The lacerations I saw earlier will not have closed in the last twelve hours – they were too deep." He'd begun unravelling my bandages now and muttered a few choice swear words once he had uncovered my soles. "This will sting a bit." He lifted my feet up and lay them back onto an absorbent pad on his lap, snapped on his surgical gloves, then started cleaning my feet with the pink solution. It burned pretty intensely, but I didn't flinch. "You okay?"

I shrugged. "I'm fine."

He went back to his task, scrubbing at my soles now. Every so often, he flicked a look back up at my face. "I must admit, I thought you'd be yelping by now. I brought some local anaesthetic in case."

"I'm not a complete baby, you know. The saltwater stings worse than that stuff when I get shredded on the reef."

Heath paused what he was doing and sat up straighter to frown down at me. "When you get *shredded*? Why the hell are you getting shredded?"

"Windsurfing and kiting aren't sports for the faint-hearted you know. Not around here. I've had my fair share of scrapes. No biggy."

Heath's gaze moved along from my feet up my legs until he sucked a sharp breath in through his teeth.

"Jesus Christ. What is all this?" He traced a long scar up the side of my calf, then focused on a slightly raised area of scarring around my knee. Leaning forward slightly, he seemed to be inspecting all the smaller scars on my feet and shins. I felt my face heat at his scrutiny of my legs. Typical that he was looking at them so closely for imperfections rather than any other reason.

"It's nothing. A mate I was surfing with in South Africa got bitten by a shark – now *that* is some insane scarring."

All the colour had now left Heath's face. He looked like he was going to be sick. "I had no idea it was so dangerous. Why the fuck does Max let you do it?"

I narrowed my eyes at him and crossed my arms over my chest. "Max does not *let* me do anything." My voice was now low with fury. "I am actually an adult you know. I can make my own decisions."

"Clearly not if your legs end up sliced to smithereens. Bloody hell, there's more on your arms too! I thought you wore a wetsuit?"

I rolled my eyes. "I wear a shorty in summer, and I didn't really need one at all in South Africa."

"Surely not all windsurfers have to take these types of risks?"

"No, they don't, but I'm not most windsurfers."

"You're not to take those types of risks again," Heath's voice was tight, and his face was still unnaturally pale.

"I think you'll find I can do what I bloody well like."

"That's ridic–"

"Don't say it!" Oh crap, I was shouting. Why did I let him rile me up so much? I tried to yank my feet back off his lap, but he grabbed my ankles to keep them in place.

"Let me just sort your feet out, Midge. We can discuss your risk-taking behaviour and your gruesome patchwork of scars after that."

I sighed and relaxed my legs. When he was satisfied I wasn't going to pull away again, Heath snapped off his gloves and replaced them with a new pair. He then tilted my foot and used the pod of glue to close the lacerations. I sat in uncomfortable silence as he put dressings over his handiwork, and as soon as he was done I pulled back my feet and tucked both legs up beside me on the sofa, away from Heath's critical gaze.

Gruesome patchwork of scars – the cheeky bastard.

I knew for a fact that most men did not consider my legs gruesome – not by a long shot. They were toned and tanned and awesome. Not that I was particularly vain. To be honest, my looks were something I had always just taken for granted. I'd been told I was beautiful from a young age, but being a tomboy who tried to keep as grubby as possible I hadn't always welcomed that news. It was as I grew into my teens and physically developed earlier than the other girls that I really started noticing how differently I was treated. The irony was that, in general, I really didn't care about my appearance or how people viewed me. I'd never had to make an effort to attract attention, and make-up and hair straighteners did not go well with salt water, so it wasn't something I had to consider too much. As long as I ran a brush through my curly blonde hair after I washed it, I was golden – that was the extent of my beauty regime. People took me as they found me. But for some reason, with Heath I *did* care. Being beautiful held very little importance to me, but being beautiful to him felt absolutely crucial.

"No sea water for at least two weeks, Midge." He was packing his bag up now, but paused to give me a stern look.

"*Two weeks?*" I hadn't thought about how all this might get between me and the sea. "That's not going to work."

"I'm sure you can manage without your ridiculous hobby for two weeks. Maybe you could take up something less dangerous?"

"It's not just a hobby, you dickhe–"

"Oh, I'm sorry. I forgot – you think of it as a *spiritual experience*. Isn't that right?"

He was smirking and my face felt like it was on fire. Oh, how I wished I'd never shared my feelings about the sea with my family and Heath, and left myself open to their relentless piss taking. Everything to them was all so black and white. There was no room for anything fanciful, like spirituality or alternative thinking. I'd been down the road of trying to open their minds so many times and I was sick of it.

I opened my mouth to tell Heath that although, yes, I did consider my time spent in and around the sea something which fed my very soul, that was not the only reason I didn't count it as just a hobby. Then I hesitated. My beachside well-being centre had been doing well over the last few months, but I wasn't ready for anyone to know the details yet, let alone my biggest critic. The last thing he saw me as was a business-woman. And if I ended up leaving the country for a few months like Bodhi wanted, I might have to close it all down or sell it anyway. I didn't want to give my family or Heath another excuse to call me a flake or a quitter.

"Whatever. The bottom line is that two weeks without sea water is just not going to work for me."

"You'll have to make it work, Midge. I'll not have my handi-work buggered about because you've got to get your feet wet. Now I'd better–" He broke off as something caught his eye on my side table. When I realised what he was seeing, I made a lunge for it, but my feet held me back and he was too quick. "What the hell?" he muttered as he looked at the leaflet clutched in his hand. "Brazil?" It was a mock-up Bodhi had printed to encourage me to say yes to his plan. On the front was an image of me on a windsurfer about five feet in the air, a huge smile on my face and my hair flying out behind me. The name 'South American Windsurfing Tours' was written underneath. This new business venture Bodhi was proposing would offer a combination of guiding and instructing off the coast of Brazil for the super-rich. I'd basically have to spend a large proportion of my year out there and I hadn't agreed to anything yet. Not that it was anything to do with Heath.

"That is none of your business, Heath." I went up onto my knees on the side of the sofa to grab the details out of his hand but lost my balance and fell forward. He caught me before I fell face down onto my coffee table and hauled me up by my armpits so I was standing on the sofa, my chest pressed against his. He made a choked noise in the back of his throat and I used his distraction to make another grab for the paperwork. It took him a few seconds, but he managed to hold it out of my reach with one arm above his head. I grabbed the arm holding the leaflet with both of my hands, but even with all my weight and strength (and years of yoga and water sports meant I was strong) I couldn't make him bend his arm. Growling in frustration, I yanked on his arm again, struggling against him and trying not to be distracted by how hard the musculature of his chest and stomach felt against my body.

"Give. Me. That. Back." I grunted out as I tried to climb up Heath's actual body to get to the papers in the hand of his outstretched arm. I did not want him to know about this. Not this. It was mine, and it was private. He had no right.

"Jesus, Midge." Heath's voice was hoarse. "Shit, calm down. Don't–" He turned us both and flipped me onto my back on the sofa with the heavy weight of his body pinning me down to restrain me. His breathing was heavy, as if he'd just run a marathon and the colour was high in his cheeks. That smell again: clean man mixed with expensive aftershave. Combine that with how the hard muscle of his body contrasted with the soft give of mine, and it was as though one of my obsessive Heath fantasies had come to life – but the reality was so much more satisfying. I was going to embarrass myself if I didn't extricate myself from this position pronto. I wriggled to get free and Heath stiffened above me.

"Don't move," he choked out. When I looked at his face I could see his jaw was clenched tight, the tendons were standing out on his neck. His eyes flew to mine and the fire in his gaze startled a shocked breath out of me. And then, suddenly, his weight was gone. Cool air replaced the warmth of his body and I was left gasping for oxygen, flat on my back on the sofa. Heath had shot around to the other side of the coffee table, a horrified look now replacing the fiery one from a moment ago.

"Shit, sorry, Midge," he muttered as he grabbed his bag with a hand that was shaking slightly. He looked back down at me, giving me one last quick scan from top to toe before closing his eyes briefly, shaking his head and then striding out of my flat, slamming the door behind him like the hounds of hell were chasing him.

I put a hand over my heart, feeling its frantic beat within my chest, and took a few deep, steadying breaths. By the time I realised Heath had taken the leaflet with him, it was too late.

Chapter 3

Law unto herself

HEATH

I rubbed the back of my neck as I took the steps up to Max and my sister's office two at a time. My night shift had been hell on earth, and I was in dire need of a shower, some sleep, and some goddamn food. The last thing I needed to do was make a pit stop on the way home. It was madness, the state I was in. But I couldn't get that bloody leaflet out of my head. Why was Yaz on the front cover of a leaflet advertising windsurfing in Brazil? Did she want to move there, leaving her family behind? And how did she even get into something like that? Although I had to admit this kind of stunt was very on-brand for Yaz. Her idea of gainful employment was flaky at best. She certainly ducked in and out of the reception job at Max and Verity's architecture firm when it suited her.

I didn't like having unanswered questions about her. In my head she was very much locked away in her own category: irresponsible, alternative, slightly crazy, an exhibitionist.

I'd always known Yaz was different. As a child she'd danced to the beat of her own drum, demonstrating early an obsession with the sea that put pretty much everything else into second place, including school and anything even vaguely serious. Back then I'd thought it charming. Like how I thought her badly hidden crush on me was just as charming – the way Yaz hung off my every word and looked at me like I was the second coming of Christ was a massive ego boost. But as the cute five-year-old grew into the almost outrageously beautiful teenager, things became a little more problematic. I knew I should view her as a little sister, but I defy any straight man, other than an actual blood relative, to not find her attractive. From the age of sixteen, she looked like a surfer chick, make-up-free version of Scarlett Johansson. Try having that level of adoration from a human so beautiful that people often stared at her open-mouthed on the street like they couldn't actually believe she was real.

Not. Easy.

In fact, over the years I began to find my fierce attraction towards Yaz to be a source of massive guilt. She had always been too young, too naïve, and too in love with me for anything to ever happen. The power balance was completely off, and anyway I wouldn't have survived past the first kiss as Max would have killed me (true story – he and his stepson Teddy train in Taekwondo; I work out, but those two would pulverise me).

Luckily I moved to London to start my rotation in emergency medicine, and only saw her sporadically over the next five years. Problem solved. Except I *missed* her. How weird was that? Then Max and Verity moved their company down to Dorset where Yaz still lived. Not long after, a consultant job came up in Bournemouth and I followed them down there. I told myself it was only natural that I would want to live near my sister and my best friend, that the lifestyle near the sea suited me more. And all of that was true... but the fact that Yaz lived in Dorset was lurking at the back of my mind too. Cue yet more guilt – guilt is one of my specialties.

Once I'd moved to Dorset I began bumping into her quite regularly. And that was when my true torture began. Yaz was even more beautiful than before, and she still looked at me as though I was the most amazing human she had ever seen, still hung off my every word.

So what was the problem? The girl thought you hung the moon; you were so attracted to her it physically hurt. Why not jog on and make your move?

Well, aside from the Max issue, Yaz was not the type of woman I wanted to have a serious relationship with. Not after my messed-up childhood with parents who, to put it mildly, didn't exactly conform to societal norms. I needed someone stable. And I wasn't about to risk my friendship with Max for a quick fling with his sister. I respected him and his family too much for that. My twin sister Verity and I *needed* our close friends. We had almost no contact with our actual family. Max's mum and dad had been parental stand-ins for us since we had first met Max at boarding school aged thirteen. He'd arrived at school as an awkward, northern fish out of water, and V and I had liked him immediately. The three of us became best friends, and V and I had been virtually adopted by Max's mum and stepdad. Verity and Max both went on to study architecture at university, and set up their own architectural business a few years after qualifying. It was natural that Verity partner with Max. His gruff northern demeanour wasn't exactly conducive to winning clients. He needed my sister's charm and connections, her natural self-assurance and keen business mind. With our eclectic but extremely posh upbringing, Verity and I could hold our own at a dinner table with celebrities, dukes, duchesses, politicians, you name it. Max was the creative backbone of the business, but Verity was the reason it survived.

So from the minute I moved to Bournemouth, I pushed my longing for Yaz to the back of my mind. The stakes were simply too high for me to risk a relationship with her, and she just didn't fit in with what I wanted in the long term (my childhood had enough that was alternative about it to last me a lifetime). But increasingly I could feel my resolve cracking.

I pushed through the door into the office and froze. Yaz was lying on a yoga mat in the middle of the office, her legs spread in an almost physically impossible V as she leaned forward so that her chest met the floor, stretching out both her arms to touch her toes on each side. There were a couple of others doing the pose with her (badly) and the entire male contingent of the office appeared to be in suspended animation, their gazes locked onto Yaz's well displayed, lycra-clad figure. *Then* she proceeded to lean all the way forward, bringing her legs behind her now and coming up onto all fours. A young guy to my right dropped his pencil, and I heard another one mutter "Jesus Christ" under his breath in a hoarse whisper. I threw a thunderous look at both of the wet-behind-the-ears little snots, and they both flushed red before turning back to what they should have been bloody well getting on with in the first place.

"Giving everyone a good show as usual I see, Midge." My own voice was hoarse now – I tried to tell myself that it was the result of dehydration from my night shift. "Bit early in the day for those types of moves, wouldn't you say?"

Yaz's head snapped around to meet my gaze. The peaceful expression on her face from a moment ago fell as she scowled at me. What was stupid and crazy was that I felt her scowl like a punch in the gut. It was the complete opposite of the dreamy way she used to look at me, and instead of feeling relief I always felt an almost crippling sense of loss.

"It's called yoga, you ignorant prick. Not that you'd know anything about it – I doubt you'd have the flexibility required with that stick permanently up your arse."

"It's not *my* arse that's on display for the entire office to gawp at."

Yaz pushed up onto her feet at this comment, her face flooding with colour and her small fists clasped at her sides. Eyes flashing, delicate jawline set at a stubborn angle. She was furious and magnificent. It took all of my will power to feign a somewhat bored expression and not to gawp myself.

"I do *not* have anything *on display*," she said through her teeth. "You can go and–"

"Heath," a soft voice cut Yaz off, and I felt a hand settle on my arm. With great effort, I turned away from Yaz to see Max's wife Mia frowning up at me. I was relieved to see the colour back in her cheeks after the weeks of morning sickness she'd endured incubating Max's spawn (anyone's physiology would be challenged by that). She was now sporting a more healthy glow and her bump was becoming more obvious by the day. "That was uncalled for."

Another kick in the gut – gentle criticism from Mia was the equivalent of a being screamed at by a sergeant major. She was generally quiet, stoic, non-judgmental – she was not the sort to push her opinions forward, not unless she felt she had no other choice. It wasn't the first time she'd objected to the way I spoke to her friend. Mia was fiercely loyal, and had become close to Yaz even before she got together with Max.

But then that was typical of Yaz. When Mia had arrived at the company, she'd been traumatised by an abusive relation-ship, something that Yaz's emotional antennae had picked up on long before anyone else. And Yaz was so warm, so empathic that Mia, as closed off as she had been at the time, still bonded with her and allowed Yaz to help her heal. There was something about Yaz that encouraged people closer. Just being around her made people feel warm, safe, listened to. Sometimes it was a little spooky – the first time she met my cousin (a Hooray Henry rugby lad who I'd thought had the emotional depth of a puddle) she made him cry after delving into his deep-seated feelings of inadequacy instilled in him by his shitty parents (not a shock – his mum was my dad's sister after all). When I asked him about it down the pub, he said he felt lighter than he had in years and that the conversation with Yaz had "freed him from his repression". He'd only spoken to her for thirty minutes max.

I looked around the office full of workers in front of whom I'd just humiliated my best friend's sister. "Sorry, Midge," I muttered. Mia gave my arm a light squeeze as Yaz threw me a disgusted look and turned back to her audience.

"Everyone, try to clench your core now with this move," she said brightly. "Tighten up those v-jay-jays, ladies. Get those groins in action, gentlemen."

"Are you here to see Max or Verity?" Mia asked me, and I cleared my throat, forcing myself to divert my attention from Yaz and her core-clenching instructions.

"Let that negative energy flow over your being. Focus on centring yourself in the moment." She was balancing on one foot now and reaching up to the ceiling with her both hands. A slither of stomach was revealed as she stretched her body upwards. The idiots trying to copy her on the mats behind were all toppling over.

Mia gave my arm another squeeze, and tore my eyes away from Yaz to look at her.

"Max."

"Right, come on then." And this small, shy, pregnant woman put her hand to my back and literally frog marched me over to Max's office. The office space itself was all open plan, although Max and Verity had their own individual offices on either side – the door and walls of each one was glass, however, which was supposed to encourage openness and break down barriers. Max was an antisocial bastard and I'm sure would have preferred to design buildings from a small underground cave for which he didn't have to pay rent or utilities, but my sister had other ideas. Verity spotted me as Mia propelled me across the office space, giving me a low wave and cocking her head to the side in question. As twins we'd always been able to communicate without words. She frowned as she glanced between Yaz and me, her disapproval of my behaviour radiating through the glass wall. I gave a small shrug before Mia marched me into Max's office and shut the door behind her, Max's eyes went wide and he sat up straight in his chair. He opened his mouth to speak, but Mia got there first.

"I have had *enough* of this shit," she said, her voice still low and quiet but now vibrating with anger. She was between me and Max, next to Max's desk, and she had her hands on her slim hips, emphasising her bump. I'd never seen such an attitude-laden pose from her before, and would have been happy for her had that attitude not been directed my way. After all that she'd been through, Mia was much more likely to shrink from confrontation rather than start an argument – it showed that she was finally starting to trust us. Max was looking at her now in shock, which rapidly melted into a pleased, proud expression with a small smile. "And you!" she turned on him. "You can wipe that smile off your face. How Heath treats Yaz is no laughing matter."

His smile dropped at that. Even though Yaz frequently drove him up the wall, he did not like anyone messing with his little sister. "What did you do?" he asked. Whilst Mia's tone had been pissed off, Max's was downright menacing.

"I didn't do anything. I was just–"

"You told her she was putting on a display and that she had her arse out."

"She does have her arse out!"

"Mia, love," Max said, standing up from his chair and approaching this new Attitude Mia with appropriate caution. His angry expression from a moment ago had faded, much to my relief. "Heath has a point. It's quite the floorshow she puts on out there. I don't think–"

"Don't call me love when I'm pissed off," she snapped. Max stopped in his approach and held his hands up in front of him in surrender. "This is part of the problem. Neither of you treats her with the respect she deserves. You both act like she's an annoying little sister." Mia sighed and her hands dropped from her hips as she turned to Max. "Do you even know why she does the yoga, aromatherapy, crystals and all that other stuff in the office?"

"Er." Max scratched his head, and I almost felt sorry for the poor bastard. There was obviously a right answer to this question. "To wind me up?" And that was not it.

"She wants *your* business to do well. She's trying to settle the nerves of *your* employees that you scare half to death. If it wasn't for Yaz, half your staff would have jumped ship by now. Neither of you appreciate her. You both act like... like *dicks*." My eyebrows shot up at this – Mia calling us dicks was so far from her normal it was a little unnerving. "And you." She pointed at me, eyes narrowed and face still flushed with anger. "You need to leave her alone now. That's *enough*. You know it's enough. Fair warning – I'll not put up with it anymore." With that, she spared us both one last filthy look, before sweeping out of the office. Max and I watched as she went directly to Yaz, grabbed her hand, and dragged her up into a hug.

"Well, it's safe to say that she's coming out of her shell," I pointed out in a dry tone. Max was back to that small smile again. The man seemed awfully pleased for someone who'd just been called a dick by his wife. But then Max was completely in love with that woman – any sign that she felt safe enough to swear at him he would take as a good sign.

"She is, in't she," he said, his voice lighter than I'd heard it in a while. Whilst I was pleased for him and Mia, I had more pressing matters to discuss. I slapped the leaflet I'd stolen from Yaz down on the desk and it skidded over to Max. He frowned down at it, then back up at me.

"What's this?"

"You tell me. This was in your sister's flat. Is she moving to Brazil?"

"And why were you in her flat?" Max's standard scowl was well and truly back on his face. Grumpy northerner restored to normal service.

I rolled my eyes. "Stand down, big guy. You're the one who asked me to pick her up from the arse-end of nowhere last week. Her feet were cut to pieces – I had to go back later and glue the lacerations."

"She didn't tell me that. I just thought she got lost after one of her hippy rallies. Why did her feet get cut up?"

"It was a rave, Max. I think she had to make a sharp exit and left her bloody shoes behind. Then she couldn't find the way out of the woods. Honestly, the girl does not give one single shit about her safety." I was on a roll now. All the worrying and obsessing about Yaz I'd done over the last week was coming out in one go. "She doesn't lock her door when she's alone in the flat. Did you know that? No peephole and no proper lock. And then there's her injuries. Not just her feet. She's covered in scars. She's like some sort of war veteran rather than a windsurfer."

"Heath, she gets a bit bashed up every now and again, but

she's got it under control. The water is her thing. Yes, there was that concussion three years ago but– "

"Concussion? What the hell?"

"She was surfing the reef, got thrown onto some rocks. Hit her head pretty hard. They stitched her up in minor injuries – had to spend the night at mine to check she didn't go doolally as it was such a hard thump to the noggin. But she's a tough 'un." Max shrugged. How the bastard could be so blasé about his little sister's safety was beyond me. The scenario he'd just recounted had made my blood run cold. She'd bashed her head on the reef hard enough to split her scalp open? She could have died. I felt like I was going to throw up.

"You have to stop her doing that shit," I said, struggling to keep the anger out of my voice.

Max frowned at me. "I've never been able to control Yaz. You know that. She's a law unto herself. And she needs that time in the water. Even when it's ball-freezingly cold, she's out there in her winter wetsuit, ripping it up. Nobody could ever separate my sister from the sea."

"I don't know what the fuss is about. It's just messing around on a board, isn't it?"

"When is the last time you saw Yaz windsurfing, Heath?"

"Oh, I don't know. The last time V and I went on hols with your fam to Spain?"

"That was ten years ago. She'd only just started out then. I'm sorry, but you have to see her out there to understand. I've only just started realising in the last few months. Mia's been on about how amazing she is."

I rolled my eyes, surprised that Max bought into all this Yaz-at-one-with-the-sea bullshit. "What about that, then?" I pointed to the leaflet and Max frowned down at them again.

"She's always been a free spirit. Maybe she feels she needs a change?" he muttered.

"A change? Max, this is Brazil we're talking about."

"Oh."

"Oh? Is that all you've got to say?"

Max sighed. "Listen, Heath, I'm sure Yaz isn't really thinking about moving to Brazil. She probably just wants to spend a few months there. But anyway, I don't know what you expect me to do about it. Yeah, I'd miss the little shit but–"

"What about how far Mia's come?" I put in, hitting him right in his weak spot. "I'm sure Mia would be upset if Yaz moved away, even if it was only for a few months. Might even hinder some of that progress she's made. Especially with the baby on the way."

Max's frown deepened as he considered that before his eyes flashed to me and they narrowed. "What's all this sudden interest in my sister? I thought you couldn't stand her. Last few years, you've treated her like an irritating gnat. She's one of the few people for whom you turn the charm *off*."

I opened my mouth to speak, then closed it again. I could feel my ears heating and knew the tips of them would be red by now – a sure-fire embarrassment gauge with me. Max's gaze darted to my ears, and he pushed up from his chair. I was six foot one and well built, but this big bastard had a couple of inches and a good few kilos on me. "I'm going to ask you again, *mate.*" His voice had dropped an octave now, and he'd crossed his arms over his chest. "What were you doing in my sister's flat?"

"And I'll tell you *again* – I was gluing her feet back together after *you* asked me to fetch her."

"So, there's nothing going on?"

"Of course not! She's like a little sister to me as well." I shifted uncomfortably for a moment as an image of Yaz in her lycra popped unbidden into my mind.

"Fine."

"That said, I think you should do something about her security and her risk-taking behaviour."

"I'm not her father, Heath. She's never taken well to me bossing her. Even my stepdad has a job of it."

"Well, you could at least find out about this Brazil thing."

"Yeah, right. I'm sure there's nothing in it, though. She goes off on tangents all the time – it never actually comes to anything. Anyway, if she was thinking of going away, I'd have thought you'd be glad. She seems to piss you off something chronic recently."

"She doesn't piss me off."

Max snorted. "Could have fooled me. Listen, I know Yaz can be an annoying little shit, but you should really lay off. If anything, it's winding my missus up and Mia's got enough going on."

For some reason Max's statement caused a flash of anger to shoot through me, so strong that I almost wanted to punch him in the face. "I don't think she's annoying."

Max's gave me a disbelieving look.

"You know as well as I do, Yaz has idolised your idiot self since she was a little scrap of a five-year-old. You didn't seem to mind before, but now it just pisses you off. To be honest, she seems to find you just as annoying as you find her nowadays, so I don't think you have to worry about discouraging her romantically anymore. Her days of mooning after you are finished. So you may as well try not to be such a bastard around her. Right?"

My mouth felt dry all of a sudden as I let Max's words sink in.

"Right," I managed to croak out. "I'd better go home and sleep. I've got another shift tonight."

Yaz didn't look up as I walked by Mia's desk and I rubbed my chest absently to soothe the ache that seemed to have settled there as I strode for the exit.

Chapter 4

She looks amazing out there

HEATH

"Are you sure this is okay?" Penny asked as we walked down from the car park to the beach. "They won't mind me just turning up?"

"Course not," I said as I slung my arm over her shoulder. She looked up at me with that quizzical look that Penny often wore, as if my casual affection was unexpected. It was the same look she'd given me yesterday at work when I asked if she wanted to come down to the beach rugby after work today. I didn't see what was so bloody confusing. I *liked* Penny. She met all my specifications for a girlfriend, therefore it made complete sense for me to invite her places. Yes, okay, maybe I hadn't actually made any sort of *real* move on her yet. It just never seemed to be the right time, or the atmosphere was off, or the setting wasn't right. But that didn't mean that I wasn't *going* to make a move. Of course I was. I was Heath Markham, for God's sake – Bournemouth's answer to George Clooney. Maybe it was just because Penny was the woman I had decided I was going to be serious about that I was finding it hard to kick things off. Yes, that probably explained it.

"Any blighter can tip up and play. Anyway, I want you to meet everyone." There it was again – that slightly baffled look. Before I could ask her about it, Teddy had jogged up to us and punched me in the arm.

"Ow, what was that for, you little shit?" I said as I slipped my arm from Penny's shoulders so I could rub the biceps of my other one. "Don't make me put you in a headlock again." I reached up and ruffled his hair. When he tried to duck away, I got him in a partial headlock, but was nearly thrown to the ground for my trouble. Twelve-year-old Teddy had been a lot easier to mess with than this great big nineteen-year-old monster. "I thought you were still at uni."

"Summer hols. Thought I'd come back to see the grumpy bastard. At least that way I get some of Mia's cooking."

Teddy was Max's stepson. Kind of. Max had never actually been married to Teddy's mother, but she'd moved in with him when Teddy was nine. When Teddy's mum tired of the quiet life in Bournemouth and left for London, Teddy was fifteen and didn't want to go with her. It'd been a rough road. Teddy had had a lot of abandonment issues, which he took out on Max for a while. Then two years ago Mia had arrived on the scene. Teddy had taught her self-defence and found out what it was like to put someone else's needs above his own. That, combined with Max's steadfast insistence that he wanted Teddy living with him, had helped Teddy to come out of the arsehole teenage stage. Now that Teddy was at uni, he came back down here any chance he could. I wasn't convinced he saw his mother more than twice a year.

"Ted, this is Penny."

"Oh right. Yeah, hi." Unfortunately, despite the lack of genetic links, Ted seemed to have developed exactly the same social skills as his stepfather. His interactions with attractive women comprised unintelligible grunts and poor eye contact. Jesus, how was this kid surviving at uni? Did he see any action at all? I just had to hope that he'd found a charming wingman, just like his stepfather before him. (I swear that man owes me nearly all his undergraduate shags.)

"Come on, this way, Penny," I said, brushing past Ted and leading Penny down towards the pitch.

"Oh dear, I thought there'd be more girls," she murmured. I wasn't used to Penny sounding nervous. She was always so self-assured. But then I only really interacted with her at work, and there she had every reason to be self-assured. Penny was an intensive care consultant and one of the most confident, capable people I knew.

"There's usually a few here," I muttered, scanning the beach for Yaz. Verity was in London. She'd told me there was some trouble with a bid they were competing for up there that wasn't going so well. Max told me that "some billionaire tosspot was giving her gip", whatever that meant.

"Don't worry," Mia said as she drew alongside us. Max had ordered her a smaller Sandbaggers top, but it still looked ridiculously large on her. "There's no tackling and these great louts can't shift their bulk very fast. We run rings around them. Hi, I'm Mia, you must be Penny. Max won't let me play now with balls flying around." Her hand went to her small bump.

"Oh congratulations!" said Penny and Mia gave her a shy smile.

"Thanks. Well, I've insisted on warming up with everyone. Max still isn't too happy about it but Heath's assured him that it's perfectly safe for me to stay active."

Penny relaxed a little after meeting Mia. They'd both been netballers before, and Mia gave Penny the whole spiel about how touch rugby is a cakewalk compared to that. Max joined our group and we all started warming up, throwing the ball around and chatting with the others. It was only after the second time a ball hit me in the face that I realised I wasn't really paying attention. My eyes kept flicking up to the bike racks and then up to the promenade. It wasn't that unusual for Yaz to be late. The woman seemed incapable of running to schedule ever, but it wasn't like her not to make it in time to start the game.

"She's not coming."

I flinched as I realised Mia was standing right next to me. She was looking at me with narrowed eyes as I turned to face her. I didn't like how she'd seemed to read my thoughts.

"What do you–?"

"Yaz. She's not coming to rugby. She's teaching."

"I wasn't thinking about... wait – teaching?"

"Yes, over there. See?" Mia turned towards the sea and pointed out at the waves, which seemed to be huge tonight. A couple of windsurfers were out there. One of them kept getting slammed by the waves and having to water-start again and again, but the other one was dipping and diving in the waves, doing jumps through the surf. I recognised that body and that long blonde hair. The way she moved through the water was almost unreal. When she flew off the edge of another wave and arced through the air in a forward loop, I stopped breathing altogether. Her body looked tiny in amongst those powerful waves. All sorts of scenarios were going through my mind – Yaz's head connecting with the mast; Yaz losing consciousness and falling into the water; Yaz coming off the board and being pulled under the surf, then being ripped to shreds by rocks lurking underneath.

"Heath!" Max's annoyed shout cut through my fevered thoughts as he slapped me on the shoulder. "What the fuck is wrong with you, mate? We're about to start! You had a stroke or something?"

The windsurfer who Yaz was teaching had fallen again. They were in deeper water past the surf, both off their boards now, and it looked as though Yaz was talking to him. Then they both manoeuvred their sails and boards to the correct position, before doing a side-by-side water-start in the middle of the sea. Yaz waited for the wind to catch her sail, then sprang back up onto the board like she was born to it. The other guy was a little shakier but got there in the end.

"See," Mia's quieter voice came from my other side and I felt her lay her hand on my arm. "She's teaching. Now the evenings are lighter. She can do more and she's getting so booked up she said she couldn't make it here tonight."

"Who's the guy out there with her?"

"Er... her student? Heath," Mia's voice dropped to a low murmur, and she stepped closer to me. "Are you okay? It's just you're kind of ignoring Penny and she's never played before. I've explained some basics but you staring out to sea like this looks a little... well, it looks a little weird."

"Who are they?" Penny's voice jerked me back to reality, and I turned to look at her. That curious look was back on her face again, and she was staring up at me with her head tilted to the side.

"Er... what?"

"Out there." She pointed out to where Yaz and her student were zipping in and out of the waves. "Those people you're staring at."

"That's my sister, Yaz," Max put in. Why did he have to pick this moment to become such a helpful, talkative bastard?

"Oh, the girl we picked up on the side of the road? The one with the cuts on her feet."

I forced myself to turn away from the sea and towards Penny.

"Yes." I cleared my throat and flicked another lightening quick glance back at the sea. "She's still being a nut job, as you can see."

Penny gasped, and I spun around just in time to see Yaz land another forward loop and then go into a crazy low jibe before shooting off in the other direction.

"Nut job? She looks amazing out there."

"Well, she shouldn't be in the sea with the damage to her feet."

Penny turned towards me and frowned. "You glued her feet three weeks ago. Surely they would have healed by now?"

I muttered some bullshit about "delayed healing with the tougher epidermis of the soles of the feet." Penny looked unconvinced, and by the time I'd looked back out at the sea, Yaz was hurtling down towards the harbour with her student in tow. I shook my head to clear it. I had to concentrate on the matter at hand and stop getting distracted by Yaz. It was bad enough that I was thinking about her an embarrassing number of hours in the day (and night if I was honest – x-rated Yaz dreams had become a nightly torture), my mind absolutely should not be wandering to her when I was with the woman I'd decided was *the one*.

I forced a smile and slung my arm over Penny's shoulders again. It felt even more awkward this time. "Right, what can I tell you about this beautiful game? I'm sure Mia here hasn't done us justice – we're pretty special, you know. This is the beach touch-rugby capital of the UK."

"Only because it's crap, so no other bastard plays it," Teddy said, rolling his eyes.

"Ah, the ignorance of youth." I took the opportunity to

release Penny so I could attempt to grab Teddy into a headlock again. That sense of wrongness left me almost immediately. "You need to respect the game, little man."

Chapter 5

My mistake, no offence

HEATH

"Are you sure you want me to come to the pub?" Penny gave me a confused smile, and I frowned.

"Of course," I told her. "Why would you think I wouldn't want you to come?"

She bit her lip and looked to the side, then gave a small shrug. "No reason I guess. I just... never mind. I could use a glass of wine."

I smiled at her and took her hand in mine for the short walk to the Pig and Whistle, ignoring how wrong and awkward it felt. As soon as we arrived at the pub, I let go of her hand to open the door and somehow just couldn't bring myself to take it again. I justified that in my mind as simply being respectful to Penny in front of my friends, but I knew that was just bullshit. We all sat at our usual tables. Penny was great, her quiet confidence and maturity shining through. She looked beautiful but understated in her sports outfit. Not like... damn it! I needed to stop letting my mind wander where it shouldn't.

I began to relax. Maybe I just needed to spend more time

with Penny? Surely then I'd start feeling something. Just as I'd convinced myself that was the case, the hairs on the back of my neck stood up as the pub door opened and some instinct had me turning to look. Her hair was still damp, but what had dried was in a disarray of messy blonde curls. There was nothing overtly sexual about her outfit. Her jeans were ripped but hung loosely off her hips, and she had obviously just thrown her t-shirt over her bikini, which was clearly visible underneath. Her hair fell in her eyes as she laughed at something the tall, long-haired man with her said, and she reached up in a fluid move-ment to pull the mass of it back into a messy bun on the top of her head. The long-haired man's face went a little slack as he watched that process. I felt my jaw clench as this dickhead focused on Yaz's chest while she was scanning the bar, completely oblivious.

I wasn't the only one noticing his leering. Another of Yaz's friends called Dee was also with them – I'd met her a few times before. She had the same water sports-obsessed, laid-back atti-tude as Yaz. But Dee didn't look so laid-back now, however. She was scowling at the long-haired guy like he was a piece of crap on her shoe. Eventually Yaz's eyes fell on our group and she smiled. Not at me, though. As was becoming a pattern now, she avoided eye contact with me completely.

"Hey there, beach-touch losers," she said, ruffling Teddy's hair as she pulled a chair out to sit. "You all remember Dee, and this is Bodhi, my soul brother and new business partner in crime."

"Hey, all," Bodhi said, taking the seat next to Yaz and pulling it so close to her he had to drape his arm over the back of her chair. Dee pulled up a chair on her other side and gave Bodhi another brief contemptuous look before smiling at the group. All three of them were sporting ripped jeans, surf t-shirts and flip-flops. Dee was dark-haired with a pretty, freckled, make-up free face. Bodhi's hair was the male version of Yaz's, with blonde streaks and a natural wave to it. He was tanned and lean. The bastard looked like he'd just stepped out of a surfing magazine. He and Yaz could be models for Billabong. My gaze dropped to where my hand was holding my beer and I realised my knuckles were white.

"What business?" I snapped. Everyone's eyes flew to me at my sharp tone. Mia was frowning.

"Yaz started a well-being business a year ago, Heath," Mia said. "She's got a studio down at the harbour."

"Well-being? What does *that* entail?" I could hear the condescension in my tone and hated myself a little for it.

"Yoga, reiki, acupuncture... that sort of thing," Yaz mumbled, still avoiding eye contact with me. "Dee's a qualified dietician, so she runs groups and individual coaching as well. We try to be as holistic as possible. We use the studio in winter, but in summer we're mostly on the beach when we can be."

"I thought you just taught a bit of windsurfing down there?" I said. I'd seen Yaz teaching before and just assumed it was the odd summer job she picked up.

Yaz shrugged. "To me the sea is part of well-being. I've been a qualified instructor for years, so it made sense to make it part of the business. A lot of my clients do yoga as strengthening for water sports, so they come to me for both."

"Yaz won't admit it, but she's the best teacher out there," Dee put in. "She's helped my windsurfing no end. I'd have never learned a heli tack if it weren't for her."

Yaz smiled at her. "You were killing it out there, hun. You didn't need me."

Dee rolled her eyes. "Killing it, my arse! I could barely get in the harness before you took me out."

"Well, it's all spiralled a bit," Yaz said, addressing the group again. "And I was having trouble managing it all as it was, hence, Bodhi. He's been a lifesaver."

"It's so good to meet you, Bodhi!" Mia (the traitor) seemed way too enthusiastic about this new dude. "Yaz has told me so much about you. I hear the business is really picking up."

Bodhi gave Mia a lazy smile. "You must be Mia. We're doing alright, thanks. The weather helps and Yaz draws quite the crowd." As he said the last, his hand that was resting on the back of Yaz's chair reached up and shook her messy bun. Yaz laughed and elbowed him in the ribs. I had to release my beer, as I was in danger of shattering the glass. He touched her hair. A red mist descended over my vision and for a moment I thought I might be in real danger of shoving the table out of the way and punching this smug fucker right in his overly tanned face.

"Shut your pie-hole, you cheesy badger," Yaz said as his fucking hand settled back into its position behind her. "You've plenty of admirers down there yourself. And anyway, we're popular because of our holistic approach and the standard of our teaching and equipment. Those new sails we bought last—"

"I bet," I couldn't help muttering into my beer, and Yaz fell silent.

"Something to say, Heath?" she asked. She was giving me eye contact now, but definitely no smile. I felt an unreasonable surge of anger.

"Any idiot can see you aren't winning clients with superior teaching techniques and fancy sails."

Yaz's face flooded with colour and her eyes flashed. "Oh really? Don't hold back, Heath. Tell us why our business is becoming more successful than any other on the harbour."

I rolled my eyes. "If you think that any bloke in a five-mile radius is bothered about how capable a teacher you are or how high quality your sails are with you standing out there in a bikini top and cut-offs, you're delusional. Tits and arse, that's what's selling your lessons and you know it. I'm sure pretty boy here draws in some birds as well, but don't delude yourself that your reputation is based on talent alone."

Silence fell on the group, broken by Bodhi's sudden burst of laughter. "Well, if it brings in the business, then I'm all for it."

I shifted uncomfortably in my seat. Yaz was staring down at her drink, her mouth drawn into a tight line. I didn't like her expression or the fact I'd been the one to put it there. Max sighed and shook his head. And Mia was glaring daggers at me. I cleared my throat.

"Listen, I didn't mean—"

"Thing is, *bro*," Dee cut in. She might still be sporting a smile, but there was a hint of steel behind her expression. "The peeps Yaz teaches aren't your average punters wanting to dabble in some water sports and add some material into their wank banks. They're some seriously hardcore players. If her teaching wasn't up to standard, they'd admire her from the shore but book up some other fucker who knew what they were doing to teach them." She shrugged. "You get a rep out there, man. If her shit wasn't tight, she wouldn't last long in this industry. Wouldn't expect a land-lover like you to understand, but the guys who come to her live and breathe the *ride*. They will not waste their time for a nice body and a pretty face."

I gave Dee and then Yaz a tight smile. "My mistake, no offence."

She nodded and shifted closer to Yaz who, after a brief hurt look which felt like a punch in the gut, went back to ignoring me. I took a deep breath in and out through my nose, resolving to just *stop*. Mia was right – I was *such* a prick.

I managed not to punch Bodhi over the course of the next hour, however sorely tempted I was. And I also didn't make any more digs at Yaz. She slowly recovered from my put down and became normal animated Yaz again. Wherever Yaz was, her presence and energy always seemed to fill the space. Even Penny was drawn into a conversation with her. About health of all things. I would have thought that they were on completely opposite ends of the spectrum when it came to their views about healthcare, but to my shock they seemed to find a surprising amount of common ground.

"Exactly!" Penny cried in a near shout. It was about as excited as I'd ever seen her. Penny's default mode seemed to be calm and serene. "That's *exactly* what I mean."

Yaz smiled at Penny and leaned forward in her chair. It felt like the entire table leaned with her. Yaz was just that magnetic a person.

"Yes. I've always thought that the medicalisation of society was out of hand. I mean, if we just–"

I tried, I really did, but I just couldn't let that one go.

"You're against the medicalisation of society?" I burst out, cutting her off and pulling the attention of the table my way. "So, I guess you think that the progress we've made in things like infectious disease – including the eradication of smallpox – or the fact we can unblock cardiac arteries now instead of just prescribing bed rest, or pull out clots from the brain to reverse a stroke, or replace joints when they're worn out from arthritis, are all a bit of a waste of time. Bloody hell, yes, of course. I don't know why I didn't think of it before. What a menace medicine has been to society. Much better if we stick with your poxy crystals – I'm sure a bit of rose quartz could sort that HIV infection right out... oh wait–"

"I'm not talking about the eradication of smallpox," Yaz interrupted in a tight voice. The excited smile had dropped from her face, and I almost wish I'd kept my mouth shut. "And I'm not saying medicine isn't a good thing. I just think that big pharma, the meat industry, the alcohol industry, the–"

"Oh God, spare me the big bad pharma talk. Pharma keeps plenty of people alive."

"Heath," Penny put in, "Yaz has got a point you know and I–"

"Christ, don't humour her. Honestly, Yaz, this alternative bullshit is getting a little old, you know. Why not try looking at something scientific or evidence based for a change?"

With that, Yaz stood up so abruptly from the table that her chair toppled over behind her and crashed to the floor. The whole pub seemed to fall silent at the noise.

"You want evidence?" The flecks of green in her brown eyes flashed, and the colour in her cheeks shone through her tan. She looked absolutely furious and so beautiful that my mouth went dry. "Yes, you can unblock arteries, you can remove clots, you can replace joints. I'm not disputing that. But maybe, just maybe, we should try to do something *before* the debris builds up in that artery, or before the joint wears out, before the patient has a stroke. Maybe my yoga classes work better for back pain than your drugs. Maybe we should put more emphasis on the only evidence-based intervention that has had the greatest effect on all of those things? Do you know the one intervention that can reverse type 2 diabetes in ninety percent of people? Lifestyle change. How we live our lives *matters*, you colossal prick. That's all I'm saying. Relying on pills and procedures *after* the fact isn't the right way to go. You know what?" She spun around and picked up the fallen chair, slamming it down on the ground with a thump. "Fuck you and your judgemental superiority. I don't need your shit, Heath Markham-hashtag-NHS-hero. Go save some lives after they've nearly popped their clogs and *I'll* try to make sure they never end up there in the first place."

There were tears in her eyes by the end of that speech and her mouth was quivering, but she held it together to deliver that parting line. All I could do was sit there with my mouth open and my eyes wide. She was bloody magnificent. So when she stormed out of the pub with Bodhi and Dee in tow, I couldn't get my brain in gear fast enough to stop her.

After a few moments of uncomfortable silence, Mia said my name, and I blinked, struggling to focus on her face for a moment.

"You promised, Heath." She was glaring at me across the table.

A rush of air left my mouth as I threw my hands up. "I'm sorry, okay. I just can't handle all that alternative crap. It really winds me up. She's an intelligent girl and–"

"It's not me you need to apologise to. And can I just say that I have never, in any interaction I've witnessed between you and Yaz, ever thought that you viewed her as intelligent."

"That's not–"

"You treat her like an ignorant child, Heath. We can't all have medical degrees, you know."

I sighed. "I'm not saying that. I just don't agree with her undermining the medical world and – "

"So, you don't think any of what she said just now holds any merit?" Penny chipped in. Ugh, they were all having a go now. "You don't think that our society relies too heavily on the medical model?"

"Well, I–"

"You like evidence-based medicine, yes?"

I nodded. She was looking fired up now.

"Well, there's almost nothing in all of medicine that has the vast, consistent, and diverse evidence base as what Yaz is advocating. There is no pill, and there never will be any pill, that can reduce the burden of chronic disease in the way that healthy lifestyle factors can. You know, the INTERHEART study estimated over 90 percent of risk for heart disease was modifiable. And that's across fifty-two countries."

"Er... what?" asked Teddy, looking thoroughly confused. "Break it down for us muggles."

Penny smiled at him. "Basically, this study showed that over ninety percent of the risk of having heart disease comes from stuff we can change about our lifestyles."

"Woah! That's nuts," Teddy said, his beer lowering slowly and his eyes wide.

"Yes, it is *nuts*," said Penny. "What's more nuts is that all doctors aren't pushing for change. We need people like Yaz to help us potentially create a massive public health revolution on a country-wide scale. To put the money into what is *actually* going to help patients."

"I'm not denying that lifestyle factors are important, but– "

"We need to *prevent* disease rather than wait for it to manifest so that doctors have to treat the symptoms."

"I'm not disputing any of that," I said in frustration. "Yaz isn't just banging on about diet and lifestyle. She's on about crystals and reiki and all this other bullshit as well."

"Yaz is a *qualified* acupuncturist, reiki therapist, yoga instructor and windsurfing instructor. I'm sure an hour with her, even if it *does* involve the odd crystal, would do most people the power of good."

I sat back in my chair, feeling deflated. "When did she qualify in all of that?" Penny had spent barely an hour with Yaz. How was it she knew more about her than I did, and I'd known her for over twenty years?

"She did all the courses over the last few years," Max said with a shrug. "I didn't even know myself, mate. She kept it on the quiet in case I took the piss. I only found out through Mia."

"They were really intense courses as well," Mia said, her

voice still stiff with anger. "She worked her socks off and all in her spare time."

"Oh... that's surprising."

"Not really," Mia said. "Not if you know her." Her voice dropped to smaller than before as she went on. "She's helped *me*, you know. More than any pills have in the past."

I gave Mia a soft look and Max put his arm around her shoulders, giving her a squeeze. There was no denying how much Yaz had helped her. Yaz's positive energy was impossible to be around without it rubbing off. She was a feel-good person. Someone who just seemed to make people happy. When I thought about it, she *did* lighten the office atmosphere at Max's business. The bastard probably owed his sister big time in terms of staff retention, and not just because the blokes wanted to stare at her arse in lycra (although that, I was sure, was a huge bonus).

"I'll apologise to her," I said to my now hostile audience.

"Yes, you will," Mia said, glaring at me again, her voice laced with steel. "Then you'll *leave her alone*. This crap you pull with her ends today."

I nodded, although my chest lurched at the idea of leaving her alone. But that was, of course, the most sensible course of action. I needed to leave Yaz alone now. To stop thinking about her, stop obsessing over her. I knew what had driven me to be so vicious tonight. It was the irritation of having her constantly on my mind, the worry I'd felt watching her on that bloody windsurfer, and the totally unreasonable homicidal thoughts I'd had when Bodhi looked like he was trying to stake his claim.

Yes, my head knew it was high time I left Yaz alone. I just hoped my heart was paying attention.

Chapter 6

I never thought you'd be cruel

HEATH

"Yaz!" I jogged across the road from my car as I saw Yaz arrive on her bike at the side of the building. Her head whipped around as she was bringing her bike to a stop. She frowned across at me briefly before turning back to her bike, propping it up against the bike rack and heading for the front door of the beachside unit. I stopped a few feet away from her and shoved my hands into my pockets. She kept her back to me as she unlocked the door.

"Er... you should really use a bike lock." As soon as the words were out, I kicked myself. What was wrong with me? I was here to apologise, for God's sake. Couldn't I stop being an arsehole for five minutes?

Yaz stopped and turned to give me a withering look that, quite frankly, I didn't know she had in her.

"If anyone is desperate enough to steal my bike, then good luck to them and may they go in peace with my blessing."

Right. She may have had a point there. Her bike looked about fifty years old and was sporting a substantial amount of rust. As I looked closer at it, I realised I remembered this bike from Yaz's childhood. It still had the large basket on the front and the streamers on the handlebars.

"Fair point," I conceded. She frowned as if I'd confused her and then shook her head.

"What do you want, Heath?"

"Woah! This is an amazing space," I said, ignoring her question as I followed her, uninvited, into a studio. We were on the seafront and the large windows had incredible views across the bay. Yaz started moving through the room, setting out diffusers with essential oils on the ledges at the side. All of a sudden the air was filled with everything Yaz, and it was such I hit that I felt a little lightheaded. I could make out lavender, tea tree oil, and something with just a hint of spice to it.

"I'll ask you again, Heath. What do you want?"

I gave a small start, realising that I had been staring into the middle distance for several seconds. Clearing my throat, I tried to focus on my reason for being here.

"I came to apologise."

Yaz looked surprised for a moment, and then she rolled her eyes. "Mia's been reading you the riot act, hasn't she? My brother is giving me the same bullshit. I'll tell you what I told him: it's all cool. I don't need an apology. You have your opinions and I have mine. No reason we can't just jog on and let it go."

"I don't want to jog on." At the back of my mind, I knew I was being completely unreasonable. The way I'd treated Yaz of late would make her suggestion the most sensible course of action. But the truth was, I didn't want to just agree to disagree and be cordial when we saw each other. I didn't want indifference from her. Yaz gave me another bewildered, annoyed look before looking over my shoulder and smiling. It felt like her smile sucked all the air out of the room, rendering me completely incapable of speech.

"Hi, beautiful ladies," Yaz said through her smile. I turned to be confronted by five women holding five babies. Some were newborns, some looked about a year old. All five women plus the two babies that weren't asleep were staring up at me. Most of the women were make-up free and had various unidentified foodstuffs on their activewear. One stood out as being surprisingly well groomed. She gave me the kind of predatory smile I was used to receiving from women in general. The others looked horrified that I was there. "Come through," Yaz ushered them in, "Heath was just *leaving*."

I raised an eyebrow. "I was?"

"Yes, you were."

"I can't stay for the class?"

Yaz narrowed her eyes and put her hands on her hips. "You want to stay for a postnatal yoga class to strengthen your pelvic floor?"

"I'm sure my pelvic floor could do with a little tune up."

One woman let out a short giggle.

"Heath, you're wearing a suit."

"He could take the jacket off," one of the more bedraggled women suggested, her gaze shifting from shock to interest as she swept my body from top to toe with her eyes.

Yaz rolled her eyes. "He'll make you guys feel uncomfortable. We're here to loosen up and let our chakras flow with positive energy. His energy is all wonky. He'll bugger it all up."

"I won't feel uncomfortable," another of the women said as her baby started gumming her face. I noticed she had one eye rimmed with eyeliner and the other without.

"His energy seems straight to me," the one with the lopsided ponytail commented with a cheeky grin. "No wonky chakra from where I'm standing."

"Well, if it's okay with these lovely ladies," I said, "then I don't see why I can't stay." There were various rather enthusiastic murmurs of agreement from the other women.

"He can go at the front," someone put in. I glanced at her and noticed her eyes were pointed at my arse. "No objection from me."

"There we go," I grinned. "You wouldn't want to be sexist about it, would you, Yaz?" I took off my jacket and pushed up my sleeves.

"He's staying," one mum said forcefully, pushing me up towards the front of the class. I winked at Yaz and she rolled her eyes, muttering about how I would "disturb the energy."

I heard one woman murmur to another that I could "disturb her energy any day." I smirked as I stole a yoga mat from the side. The smirk was quickly wiped off my face as I tried to follow a series of yoga moves that appeared to require the level of flexibility of a contortionist. It took all my efforts not to do myself an injury. And with Yaz proving just how flexible she was directly in front of me, I was in danger of a very unchild-friendly reaction. Preventing that was sucking quite a bit of my attention. When I lost my balance and nearly squashed a baby who had crawled under my downward facing dog, I gave up and started laughing. Another baby got in on the action, standing on wobbly but sturdy little legs before sitting his butt down right on my head.

"I'm so sorry," his harried mum said as I manoeuvred the baby off my head and sat up.

"It's fine," I told her with a smile. She stared up at me and her eyes went unfocused for a moment.

"You're really beautiful," she said under her breath before her face flushed bright red. "Sorry, sleep deprivation seems to have melted the filter between my brain and my mouth."

"Heath," Yaz's uncharacteristically sharp tone echoed

around the studio. "You're obstructing Gayle's view. Maybe it's time you left." I glanced back at Gayle behind me. She was fast asleep on her mat. Her baby was one of the active ones that had attacked me, and he was now heading her way. Before he could wake up his mum, I swept him up in my arms and moved to the side of the room. I became like the pied piper of babies then. All the mobile ones crawled my way. I decided the best plan of action was to lie on a yoga mat and let them use me as their own personal soft play. There was a fair bit of drool and snot involved, but I counted myself lucky that nobody vomited.

"Er... Yaz?" one mum called. I looked over at Yaz and my eyes met hers. She had a similar dazed expression to the mum earlier as she watched me. "Yaz! I don't think we can hold this position for much longer!" Yaz's head snapped around and her face flooded with colour under her tan. As she moved into a new position, one of the newborns started crying. Before the mum could pick her baby up, Yaz stepped over to them and offered to take her. She then performed the unlikely feat of completing the rest of the yoga class, splits and everything, with a baby nestled into her chest.

Yaz

"Heath, I really don't have the energy for this."

The last of my new mum yoga ladies had left. I'd had to practically push Gayle out of the door in the end. I could cut the post-natal hormones in the studio with a knife. None of these poor ladies were ready for Heath, and certainly not a Heath who was lying on the floor playing with their babies. Getting that image out of my own head would be a problem.

"I don't know why you're still here, but I've got a full day so..."

"I'm not leaving until you accept my apology." He was back

to looking stubborn, and I was losing my patience, which just wasn't me. I was centred, I was Zen, I was in control. I didn't lose my shit or raise my voice. I didn't let other people annoy me. But when it came to Heath...

"You can shove your apology up your arse." There, I'd said it. It felt good. "You're only doing it to appease Mia and my brother."

"That's not why I'm doing it. I really regret saying–"

"You regret telling me what you really think of me because it made you look like a bully, and it pissed your best friend off."

"Yaz that's not–"

"It doesn't matter, okay? You can't upset me anymore. Go back to your super important life and let me go back to mine. I know we can't completely avoid each other, but we can at least be civil."

His dark eyes flashed, and he stepped into my personal space. "Will you let me speak? I'm trying to explain that–"

"You know what? I'm tired of you mansplaining *everything* to me. I'm over you now and I–"

"You're over me?" Heath shifted even closer, and I felt another surge of heat in my cheeks. Why did I say that? I couldn't *think* straight with him this close.

"You know what I mean." My voice lost its heat in my embarrassment and dropped to a whisper. "I'm not a teenager anymore."

"I know that." Heath's voice had also dropped lower. I looked up into his eyes and his pupils were dilated as he stared into mine. Something passed between us in those few seconds, as if there was a magnetic force pulling us together. We both moved at the same time. Heath's hands came to either side of my face, mine went around his back and he was kissing me. As his lips moved against mine, my brain short-circuited in a haze of pent-up lust. All my frantic teenage fantasies were coming true. I forgot that I'd hated him a moment ago. I forgot that he'd embarrassed me, humiliated me, that he didn't respect me. To my shame, I even forgot that he had a girlfriend. All I could think about was how to get closer to him. I pressed my body into his and pushed my hand up under his shirt to feel the muscles of his back. He made a low sound in the back of his throat as one of his hands slipped into my hair, the other splaying the middle of my back to pull me even closer. If the door of the studio hadn't opened at that moment, I seriously think I would have climbed him like a spider monkey. Instead, I flinched at the creak of the hinges and leapt away from Heath at warp speed.

"Oh... I–" Barry, one of my clients, stood there looking mortified, the poor man. A couple of others filled the open doorway behind him, and he turned to shoo them out. "Yaz seems to be a little busy right now. Let's give her a moment to–"

"Bazza, it's fine–" I said just as Heath said, "That'd be great."

I flashed him an annoyed look and his mouth set in a stubborn line.

"Heath is *leaving*."

"I'm not going to–" Heath started to say, and Barry continued to usher the others out of the door. I'd officially had enough of this nonsense. I marched forward and grabbed his arms to drag him to the corner of the studio.

"Get out," I whisper-hissed at him.

"Yaz, listen–"

"No, you listen, you arrogant bastard. This is my place of work. You can't come here, demand to speak to me, and humiliate me in front of clients. I don't come to your hospital and embarrass you. Do I? Now, I don't know what you're playing at with this new method of torturing me, but it's *cruel*, Heath.

You've been a prick to me in recent years, but I *never* thought you'd be cruel."

"Shit, no, Yaz," he said, stepping towards me with a pained expression on his face. I took a larger one back, and he held his hands up in surrender. "I'm not trying to humiliate you. I – I... Jesus, I don't know what I'm doing, to be honest. I'm sorry. But – but we need to–"

He looked so confused and lost that I did believe then that he wasn't playing a game. It was also very obvious that he hadn't meant to kiss me. That magnetic pull had been impossible for him to ignore, either. But he wasn't happy about it. No, he looked conflicted and genuinely shaken. Something that had been my fantasy for over a decade had left Heath looking like he was going to be sick. What a confidence boost.

"Just get out." I could hear the defeat in my own voice now. I really could not handle any more from this man today. Heath must have heard it too because after he lifted a hand towards me which I flinched away from, he sighed and gave a slow nod.

"Okay, okay. I'll go. I–I really am sorry, Yaz."

I didn't know if he was apologising for the pub or for what had just happened in the studio. Either way, regret was written all over his face as he turned to leave.

"Dr Markham?" I heard Barry say as Heath opened the door. "You won't remember me, but I saw you a couple of months ago in A&E. I'd had a heart attack. You sorted me out."

"Oh, yes. Of course I remember you, Mr Taylor," Heath said smoothly as he stepped back to let Barry and the others into the studio. "How are you doing?"

"Wake up call for me. Sorted myself out now. I'm not diabetic now, you know? Thanks to Dee and this one – lifestyle change and all that." Barry pointed over at me with a huge smile on his face. Barry was one of my biggest fans. "You two have that in common. You both saved my life."

I expected Heath to give Barry a patronising whatever-you-say smile, and me a subtle eye roll. Instead, he looked between me and his ex-patient with a new curiosity in his expression.

"Not sure I did that much for you, old chap," Heath said after a slight pause. "I just made sure you got treatment for the problem. Yaz, I assume, is making sure the problem never happens again."

"Er... right," Barry said, giving Heath a bemused smile as he strode past him and out of the door.

I blinked after the departing Heath in confusion. What was that?

Chapter 7

In love with someone else

HEATH

"Hey, Penny. You mind if I come in a sec?"

Penny looked up at me from her computer. She was wearing a silk shirt with a pencil skirt and high heels, and her hair was back in an immaculate bun. Her make-up was perfectly applied. Her black-framed glasses added to the effect. Objectively, she was gorgeous. Anyone could see that, I told myself.

She smiled a wary smile and leant back into her chair. "Oh, sure. How's everything in ED?"

"Yeah, fine. I just came to apologise for the other night. Not sure what got into me, to be honest."

Penny reached up and took her glasses off, levelling me with a shrewd stare and sweeping out her hand to indicate for me to sit in the available chair.

"Don't you?" She sounded genuinely curious.

I shrugged. "Long hours, and I haven't been sleeping. It's no excuse, but I didn't mean to behave like a tosser and make you feel uncomfortable."

60

She tilted her head to the side. "It's not really me you made uncomfortable, Heath."

"Well, you were there as my date and so–"

"I was?" Penny's perfectly shaped eyebrows were raised in surprise.

"Well, yes, of course."

"It didn't seem that way to me."

"We're dating," I said firmly, annoyed that she was now being deliberately obtuse. Penny sighed.

"Heath, you're not remotely attracted to me."

I faltered for a moment before regaining the power of speech. "That's... that's not true."

Penny pinned me with a shrewd stare and stood up. "Right then," she said as she marched around her desk and right up into my personal space. "Kiss me."

"Er... what?"

"If you're so attracted to me, then kiss me."

"Well, I–"

"Because you have made no move to kiss me so far. You hold my hand or put your arm around my shoulders in the most perfunctory manner, as if you're going through the motions. I knew from the very first time we went out that you had absolutely no interest in me sexually, yet you continued to ask me out. I *am* attracted to you, by the way. Not that you would have noticed."

I frowned at her and puffed out a breath. "Why do you even agree to go out with me if you're so convinced I'm not really interested?"

"Heath, you're bloody gorgeous. You're charming, fun – of *course* I agreed to go out with you. It's been confusing, but that doesn't mean it hasn't been fun."

"But I–"

"Go on then, kiss me." Penny put her hands on her hips.

Her tone was full of challenge, almost like she was daring me to do something.

"I–"

"You see," she said, all smug as if she'd just proved her point. "You can't even–"

I cut her off mid-sentence. Grabbed her round the waist, pulled her into me and kissed her, hard. She melted into me, her hands went into my hair and I felt... nothing. When we broke apart, I took a rapid step back and shoved my hands into my pockets. She looked up at me with a dazed expression for a moment before clearing her throat and smoothing down the front of her skirt.

"Point proven." Her tone was clipped, and I immediately felt like a colossal bastard.

"Penny, I'm so sorry. I don't know what's going on with me. I really, *really* want to–"

Penny's expression softened. "You really want to like me. I'm not sure why, but you think you *should* like me, or at least someone similar to me. I think in your mind there's some sort of list or criteria a woman has to fulfil in order to be considered dating material."

"No, that's not–"

"I'm sure you have your reasons, but that's not the way the world works."

The reality was that Penny had come uncomfortably close to the truth. I did have a list of criteria. In fact, it wasn't even a mental list – it was a word document on my laptop. At university and even throughout my training in my twenties, I hadn't really bothered that much with The List. I wasn't interested in settling down then, so the women I was with didn't have to live up to it. But now, over the last couple of years, I'd decided that if I wanted to have a family and settle down I needed to get The List out again. I had my reasons.

God, did I have my reasons. But I wasn't going to get into that with Penny.

I sighed. "I really do like you, Penny. But you're right, I don't seem to like you that way. I'm so sorry – I've behaved like the most unbelievable wanker."

"It's fine," she said, waving her hand in the air. "I had a good time – you're an entertaining guy. Even if you *were* attracted to me, it would never have worked."

"Why not?"

"Heath, you're in love with someone else."

I RUBBED MY CHEST AS I MOVED THROUGH THE department to resus. This ache had been building there for the last few months. I had thought it might be gastritis and had tried everything to ease it – antacids, change in diet. I'd even gone so far as having a heart tracing and a stress echocardiogram from one of my cardiology mates, but everything was fine. I just couldn't shake this horrible feeling. As well as the chest weirdness, there was another strange sensation that had crept in – one that almost felt like I was falling. Like I was out of control. I hadn't felt like that since childhood, and it wasn't something I relished re-experiencing. The fact I couldn't sleep didn't help. Whenever I managed to nod off, I had vivid dreams filled with curly blonde hair, green eyes, ripped cut-off jeans, soft lips... I would wake up drenched in sweat, ridiculously frustrated and wracked with guilt. It was two weeks since that day in Yaz's studio and my obsession with her was only growing. Pennygate had not helped at all. Of course, Penny was wrong. Me, in love? With Yaz? Ugh, there was that bloody pain again. Maybe I needed a gastroscopy?

"Okay, so I'm worried about a case in majors. Can I run it

past you?" asked Josh, the twitchy, anxiety-ridden senior registrar. This guy was not suited to emergency medicine. Last week he'd asked a vascular consultant to review what Josh had believed was a possible case of gangrene. Turned out the patient had a verruca. The vascular consultant was not amused. Josh's response was that you can't be too careful. Apparently he'd heard of a case of necrotising fasciitis starting in a similar way ("They had to chop the guy's knob off in the end, mate," he'd told me in a worried tone). I'd tried again and again to encourage him to use his own clinical judgement – actually, scrap that, not just clinical judgement, but common bloody sense.

"Go on then," I said, leaning against the central hub desk and preparing myself for a convoluted story, likely including a list of all the patient's pets over the last decade (I'm not even joking – that was exactly what Josh did with the last asthmatic he presented to me).

"Okay, so recurrent falls, ninety-one. Tripped today. Denies loss of consciousness, but I really think that he might have..." I let Josh drone on as I snatched the notes out of his hands and headed towards the patient's cubicle. I'd found from bitter experience it was better to take the history from the patient myself than to listen to Josh's endless monologues where he postulates various medical theories whilst often missing the point entirely. But before I made it round the corner, Josh stopped me with a hand to my arm and lowered his voice. "Just to warn you before you go in. There's a woman in there with him and she's... well, you'll see what I mean. I try to be professional at all times. You *know* I do."

"Yes, Josh. I am well aware of your professionalism." Josh had written a five-page entry into his learning log for his appraisal about a possible episode of overfamiliarity with a health care assistant. He was worried he may have 'abused his position' – the poor girl only asked him out for a drink. The half-wit should have just said yes and been flattered. But *no*, he has to bore me as his educational supervisor with his non-existent ethical dilemma. He'll never get laid at this rate. He cleared his throat. "Well. The lady is..." a trickle of sweat made its way down his forehead and I frowned.

"Given you a hard time, has she?"

"No, no... it's just that–" he trailed off and gave a helpless shrug.

"Alright, mate," Tim, one of the nurses, greeted me and I gave him a wave. But as he walked away, something caught his attention in one of the cubicles and he did a double take. Still fixated on whatever he was staring at, Tim nearly tripped over the phlebotomy tray in front of him. When I glanced over at the desk, a couple of the orthopaedic consultants were also staring past Tim into the same cubicle. One muttered to the other and a slow smirk spread over his face.

"What are all those buggers staring at?" I muttered.

"You'll see," Josh said darkly as he trotted after me around the corner. Then I saw her and it all made sense. Blonde curls everywhere as if she'd let them air dry from the sea. Loose white Billabong t-shirt, which was falling off one tanned shoulder and so old it was nearly see-through and doing nothing to hide the bright bikini underneath. Flip-flops and, of course, the frayed denim shorts that had seen better days revealing most of the toned, tanned legs. She was crouched, talking to an elderly man in a chair, smiling at him and filling the whole department with her energy. Her head turned as I approached, and her smile fell. That aching feeling was back in my chest again.

Chapter 8

What kind of man are you?

HEATH

"Great," I heard Yaz say under her breath, her tone implying my presence here was anything but.

"What are you doing here?" I demanded.

She stiffened at the accusation in my tone, and I immediately wanted to claw the words back. Where was my natural, effortless charm that seemed to be so easy to wield with everyone else?

"You know Miss Hardcastle?" Josh asked me with a hint of reverence.

"Josh, I've told you five times already to call me Yaz." She gave Josh a patient smile, which fell again when she looked at me. "I'm here because Bryn is my friend, and I was the one who found him. He lives in the flat below mine."

"Oi! I know you," Bryn shouted at me, waving his stick in the air. "You're the bugger that carried my Yaz up to her flat. Taking advantage of her."

The department went suspiciously quiet. Yaz stood up and looked up to the ceiling, seeking patience.

I heard one orthopod behind me mutter, "Typical. That jammy bastard always lands on his feet." Josh was looking up at me with a mixture of horror and respect.

"Mr Pickering," I said through a forced smile as I moved into the cubicle and ducked to avoid the still waving stick. "As I explained before, I was merely transporting Yaz because of her injured feet. There was no impropriety, I assure you."

Bryn snorted. "A likely story. I know a gadabout when I sees one."

Noticing that the entire department was still staring this way, I shook my head in annoyance, ushered Josh into the cubicle and pulled the curtain to shut out prying eyes.

"My gadabout activities aside, Mr Pickering. Can we discuss why you're here today? I'm Dr Markham, but please call me Heath."

"I brought Bryn his shopping and found him on the floor."

"Tripped over Doris," Bryn grumbled, still eyeing me with suspicion.

"His cat," Yaz explained.

"Landed on my feet when this one moved in," Bryn said, gesturing towards Yaz. "Look after me, don't you, love? Not sure what I'd have done if you hadn't popped in today."

"She's quite a girl, Mr Pickering," I agreed, and his expression softened from his former scowl at me.

"Well, at least you're not stupid," he said. "Now then Gadabout – this young lad has been very thorough. I've had the works here, haven't I, Yaz? All sorts of machines hooked up to me. Blood tests. The lot. Well, that's all fine and dandy, but I should be getting on home now to feed Doris."

"Bryn is tired," Yaz explained. "He just wants to go home. Josh here has been *very* thorough, but Bryn's fine. I can call us a taxi."

"I was just saying to Miss Hardcastle," Josh leapt in, and

Yaz rolled her eyes at his repeated use of her surname, "that there are some safety issues to explore and– "

"You feeling alright now, Bryn?" I asked.

"Right as rain. I've a beautiful lass wants to take me home. I've had a cuppa and a biscuit. I'm all set."

"Could you do me a favour and walk for me?" I asked as I pulled back the cubicle curtain.

Bryn grabbed hold of his stick and stood up. Yaz hovered for a moment but let him get his balance. He made slow but steady progress over towards the central hub with Yaz next to him. Much to my annoyance, the orthopaedic surgeons all stopped their conversation to watch her. Their eyes dropped to her arse as she walked back with Josh and I heard one of them mutter, "Told you Markham's a jammy bastard," under his breath.

"Two more NOFs on the board if you haven't seen yet, lads," I called to them once I caught their eye. NOF stands for 'neck of femur fracture', and their emergency list was full of them. "Why don't you jog on with that?"

Ruben, renowned player and all-round prick, winked at me and his registrar gave me an unsubtle thumbs up before they both set off into the department.

Meanwhile, Bryn made it back again and lowered himself into his chair.

"Right, well – I agree with Yaz. It's high time we get you back to your cat."

Bryn gave me a relieved smile, the wrinkles at the corners of his faded blue eyes multiplying. "You may be a gadabout, but you're still a good lad underneath."

"B–but he's not safe at home," Josh spluttered. "This isn't the first time he's fallen. There's the issue of the cat being a hazard. He should have an occupational therapy assessment in his home before he's–"

"Yaz, can you get a bell for the cat?" I asked, and she nodded straight away. "The OT can get out to Bryn tomorrow. Problem solved."

"He really *is* exhausted," Yaz put in.

"Don't fuss now," Bryn said, but she laid her hand over his and crouched back down next to him.

"You are, you stubborn old sod. We need to get you home."

"There will still be significant risk," Josh said, looking flustered as he tried to avoid eye contact with Yaz. Unfortunately his gaze settled on her chest before he flinched and averted it to the much safer territory of mine – but not before he blushed bright red, no doubt thinking up yet another log entry on professionalism to bore me with. "He shouldn't be allowed to–"

"*Allowed* to?" My eyebrows went up as I turned fully towards Josh. "Excuse us for a moment," I said to Yaz and Bryn before leading Josh away from the cubicle and back to the central hub. "Bryn doesn't need us to *allow* him to do anything," I told Josh in a low voice once we were out of earshot. "You do realise that if he wants to go home, he is perfectly entitled to make that decision himself?"

"I just thought it might be safer if he was admitted while we established how safe his home is for him to be in and minimise the risk."

"Bryn is not a child. He has no cognitive impairment. He wants to go home to his cat and we need to facilitate that."

"But the risk–"

"What do you think the risk to Bryn would be if we admitted him?"

"Well–"

"Hospital acquired infections, deconditioning, loss of independence. Admission is more of a risk to him than his cat."

"Right," Josh muttered, his face flushing a little. "I just... well I–"

I rolled my eyes and started back towards the cubicle, with Josh trailing behind me.

"Right," he said, once we were back in front of Bryn. "Sorry about that. Of course, you can go home."

"Don't worry yourself over it, lad," Bryn put in, patting Josh's hand like he was reassuring a child. "At least I've had a good old MOT."

"Okay, I'll sort out the discharge papers," Josh said, more flustered than ever now. Another trickle of sweat made it down his forehead. "I d–didn't mean to imply that you don't have the capacity to make your own choice." The poor man looked on the verge of tears now. "It's just... I'm not good with risk and–"

"You've done a great job with Bryn," Yaz said as she moved towards Josh and laid her hand on his arm. He froze and stopped breathing altogether. She was smiling at him again. Josh looked as though he might pass out. "You need to chill, hun. I'll make sure he's okay. He doesn't want to stay. Freedom is oxygen for the soul. Bryn's not willing to give that up. Not yet."

"Right, right. Thanks. I'll just go and write this all up." He lurched out of the cubicle and practically sprinted back to the hub.

"Is he okay?" Yaz asked, frowning after poor Josh. "He seems a bit too tightly wound. His aura's all wonky. Maybe I should recommend some breathing exercises or give him a free yoga session–"

"He wouldn't survive you in your cat woman get-up, young lady," Bryn said with a chuckle. "Leave the poor lad alone. You nearly gave him a heart attack. At least this one's going to let us get back to Doris." Bryn nodded to me, and I returned his smile. Yaz flicked me a reluctantly grateful look.

"Yeah, thanks," she said in a flat tone that did not in any way sound grateful.

"Woah," Bryn said through another chuckle. "Doesn't look like you're her favourite person, Gadabout. I've never heard my Yaz take that tone before."

"Quite," I replied in a tight voice, managing a smile for Bryn.

Yaz ignored Bryn's comments and started packing up his stuff into a carrier bag. "Twitchy Twitcherson was gearing up to make Bryn stay in overnight," she said. "He'll be right once I get him home. I was just worried the old bugger might have broken his hip."

"Take more than a slip up to break my hip, you cheeky mare."

"Bryn, you were on the floor when I arrived. You couldn't reach the phone."

"Bloody cat," Bryn mumbled, and Yaz rolled her eyes.

"Anyway," she said, turning to me again. "I am grateful. Bryn would die if he had to stay here."

Yaz probably didn't know how close to the truth she actually was. Hospitals were not safe places for people like Bryn.

"Come on then, love," she said to Bryn, smoothing back his white hair and then straightening his bow tie. "Let's get you home and get a brew on."

"My shift's finishing now. I'll take you both."

Green eyes and faded blue eyes fixed on me – one set horrified, the other still twinkling with mischief.

"Sounds good," Bryn said at the same time Yaz gave an emphatic "No!"

"I'll not go in a taxi. I don't want them lot knowing my personal information."

"Bryn, what personal information are you going to give a taxi driver?"

"He'll know my address."

Yaz crossed her arms over her chest. "He won't care about your address."

"Mavis at the day centre had her identity stolen by some chancer what told her he were from the bank. Sharp lady Mavis. If it can happen to her, it can happen to anyone. I'll not risk some cabbie bastard knowing my address."

"Can't be too careful," I agreed with Bryn, and Yaz narrowed her eyes at me.

We made our way out of the department at Bryn's speed, which gave my colleagues and those orthopaedic tosspots plenty of time to give me knowing smirks and not-so-subtle thumbs ups. I even caught a low muttered "Jesus Christ" from Chris the radiographer as we passed. I waved my hand to cut off his eye line to Yaz's chest and then gave him a one-finger salute, to which he suppressed a laugh.

"Bloody 'ell, lad," Bryn said as I pulled up to the entrance in the Porsche. "I *knew* you were a gadabout. If this car isn't designed to get you into lasses' knickers, then I'm a monkey's uncle."

"Bryn!" Yaz admonished as she helped him into the front seat.

"I'm only telling it how I see it, love," Bryn said. "Anyway, we all know this kind of nonsense won't work on you, mind. Will it?" He turned to me as Yaz climbed into the back. "Yaz doesn't like cars." He chuckled. "You're going to have to sort something else out to impress her, I'm afraid."

"This is his second car," Yaz muttered darkly as if owning more than one serviceable vehicle was akin to mass murder. "He's clearly compensating for something." I shot her an annoyed look in the mirror but she ignored me. "And anyway Heath has no interest in impressing me, you old devil," Yaz said, slapping his shoulder lightly from the back seat.

"What kind of man *are* you?" Bryn asked in surprise. "If I

was seventy years younger, I'd make sure I was impressing a young lady like my Yazmin."

"How about we go back to the portion of the day when you were so shaken up that you shut your trap for once, hey?" Yaz said and Bryn snorted.

"Take more than tripping over the cat to shut me up, young lady."

The five minutes of uncomfortable silence that followed as I drove them both home were excruciating. I'd never known Yaz so quiet. I rubbed my aching chest as we pulled up in front of their building. Before I had fully come to a stop, Yaz opened the back door and leapt out onto the road. She'd yanked open Bryn's door and started helping him out of the car before I even had my seatbelt off. As I came around to the other side to help Yaz extract Bryn, I was beginning to see the drawbacks of a low-slung sports car – not exactly conducive to a smooth exit when you're ninety-one years old. Once Bryn was up and had his stick, he swatted us away.

"Don't fuss over me. I fought in three wars – I can make it to my own bastard front door." I ignored Yaz's frown and gestures that I should leave, and followed them into the building. We settled Bryn in his ground-floor flat with a cup of tea and a biscuit. Apparently he had carers coming at seven to get him his supper. Bryn shooed her away several times, but it was obvious he enjoyed Yaz fussing over him. Eventually he grabbed the remote to turn up the volume of his television to an antisocial level before falling asleep in his chair with a biscuit halfway to his mouth. Yaz took the biscuit away, put a blanket over his legs, smoothed his crazy hair back and gave him a kiss on his forehead before we left the flat and locked up with a key that she put in a small key safe next to his door. Once that was done, I opened my mouth to speak, but Yaz was already jogging away toward her flat.

"What are you doing?" Yaz turned to me on the stairs as I followed her up.

"We need to talk."

"No, we don't. That's the *last* thing we need to do. In fact, I think you and I should avoid conversation whenever possible."

"Please, Yaz, let's just clear the air. It's not like we can avoid each other forever. My sister and your brother – my best friend – own a business together. Can we... can we be grown-ups about this?"

"You've made your opinion about my capacity for adulting pretty clear in recent years, Heath. I don't see why I shouldn't live *down* to your expectations again." She unlocked the door and was about to slam it in my face when I reached out my hand to stop her.

"I've said I'm sorry for that. Listen, I can help with Bryn. I've got the contact details for the community team with physios and OTs to come out and help him." Truth was that I had already tasked Josh with contacting the multidisciplinary team about Bryn before I left the hospital. But, ruthless bastard that I was, I decided Yaz didn't need to know that at this stage.

She sighed. "Five minutes."

I nodded and followed her into the flat.

Chapter 9

That's it, isn't it?

HEATH

I was struck again by the smell – lavender and other essential oils lightly fragranced the air. It was like a dose of concentrated Yaz and I found it a little difficult to think. Her coffee table was still covered in crystals, herbs and other various nicknacks. My house was all about order – clean lines, uniform colour. I had a housekeeper who made sure everything was in its proper place. My shirts were always perfectly ironed, my kitchen surfaces were completely free of any stuff – even the toaster was cleverly hidden. The meagre kitchen surfaces Yaz had available were bursting with appliances, old-fashioned weighing scales, colourful cake stands. It wasn't a mess as such – more a bright, colourful, cluttered, too-small environment with more than a hint of chaos.

Even the walls were covered with *stuff* – mostly a mishmash of frames with photos of family and friends. Bodhi had his arm around Yaz in one of them – they were standing barefoot on the beach in front of their windsurfing equipment. Yaz was staring straight at the camera, smiling that huge, radiant grin which always seemed to light up any setting, but Bodhi was staring at Yaz with a self-satisfied grin on his face as if he'd already managed to get into her knickers. I had the irrational urge to rip it off the wall and stamp on it like a three-year-old.

"Well?" Yaz said as she put the kettle on and got two cups down from her extensive collection on the wall.

I cleared my throat and tore my eyes away from that bloody photo.

"Okay, I've behaved like a complete bastard. I don't know what's come over me lately. Penny gave me a right bollocking after you left that night. And then when I tried to apologise at your studio, I ballsed that up as well and I was..." I shifted my feet and looked to the side. "I was completely inappropriate with you. That was unforgivable. But I haven't been sleeping recently and I think my judgement isn't quite right, which is no excuse. I'm not making an excuse. I just—"

"Heath, I'm going to say this one more time." Yaz's tone was that of complete exasperation, like she had come to the end of her tether with me. "If I have to repeat myself again, I honestly might lose it. I'm an *adult*. You were *not* inappropriate. I snogged you back, you daft bugger. Apologise for behaving like an insufferable prick, but don't apologise like I'm a child you took advantage of. Let's cut the crap, okay? I know you know I've fantasised about you for years. My entire puberty is littered with fervent, intense fantasies about being with you. I think it's safe to say that if presented with any opportunity of snogging you or in fact shagging you, my body is hard wired to say yes. If anything, *you* should be scared of *me*. The number of times I've spent thinking about you that way, I'd probably eat you alive given half the chance."

My mouth had gone completely dry and there was a faint ringing in my ears. So much blood had travelled south of my belt I feared I might pass out. Yaz had always been direct, but I never thought she would address that particular elephant in the room.

"Right," I said, and I had to clear my throat as my voice was so tight. "I... er, right."

It didn't seem that I was capable of further words. What should have happened at this juncture was that I should have left the flat. But somehow my feet were not cooperating with my brain's feeble attempt to get them to move to the exit. Yaz was still pouring and stirring the tea as if she regularly told people they had starred in all her teenage fantasies and that she would, in fact, eat them alive. The prospect of being eaten alive by this woman and what that might entail was almost too much for my physiology to handle. I took a couple of steps towards her. She looked up from the cups to me, then she froze.

"Heath?" her voice was tentative, barely above a whisper. I took another step – my conscience screaming at me to get the fuck out of there, but my entire being drawn to her like a moth to a flame. Another couple of steps and I was right in front of her, close enough for my hand, which was trembling slightly, to come up the side of her face and my thumb to sweep over her lips. She exhaled a shaky breath, her pupils so dilated now that there was only a thin ring of green around the edges.

"You still think about me... like that?" My own voice was low and husky as I searched her beautiful face. She nodded, her cheek moving against my hand, and I leaned down so that my forehead was resting against hers. That ache in my chest seemed to ease the closer I was to her, as if keeping my distance was a physical hardship that had gone unacknowledged until now. "I think about you as well. All the time. I dream about you at night, daydream during the day. How soft your skin would be, how your body would feel under mine."

A small sound escaped her lips as she stared up at me, her

face flushing and her body moving towards me just a fraction. And that was it. Any control I might have had was decimated. My entire existence centred on being close to this woman. I used my hand to tilt her face back and my lips fell on hers. It wasn't light or gentle like before in her studio. No, this time it was wild and crazy and totally out of control. One of my hands moved to her back, the other to under her thigh to lift her up onto the kitchen counter so that her face was level with mine. I kissed from her lips down her neck and along her collarbone as she slid her hand under my t-shirt to feel the skin of my back.

"Oh, God," I muttered against her skin. "I can't stop. God help me, I can't stop."

"Don't you dare stop," she said, her voice strained with need. "I'll die if you stop now." Pulling back enough to scan her flushed face and noting the fierce desire in her expression, I yanked her thin t-shirt over her head in one swift move, dislodging her mass of hair from its topknot and allowing it to cascade over her shoulders and down her back. I looked down at her bikini-clad torso – those perfect breasts and that flat, tanned stomach and my breath left me in a whoosh.

"You are so beautiful," I managed to get out in a hoarse voice as I reached up to the strings of her bikini top behind her neck. "I've thought about doing this so many times." I gave the bow a pull, and she unclipped the strap at the back. I barely had time to take in the perfection in front of me before she was yanking my t-shirt over my head and chucking it and her bikini top to the side. She spent a few moments tracing my chest, and I shivered under her touch before she pressed her soft body against mine and kissed me again.

"Bedroom," she said between kisses, and I lifted her up with her legs wrapped around my hips. A few of her crystals fell to the floor, but neither of us took any notice. I had to navigate through way too many pieces of random furniture on the way to her bedroom, the ceiling of which was in no way designed to accommodate a man over six feet tall. I laid her on the bed and hovered over her as my hips fell between her legs. She moved against me and I let out a low groan.

"Jesus, Midge, don't do that. I can't–"

"I *need* you." Her voice cracked at the end, as though she was in some sort of physical pain. And again, that fuse in my brain short-circuited. I moved against her beautiful body and her shallow breathing was all I could hear in the room. The rest of our clothes came off in a frenzied joint effort until we were skin on skin, finally. It was then I took my time to learn everything about her body: where she needed pressure, where she needed to be touched with my hands and my mouth until I could tell that she was right on the edge. She was in such a state that she yanked me up over her. "Please Heath," she begged. "Now. I want it to be with you. Not without you. I'm so tired of being without *you*."

I hovered over her, using both hands to push her hair back from her beautiful face. Her cheeks were flushed, her expression sharp with need. I reached into the pocket of my discarded trousers to extract a condom from my wallet. Once I was ready, I turned back to her and pressed my weight against her again.

"Are you sure?" I asked, my voice ragged.

"Heath, now!" she snapped as one of her hands went around the back of my neck and the other to the muscles of my back. Her lips parted as my hips surged forward and I kissed her again. The relief of finally, finally being part of her like this. Finally being as close to her as my body had been craving to be for so long. The relief of that was almost overwhelming. I pulled back to look down at her face and I could see the same emotions in her expression – awe, ecstasy, need. We moved together, our eyes still locked as our movements became more and more frantic and primal. I watched her push over the edge and let go, triggering me to do the same. It was hands down the most intense experience of my life.

I collapsed on top of her, letting her take my full weight for a moment before realising I should probably allow her to breathe, shifting over and gathering her limp body into mine so she was tucked into my side with her arm slung across my chest. As I lay there, an extraordinary sense of peace swept over me. *So this is what it's meant to feel like?* I thought. *This right here is what I've needed all along.* There had never been any sense in fighting it. Okay, maybe she was my best friend's little sister and maybe she represented everything I'd told myself I should avoid – but there was no getting away from the fact that I could not stay away from this woman. I would just have to accept that she was my future. I was pretty sure I could over-look some of her flaws, and anyway, there was no going back now. Max would skin me alive if he knew I shagged his sister and walked away. I'd just have to make the best of it. And feeling her soft body against mine, her glorious hair spread out over my shoulder, and the feel of her breathing against my chest was certainly softening the blow. In fact, rather than feeling trapped, I was suddenly feeling an overwhelming sense of well-being for the first time in months. That aching sensation in my chest had eased completely. I smiled at the ceiling as I gave Yaz's shoulder a squeeze.

Yaz let out a puff of air and I felt her previously boneless and compliant body stiffen next to mine. "That was... er... I–"

"That was amazing," I told her, pulling her now slightly resistant body more into mine.

"You – you think?" Her voice had more than a hint of uncertainty to it.

"Don't you?"

"Well, yes, of course I do. But then you've literally just topped all my teenage fantasies in one fell swoop. It's just that... well, where do we go from here?"

"Well, that's it, isn't it?" I said in a firm tone. "We're together."

"Er... what?"

Chapter 10

Make the best of it

HEATH

"There's no going back now." My voice was resigned, but I couldn't keep the smile off my face. "Of course, it'll be best if we tell Max and Verity as soon as possible. I wouldn't want them finding out any other way. We should probably give Max a ring in a–"

"You want to ring *my brother* and tell him we've just had a cheeky shag?" Her voice was rising in disbelief. "Are you *insane?*"

"Yaz, I will not tell him anything of the sort. I'll tell him we're together. A couple. As long as he knows we're serious about each other, he won't be pissed off. He'll probably be pleased."

"A couple?"

"Yes."

"So... we're a couple now?"

Her voice was edging out of blissed-out confusion and become tinged with annoyance.

"Of course we are," I explained with what I felt was the

utmost patience. "I'm not a *total* bastard, you know. I wouldn't shag my best friend's little sister, who's had a crush on me since she was five, and just bugger off."

"So, *you're* making that decision, are you?"

I paused and shifted so I was turned into her, leaning up on my elbow, and could see her face. She was flushed and her lips were swollen from my kisses. Her pupils were still huge, but she had the beginnings of a frown on her forehead.

"That's really the only decision I *can* make. But I'm willing to make the best of it."

"You're willing to *make the best of it*?" Genuine anger flared in her eyes now and I realised that I perhaps wasn't couching this in the most flattering terms. In my defence, the most mind-blowing sex I'd ever experienced in my life had just utterly scrambled my brain. No wonder I wasn't quite firing on all cylinders.

"I mean, well... we've done it now. We may as well..."

"*May as well?*" She pulled back from me and I wasn't quick enough to stop her retreat.

"Yaz, come back here. What are you doing?"

I reached for her, but she scrambled over to the other side of the bed and was pulling on her clothes. I must say that now I had made the decision to be with her and not fight this pull any longer, I didn't see the point of clothes for *either* of us for a good long time.

"You know what, Heath?" She'd pulled up her shorts and was shoving a t-shirt over her head now. The heightened colour in her cheeks from a moment ago had receded, leaving her looking pale under her tan. "You've this reputation for being the ultimate charmer. The great wooer of womankind. I have to say I've not seen much evidence of that here. Telling someone you *may as well* enter a relationship with them because you couldn't stop yourself from shagging them isn't exactly charming in my book."

I sighed and was about to say something, but she slammed out of the room before I could speak. That ache was back in my chest as I pulled on my jeans to prowl after her. I had a feeling I may have cocked that up, big style. But she was in love with me, damn it. She had been for years. In my arrogance, I was fairly sure I could claw it back.

When I made it out of the bedroom, I could see her leaning over the kitchen counter with her back to me and her hands braced on the granite surface.

"Listen, I'm sorry, okay?" I said, trying to soften my tone and not let any of my frustration leak into it. "I may not have put that in the right way, but you've got to understand that... well, this was never in my plan. There are things that I..." I broke off, unable to explain how much being with her frightened me. That what I really needed was someone who didn't invoke all of these *feelings*. Someone who was safe, reliable, stable. If I went into the whys and wherefores of that, I'd have to go down some pretty gruesome roads. And I wasn't about to do that anytime soon. "You can't expect me to be my full, charming self when I'm just coming around to the idea of 'us' as a couple. It's come as a bit of a shock to me, but now that it's happened, I–"

"You don't even like me." Yaz's voice was so hollow and devoid of emotion it actually sent a shiver of foreboding down my spine.

"What are you talking about, Midge?" I let out a nervous laugh as I made my way towards her. She still hadn't turned around to look at me. "Of course I like you. I think I just proved how very much I like you, very thoroughly."

"All you've proved is that you liked having sex with me."

"No, no, that's not what I–"

She whirled around and my voice cut off when I saw her tear-streaked face.

"Do you think I'm not aware of the way I look, Heath?"

"I–"

"I've had men stare at me since I was thirteen. Bad pick-up lines and male attention are a way of life for me. I'm *well aware* of the way I look. Just because you enjoyed having sex with me and can't stay away from me because of physical attraction does not sell me on a relationship with you. Not by a long way."

"That's not what I meant. You're taking this totally the wrong way. I didn't–"

"Did you imagine I would be happy that you liked me *despite* yourself and your intentions to find a suitable woman? That I obviously don't measure up to your ideal, but that you're willing to make the best of a bad job? I used to think you were such a gentleman. Dead posh, charming, perfect. Well, I can see now that you're anything but a gentleman. A *real* gentleman would never have spoken to me the way you just did."

My stomach hollowed out, and I thought for a moment I might be sick. It was true, I prided myself on how I treated people, especially women. I was the guy who walked on the traffic side of the pavement, who pulled out the chair for my date, who held open doors. But all that was just bullshit, wasn't it? If I could hurt a woman who meant as much to me as Yaz did, then I wasn't a gentleman at all. I never had been.

What had made me think I could speak to Yaz like that? It never occurred to me she would turn me down. She'd been in love with me for so long that I didn't even think that would be possible for her. I was beginning to see that the way I'd acted, not just today but over the last few years, had probably killed her feelings for me. Just as I was coming round to the fact that she was the woman meant for me, she was concluding that I was the last man on earth she would want to be with.

"Yaz, please. Let me explain."

"Nothing you could say will make me forget what you've just said to me. I won't *ever* forget it. I'll carry this with me for the rest of my life. What will never ever happen is us becoming a couple. You can shove that idea and your unbelievable arrogance where the sun doesn't shine."

"Midge, let's just talk for a moment." I took a couple more steps forward, closing the gap between us and lifted my hand to take hers, but she flinched away from me, her head jerking from side to side as she leapt back and slammed her hip against the granite worktop. I winced as her face creased in pain. "Please, Midge," I said, taking another tentative step forward but stopping as she held a hand up to ward me off. She was reduced to actually warding me off. I didn't think I'd ever felt like such an unbelievable bastard in my life.

"Get. Out." Her tears had dried now and her voice was vibrating with anger.

"If you just let me—"

"Get out. Get out. *Get out!*" Yaz screamed the last so loudly that she went red in the face. I'd never heard her raise her voice before.

"Okay, okay," I said softly, taking a step back and holding my hands up in front of me in surrender. "I can see you're going to need some space. We can talk later when you're—"

"We will *never* speak about this *ever* again." She slashed a hand through the air to make her point, as if that could erase what had just happened from existence. "And if you tell my brother or anyone else, I will *never* forgive you." I had a feeling that whether or not I told Max about this, forgiveness was going to be in very short supply from Yaz. I didn't like the look of her now pale face and tight features. I certainly didn't want to leave her like this. But I could see that anything I said now was just going to make the situation worse. I needed to leave and regroup so I could assess how I could have possibly fucked this up so utterly. "Now, this is my space. My flat is *my* space. I decide who I let in. If I want you to leave, you leave right fucking now. That is my decision to make, not yours. Understand?"

"Yes, of course." I moved back towards the door. Keeping my eyes on her as I went. Her mouth was a tight line and her arms were straight down by her sides with her small fists clenched so tightly her knuckles were white. When I finally made it to the front door, let myself out and closed it behind me, I paused in the corridor for a minute. The faint sob I could hear from the other side of the wood tore through me like a knife. What had I done? And how was I ever going to make it right?

Chapter 11

Prettier without it

Yaz

"But I look eighteen!" I whined.

Max took in my outfit and rolled his eyes. "You look eleven. In fact, no, I take that back. You look even younger than eleven with Mam's make-up on your face."

It was on the back of that mortifying comment that Heath strolled onto the terrace, closely followed by Verity. The twins were like something out of a magazine: Heath, in his white fitted linen shirt and chinos, had a deep tan and light hazel streaks in his dark brown hair; Verity, with her long white summer dress and glossy dark hair, was his female counterpart – both the male and female sides of the same coin. They looked perfectly at home here in glamorous Saint Tropez, as they should – this house we were all staying in was just another one of their family's many holiday homes, after all.

"Hey, Midge," Heath said, smiling at me and then ruffling the hair it had taken me over an hour to tame into what I'd hoped was a sophisticated "updo". His ruffling reduced it to no more than a messy bun. But that he'd touched my hair was enough to make my month. "You did good today once you got that skinny butt in gear."

Earlier on at the beach, Heath had taken the time to teach me how to surf. I knew it was just because he felt sorry for me, seeing as I had just been sitting on my own like a sad sack on the sand when he found me that afternoon. I'd been thrilled when Mum and Dad told me we were taking up the offer to stay at Heath's family villa in Saint Tropez. We'd never gone on a foreign holiday before. But the reality was that Mum and Dad were treating it as some sort of second honeymoon. Max and Verity were only interested in the local architecture and galleries, and there was nobody my age for me to play with. A bronzed, sculpted Heath jogging up to me with a couple of surfboards and offering to teach me had been one of the best moments of my life up until then. And I had impressed him. He'd praised me. I was a strong swimmer, and I'd taken to surfing quickly. He told me I was a natural. In my normal life, nobody really dished out praise to me that often. Academics were not my strong suit (not like they were for Max) and I'd barely scraped through at school. Daydreaming was not something my family considered a skill. So Heath's teasing praise, his ability to pick me straight up above his head and then chuck me through the air into the water while I giggled helplessly, or to pluck me out of a wave which had sucked me under when I fell off my board, had cemented him as one of the heroes of my life so far.

"Yazmin, darling. What on earth have you done to your face?" Verity was squinting at me. "I'd suggest a slightly more neutral shade at your age."

I felt my face heat up. This was the only lipstick my mother had.

"Oh shit, sorry," Verity said in a softer tone. "I didn't mean to embarrass you. Listen, maybe I could teach you how to apply make-up. I've got some much better–"

"Yaz doesn't need any of that slap you wear, V," Heath said, frowning at his sister. "She's prettier without it." He gave me a wink, and I nearly melted onto the floor. At eleven, I was only just really starting to have vague feelings about boys. But all of those burgeoning realisations were swamped by the absolute desperate longing I felt for Heath. For someone yet to even have a crush on a boy my age, the feeling was almost frightening in its intensity. In my mind, there was nobody kinder, funnier, more beautiful than him. No boy band member, no movie star, and certainly nobody else I knew in real life. *And* he was training to be a doctor so that he could help people. Could he *be* any more perfect?

"Yazmin!" Mum's voice cut into my thoughts of Heath's perfection. "Come on, love. We'll be late for the restaurant."

"I'm not going, Mum," I said, setting my jaw at a stubborn angle. "I'm going out with Max and this lot."

Dad followed Mum out onto the terrace, greeting the others and doing his standard "thank you so much" to Heath and Verity. Dad just couldn't get over the level of luxury in the villa or the fact that we were staying here for free. His gratitude seemed to make the twins uncomfortable.

"Don't be ridiculous, love," Mum said with a nervous laugh. "You can stuff your bra all you want, but you're still a child – they don't need you tagging along. You'll come along with me and your dad."

I felt heat hit my face as humiliation washed over me. Truth was, at that age I didn't even need a bra, so, in order to seem more grown up I had worn the one padded bra I'd convinced Mum to buy me in M&S. I was only just realising how transparent that effort was, seeing as I'd been flat as a pancake in a swimming costume all day. My eyes stung and I had to blink back the threatening tears. Max bursting into laughter didn't help the situation. Even Verity, who was normally so kind in her no-nonsense, posh way, was holding back a smile with little success. But Heath wasn't laughing or smiling. When I flicked him an embarrassed glance, he was frowning at my mother. His expression softened when he caught my eye.

"Listen, why doesn't Midge stay with us?" Heath said after a couple of embarrassing seconds had passed. "I don't fancy another night out, anyway. We can order take-away paella and play Monopoly here."

"What are you on about?" Max snapped. "We're meeting *people* at the club. Remember?" I knew exactly which 'people' Max was referring to. I'd seen the ultra glamourous, bikini-clad women they'd been flirting with at the beach. Heath shrugged as if the supermodel who'd been all over him today wasn't the most beautiful woman he must have seen in his whole life.

"Well, that suits me," Verity said, flopping down into the padded wicker chair on the balcony. She never seemed to consider men worth the effort, and certainly didn't have to go out of her way to track suitable ones down.

"We really can't let you–" Dad said, but Heath cut him off.

"Honestly, Aubrey," he said. That he used my dad's first name just highlighted how much of an adult he was and made me feel even more like a stupid kid. "It's no trouble. You two go out and have some alone time. Midge will be good with us."

After a bit more half-hearted protesting from my parents, they eventually left. I wanted the ground to swallow me up. Max was scowling at me. He muttered something that may have been *cock-blocking little shit* under his breath before he stalked into the kitchen to retrieve a beer. Verity was still lounging in her chair like it was all the same to her, whatever they did, and Heath was looking at me and my red face with an expression that looked suspiciously like pity.

"You don't have to stay here, you know," I told them all once Max had returned with his beer, pointedly not bringing Heath or V a drink. "I'm not a baby. I'll be fine on my own." I'd given up the idea that I might be able to go out with them tonight. My earlier confidence had been totally decimated.

"Mam would skin me alive," Max muttered, flopping down in the chair next to Verity.

"I wouldn't say anything."

Max snorted. "A likely story. You've a wider mouth than the Dartford Tunnel." I could tell that Max was already a couple of beers into his night, given that his accent had thickened. It was just one more thing that separated us: Max had a northern accent like Mum, having lived in Yorkshire until he was ten and only moved to the south after Mum left his dad and married mine. He was hardened in a way I wasn't, given that his dad had been abusive while mine was anything but. Max was also practical, almost to a fault, whilst I had my head in the clouds. I knew Max loved me, but I also knew he resented the fact that my life had been comparatively easy. I felt a wave of guilt now that his spoilt little sister had stopped him from having a good time.

"Listen, Midge," Heath said, ignoring Max's grumpiness to look at me. "I can't be arsed to go out anyway. We'll all have a far superior time vegging out and playing Monopoly." Max snorted again and Heath looked at me, gave me a wink and rolled his eyes.

"You've never *vegged out* in your life. Or eaten takeaway," Verity put in.

"Well, it's lucky then that our parents have a stock of very good Rioja in the cellar and that I'm mates with the owner of the Michelin-starred restaurant round the corner, isn't it?"

And then, with all his charm and easy company, the good food he ordered and the wine he dug out of the cellar, he thawed out Max's attitude to the point that we did all play Monopoly together. Max even muttered a slightly forced "Sorry I was a dick" to me later, after reluctantly admitting how much fun he'd had. At the end of the night, I plucked up the courage to apologise to Heath. He'd turned to me in the corridor and looked down at me with that movie star smile that took my breath away.

"I had much more fun with you, Midge, than I would have had with any of those French birds." Then he ruffled my hair before leaning down to kiss my cheek. I was still standing in the corridor, face hot with my hand on my cheek, when my parents came bustling in through the door a few minutes later.

PRESENT

Yaz

As I lay face down on my bed, sobbing into my pillow, I realised that that had been it for me back then. I'd fallen in love. Hopelessly and completely in love. And no boy since had ever measured up to Heath giving me that light kiss on my cheek all those years ago. Not until this afternoon. I sat up in bed and scrubbed away the tears that I didn't seem to be able to force down. Okay, so Heath had been kind to me as a child and that had led to this abnormal fixation on him. But I had to accept that either the man I'd fallen for had changed beyond recognition, or maybe he'd never really existed. Enough was enough. I needed some self-respect.

Never in my plan.

Not really the type of woman I'm looking for.

Coming around to the idea of 'us'.

Heath's words floated through my brain, and I had to stifle

another sob. Years of dreams about this man declaring his undying love for me had been shattered by the awful reality of him sounding casually resigned to a relationship *despite his better judgement,* purely because he was too attracted to me to stay away. Saying he had too much respect for Max to leave me high and dry after a one-night stand. Well, at least he has respect for one member of my family, because it was certainly in short supply when he was speaking to *me.* And there was no point him worrying about Max. I was never telling Max about this. I was telling no one about this. And Heath could take his self-sacrificing arse off to find the type of woman he was actually looking for, because this woman was never speaking to him again.

Chapter 12

Haven't you ever been blocked before?

HEATH

"What does it mean when you send a text, but it doesn't say delivered underneath it?"

I had just interrupted Josh explaining his latest anxiety-riddled reflective entry in his portfolio. He looked up from his notes and frowned at me.

"Er–"

"I think my bloody phone's playing up," I muttered as I looked back down at the screen, which was filled with a string of texts to Yaz, all of which did not have the delivered message after them. Josh let out a nervous, quickly muffled snort of laughter and I abandoned gazing at my phone to narrow my eyes at him.

"The phone's fine," he said, his lips twitching for some reason.

"Then why can't I get any messages to go through?"

"Haven't you ever been blocked before?"

"Blocked? What the bloody hell do you mean *blocked*?"

Josh shrugged. "I mean that when a text won't deliver to

someone's phone, it's because they've blocked you. What happens when you ring the number? Does it like just ring once and then go to voicemail?"

I felt heat creep up my neck as I bristled in indignation. "I have not been blocked! That's something that happens to... to stalkers and weirdos."

Josh did laugh this time but stopped abruptly when I shot him a murderous look.

"Right, well," Josh paused and cleared his throat, eyeing me with a nervous expression. "I hate to break it to you, but it happens plenty to us normal blokes. My ex blocked me rather than tell me she wanted to break up. Ghosted me. And I was blocked by the last person I went on a date with the minute we parted ways – I mean I had only taken her out for a Nando's, which may have been an error. She was wearing a dress and heels, so it's possible I misjudged that one slightly. My nan even blocked me once for being too needy. Anyway, welcome to my world."

I stared down at my phone and felt the heat in my neck seep up into my face. Women did not block me. I didn't think a woman had ever rejected me in my entire life. Women returned my texts, they answered my calls. To be honest, it was more common for them to be the ones calling me rather than the other way around.

"Damn it," I muttered at my phone, forgetting Josh was hovering next to me. "How the hell am I going to get to speak to her now?"

"Er..." Josh ventured tentatively.

I flashed Josh an annoyed look, and he swallowed nervously. Seriously, the man needed to grow a bloody backbone.

"Well, if she's *blocked you,* then she probably doesn't want to speak to you. Take it from a former blockee – you'd be better off leaving her alone."

"Some bird blocked you, mate?" Ruben, the orthopaedic consultant, said as he sauntered over to the central desk. He was grinning from ear to ear, the bastard. "Losing your touch, are you?"

"Bugger off, Ruben," I said, shoving my phone into my back pocket and standing up from my stool. "It's complicated."

"If a woman blocks you, then you really should respect that, you know," said my colleague Liz, as she approached the desk behind Ruben.

"I'm not some bloody stalker," I said through gritted teeth.

"I'm not suggesting that. I'm just saying that you've got to respect boundaries. You can't–"

"She's in love with me, okay!" I burst out, then immediately regretted it when Ruben's smile widened and Liz's frown deepened.

"Funny way of showing it, Casanova," Ruben put in. He was thoroughly enjoying this. I knew he was still holding a grudge from the recovery staff voting me "most fuckable" three years ago. I'd kept the title despite his best efforts with his open shirt collars, shameless flirting and grotesque displays of arm muscles. He'd even strutted through the department in his cycling lycra a couple of times – if anything, it put them off.

"Sometimes signals can be confusing," Liz told me in a serious tone, and I groaned. Liz had teenagers at home and she was speaking to me like I was one of them. "But we have to respect other people's decisions otherwise all the lines of consent become blurred and we can–"

"Oh my *God*. I'm not some creepy stalker. You don't understand."

"Just to say – that's exactly the kind of thing a creepy stalker would say," Liz said with an apologetic shrug.

"Oh wow. I can't wait to tell the recovery staff, mate," said Ruben. "Your approval rating will be right in the shit after this."

I rolled my eyes and pushed up from my stool. "Liz, shall we handover the patient?"

"Right, of course. We can talk about this later."

I kept my mouth shut. I would not be talking to Liz about my private life later or receiving another lecture, but I needed to get her off the main floor before the whole department thought I was some sort of leech that couldn't take no for an answer.

"Let's go to the office."

"But—"

"Josh, you can come too. I'll hear about your latest crisis of confidence in there."

Liz and I started moving towards the office with Josh trailing after us. Ruben's laughter echoed around the department as we went.

Blocked. Blocked! I had a flashback of a thirteen-year-old Yaz looking up at me like I was the saviour of the modern world when I told the Hardcastles about my first week on the wards working as a doctor. I remembered her smile that lit up the room when I'd arrive at her house to pick Max up; the joy on her face when I offered to let her tag along to the pub as long as she stuck to lemonade; or her expression when I made Max let her watch a film and eat pizza with us. Then there was that day when she was eleven and I'd taught her to surf in Saint Tropez – just before we arrived back at the villa she'd looked up at me with unbridled adoration, her expression so earnest as she put her small hand on my arm and told me, "You are the kindest most... most wonderful man I've ever met in my life." She then turned bright red and sprinted away before I could get out my reply, but those words had stayed with me.

That eleven-year-old's high regard has always meant something to me. The fact was, I wasn't always a good person. Especially not at twenty-one. I was an over-privileged, entitled shithead a lot of the time. Back then I treated women like crap. I was ambitious and put my career ahead of anything else. Yes, given my childhood there were excuses I could make for myself. Reasons for the emotional detachment. With the childhood Verity and I had had it was a wonder we were able to form any successful relationships full stop. I had thought that was improving over the years. But I'd certainly displayed a record level of arrogance, emotional stupidity, and insensitivity in my recent interactions with Yaz.

I couldn't get over the look on her face after I'd told her we "may as well" be together. It was as though the scales had finally fallen from her eyes where I was concerned, and she was seeing me for the first time as the horrible callous human I really was. Being well and truly knocked off that pedestal was harder than I realised. And to make matters worse, if I thought my obsessional craving for her would diminish after actually being with her, I was sorely mistaken. Staying away from her, not being even able to contact her, was now an actual source of physical pain. I wasn't eating, I couldn't sleep, I couldn't concentrate on anything. I *needed* to see her. I needed to make it right and take that awful look off her face. But seeing as I was bloody well blocked, ringing her didn't seem to be an option. I would have to be creative. It wasn't like I had never had to work for anything in my life before. Okay, so women had never required much effort on my part, but I was capable of it, surely. I just had to work out a way to speak to her without seeming desperate.

∽

"You seem a little desperate, mate," Bodhi said with a smirk.

I was seriously going to punch this bastard in the face. It had been over a week since Yaz had blocked me, and it was proving harder than I anticipated to get anywhere near her. I'd visited her flat twice – neither time with any success. In fact, on the second visit, Bryn had even taken it upon himself to come out into the corridor, waving his stick in my face and telling me to bugger off. I'd thought the old boy had warmed to me after the last time, but he seemed to have had a rather extreme change of heart.

"I'm so sorry to have disturbed you, Mr Pickering," I'd said, "but if you would be kind enough to tell Yazmin that I called round, I just– "

"I might be old but I've still all my marbles, kid," he interrupted me. "She's not been right since you brought us home. I'll not have some young buck upset my Yaz. She didn't crack a smile once when she brought me my shopping this week. Didn't even want to stay for *Countdown* and she *always* stays for *Countdown*. It's like you've drained the life right out of her. Now, bugger off."

I hadn't gone back there since. Bryn looked like he really would do himself an injury if he swung that stick around much more – I didn't want his broken hip on my conscience as well as everything else. My new tactic was to hang around Max and Verity's office and to drop into Max and Mia's house unannounced. But there were only so many times I could do that without looking suspicious. Last night I'd stayed for dinner. I think Mia could tell I was down (although thankfully she didn't know why – if she knew *that* I was quite sure she would not be serving me chicken casserole and giving me sympathetic looks) and she was trying to make me feel better. Max, not having quite the tact of his wife, put up with me for the first couple of nights but after I'd eaten Mia's cooking for the third night in a row he lost his patience. After supper, he took Mia by the hand and headed towards the stairs.

"Er... what are we doing tonight, guys? A film?" I asked.

"There's nowt *we'll* doing, you tosser. *I'm* going upstairs with my wife," Max snapped.

"Max!" Mia squeaked, swatting him on the arm as her face flooded with colour.

"I don't think that's really my scene, so I'll just stay down here and maybe we– "

"Get out of my house!" he yelled in exasperation.

"Max," hissed Mia as she was tugged along behind him up the stairs. She didn't seem to be putting up much of a fight, truth be told.

"Love, you're one that said earlier that you wanted to–"

"Shut *up!*" Mia reached up and put her hand over his mouth. Her face was still red, but she was suppressing a smile. "You've got no tact, you big oaf."

"You love this big oaf," he smiled down at her, then bent to scoop her up off the ground to carry her, pregnant and all, up the stairs. "Let yourself out, dickhead," he shouted behind him.

"Sorry, Heath," Mia's voice trailed off into giggles as they disappeared from sight.

So, it looked like hanging out at Max and Mia's wasn't an option. I needed to choose a different potential-run-in-with-Yaz location. Which is what led me to the beach at the harbour, standing next to Bodhi the *Point Break* wannabe and waiting for Yaz to come off the water.

"Shouldn't you be out there helping?" I asked him.

Yaz was currently supervising about five kids on wind-surfers. Some were getting the hang of it, but most were floundering. I watched as one kid wobbled and dropped the sail for the third time. His shout of annoyance was loud enough for us to hear from the shore as he listed to the side and fell off the board completely. Yaz immediately steered her windsurfer over to him. When she reached him, she let her sail fall into the water and sat on her board. The kid emerged from the sea, his movements angry. He then slapped the water before clambering back onto his board. He stood up again and tried to yank the sail out of the water, but the same thing happened again. This time, when he got back onto his board, Yaz leaned over and pulled his rigging towards her. I could see her mouth moving. The kid was giving jerky nods. I heard him shout again and saw Yaz gesture for him to sit on his board as well. He slumped down to sitting and his board rocked underneath him. Yaz used both hands to steady his board and manoeuvred it so they were facing each other, then she put her hands onto his shoulders. The boy looked tense for a few moments, but as he listened to whatever Yaz was saying he seemed to relax his stiff posture. A couple more nods later and Yaz smiled at him. His eyes went wide, and I knew in that moment the only thing he was seeing was this beautiful woman lighting up his world. Before long his shoulders were shaking, and I realized she'd managed to make him laugh. As she pushed away the boy stood up on his board. His movements were no longer jerky with anger so he could balance better than before, pulling up the sail and making wobbly progress across the harbour.

"Don't know how she puts up with them," Bodhi commented. "That's why I'm staying on the shore as lifeguard, ready to man the rescue boat. The little bastards are all so whiny. Pay is total shit as well. We'd be much better off sticking to the rich arseholes who wanna impress their mates with their extreme sports skills. But, you know Yaz – she's a sucker for a kid. Says it's a crying shame there's not a better academy set up for them here. To be honest, I'd prefer the little bastards stayed out of my water. Can't tell Yaz that, though."

Of course Yaz wanted to teach kids to windsurf. I could still picture her grateful, earnest face after I'd done the same for her all those years ago with surfing. Yet again my stomach hollowed out, and I felt a little ill. How long until I could claw back that level of regard from her? Was it even possible?

"So, you don't say any of this to her, then?" I asked, keeping an eye on Yaz as she made her way out to a girl who was trying to tack. The wetsuit Yaz had on was hot-pink and black. It had long arms, but the legs ended high on her tanned thighs. Her wet hair was piled on top of her head. She looked incredible.

Bodhi let out a bark of laughter. "Not a chance, mate. Got to keep her sweet. She's good for business. If she knew I'm eventually planning to can the kid side of things, I doubt she'd work with me." He shrugged. "She turned down enough offers before me and those poor bastards are now losing all their business to us. If they'd agreed to the kid thing, they wouldn't be totally fucked now."

"Don't you think that's a little disingenuous?"

"It's shady as fuck, but there's no other way to work with her and I certainly don't want to be in competition with her."

"Aren't you worried I'll tell her what you've just said?"

Bodhi snorted a laugh and slapped me on the back. I had the overwhelming urge again to punch him in the face. "Don't think I need to worry about that. She hates you, fella. Doesn't matter what I tell you – she wouldn't believe a word you said. Must say, I know I can be a bit of a prick, but *you* really took the prize didn't you?"

I crossed my arms over my chest and stared out to sea. How had I managed to get myself into a position where I was being lectured by this pathetic specimen of humanity?

"Anyway, once I convince her about Brazil, we'll be out of the country for six months of the year anyway, so it won't matter."

"What?" My voice rose in surprise and he smiled a smug little smile at me.

"Hasn't told you, has she? That's the direction the business is going in. Big waves in Brazil. Ultimate guided windsurfing adventures. None of this pissing about with kids in shitty Poole Harbour. We'll be living the high life funded by the super-rich."

I uncrossed my arms and took a step back. I could actually feel the colour draining out of my face. Yaz hadn't mentioned the leaflet I'd seen in her flat again – I'd assumed it was off the boil now. "She can't leave for Brazil."

"Why not? Nothing tying her here."

"Her family's here. All her friends. People she cares about. What about her yoga classes and her alternative therapies?"

He let out another bark of laughter. "All that bullshit will have to be put on hold. Other than the yoga – we need that for strengthening and balance. Anyway, the money she makes from that is pocket change compared to the fees we'll charge for the guiding. Most of that crap she does for free, anyway."

"For free?"

"Do you really think Yaz charges a load of old age pensioners the full rate for a yoga class? Or even those un-yummy mummies who drag their fat arses there every week?" He snorted. "She's all about giving back to the community. Least savvy business mind I've ever come across. But she's in business with me now, so all that's going to change."

"You're taking advantage of her."

"I'm going to make us both rich, you idiot. It's not like I'm exploiting her as an employee – she'll be in business with me 50/50 split. And we'll be raking it in, you mark my words. You wouldn't believe the prices we'll be charging in September."

"September?"

"That's when we leave for Brazil. Six months out there, then we'll rethink."

"Yaz has already agreed to Brazil?"

"Well, she hasn't exactly agreed yet. Money doesn't seem to be the motivator with her. Last time we spoke about it she was wondering how fulfilling it would be." He let out another bark of laughter. "I mean *fulfilling*, what a joke. You've got the best environment for water sports in the world out there. She'll be guiding competent windsurfers down beautiful coastline. Constant adrenaline, constantly doing what she loves on the water. Loads of cash. What's the problem? Well, she's warmed up a bit to the idea this week, so there is hope."

Great. This was just fucking great. Yaz was going to leave for Brazil of all places. For six months. And it didn't take too much intelligence to guess exactly what had prompted her recent change of heart about leaving.

"Yo! Bodhi!" a man shouted as he came jogging up to us. He was also sporting overlong hair and wearing board shorts with a rash vest. "You going out in that storm that's coming in? It's gonna be motherfucking insane."

"Bloody hell," I muttered as I followed the direction this guy was pointing in. There were some serious black clouds coming in from the sea. The wind was picking up as well.

"We've gotta leave now though, dude," the rash-vest guy said. "We can launch from the beach side."

Bodhi flicked a glance at Yaz, who was still out there with the kids. "Ah, she'll be right," he muttered under his breath. "Okay, Roach, let's kill it."

As he turned to follow *Roach*, I caught hold of his arm to stop him. "Aren't you supposed to be helping Yaz?"

"She's run over time, anyway. The kids'll come in any minute."

"That storm is coming now. She shouldn't have to get all the– "

"Not my problem, bro. You're so hot for her, you try to get the kids in."

"Wow, nice attitude."

"Look, I'm not the one that needs to butter her up. All I need to do is stay in business with her. I've tried getting in her pants and that pussy is closed for bros."

I rolled my eyes. "She's not a lesbian."

"Hmm-kay, whatever. Not many heterosexual ladies turn this down." He made a sweeping gesture from his face to his body, as if demonstrating that any straight woman would be mad to turn down such a magnificent specimen of a man. Wow, this guy was truly horrific. How had he managed to hide it from Yaz? This was the total opposite of how he came across at the pub. He slapped my shoulder. "You want to waste your time trying to butter her muffin, be my guest. I've got some waves to ride."

Chapter 13

Please, just give me a chance

HEATH

With Bodhi gone, I was left alone staring out at Yaz and the kids as the rain started and the wind rustled the trees behind me. It was only a few moments before everything closed in. The howling gale and sheet rain made it difficult to even make out all the children. Shielding my eyes from the rain, I saw Yaz dragging three rigs, with kids in tow, towards the shore. There were two other children following behind.

"Has he left her again?" I heard a shout next to me against the wind, and turned to see Dee jogging up to the shoreline in a wetsuit with a kite bag over her shoulder.

"Does he often bail on her when she's teaching?" I yelled back when she drew up next to me.

"I've seen Yaz dragging all the equipment in by herself more times than I can count over the last month," she said. "He's a lazy git, if you ask me."

"Haven't you spoken to Yaz about it?"

Dee shrugged. "That girl lacks self-esteem. I've told her he should pitch in more, but she's worried if she asks too much of

107

him he'll abandon the business. She won't believe me that she doesn't need him helping her at all. Nobody comes here for Bodhi. I don't know who's made her feel that she should accept his bullshit," Dee gave me a significant look at this point. "She doesn't seem to have a whole lot of support from her family or any other backers either, so she feels without Bodhi she'd be a bit lost."

My chest felt tight. I was seeing for the first time that Yaz was very much on her own. All her family, and I for that matter, did was erode her self-esteem to the point where she felt she should 'accept bullshit'.

"Crap, I'd better go in," Dee said, before wading into the water, leaving me on the water's edge. I hesitated a moment and then, cursing under my breath, kicked off my shoes and followed her. The reason Poole Harbour is so good for learning to windsurf is because of how shallow the water is. Even a good fifty yards from the shoreline, it was still only up to my waist. I made it out to the furthest kid who was attempting to heave her rig against the rain and wind. I shouted that I was a friend of Yaz's, then told her to hold on to the board. I dragged her rig and board over to the next kid and told her the same. Then I pulled both rigs, with kids attached, to the shore. Yaz met me halfway. She and Dee had already managed to get most of the other kids and their rigs to shore – they were now huddled under the shelter of the canopy with Dee.

"What are you doing here?" she yelled over the wind as she grabbed one rig, smiling at both the children before she scowled at me. The wind had picked up speed now and the sail of one rig suddenly flipped over the board and smacked Yaz on the shoulder.

"Midge! Are you okay?" I was desperately trying to keep hold of both boards when all I wanted to do was to go to her and check her bloody arm wasn't broken.

"I'm fine," she yelled. I'd seen her flinch of pain as the mast came down, though. She wasn't fine and now I could see she wasn't using that arm. But all her focus was on the children. She moved past me and manoeuvred both girls so they were holding onto the foot straps of each of their rigs. Then she wrestled one of the rigs from me. The wind was so strong that I had to let her take it or risk losing hold of them. We dragged both rigs and children to the shore. As soon as we got there, she bundled the other two up into towels and Dry Robes under the canopy and thanked Dee, insisting that she head out to go kiting. Parents had started to arrive now. Yaz was talking to them. One dad spoke mostly to her chest. I crossed my arms over mine and stared at them until pervy dad noticed me. When he did, he jerked his chin up and gave me a weak smile before hustling his kid away. Once the last child had left, Yaz walked back towards me and the rigging. The rain was nearly horizontal now, and the wind had whipped some of her hair free of the elastic band.

"How's your shoulder?" I said, instinctively reaching towards her to check that the joint was okay, but freezing when she flinched away from me. That hollow feeling was back.

"Where's Bodhi?" she snapped as she struggled with the rigging of one of the kid's windsurfers.

"He flaked – went to 'catch some waves'. Real reliable guy you're in business with."

"You don't know him." She shot me an angry look and went back to what she was doing, but I could see the red stain on her wet cheeks.

I wasn't about to argue with her about Bodhi – that would be counterproductive. She rolled her shoulder a couple of times before bending down to roll up the sail, which was blowing in the wind.

"You shouldn't be doing that, Yaz. You're hurt."

She straightened from what she was doing and put her foot on top of the sail to stop it blowing away. "Listen, thank you for helping me get the girls in," she said through gritted teeth, sounding anything but grateful. "But you can go. Now."

The wind was dying down now, but the rain was still pelting us. "I'll help you pack this all up. Then you need to let me look at your shoulder."

"I don't *need* to do anything. Why are you even here? I don't want your negative energy pulling my chakras out of whack. Bugger off."

I was proud of myself for suppressing an eye roll and holding in a short laugh. In Yaz language, "negatively affecting her chakras" was a serious insult.

"I wanted to talk to you and you're not answering my calls."

"Listen, if you're worried that I'm going to tell Max about... what happened – I told you I won't breathe a word. The last thing I want him to know is that I was a notch on your bedpost."

"You're not a notch on my bedpost! I don't–"

"Oh my God, spare me, please. Go and peddle your bull-shit to someone who wants to listen to it. So, we had sex. Big deal."

"It *is* a big deal. I told you I–"

She stopped what she was doing and her eyes flashed as she looked up at me. "If you mention your pathetic offer of a pity relationship ever again, I shall forget my oath on non-violence I made at the last solstice and hang your balls from my kitesurfer."

"Yaz–"

"I mean it, Heath." The anger faded from her voice now, making it all the more heart-wrenching to hear. "I can't take any more of that from you. Don't go there again. You've no idea how much it costs me."

I took a deep breath in and let it out slowly. Rivers of water were rolling down her face and dripping off her nose and eyelashes as the rain continued to pound down on us. She looked so beautiful it almost took my breath away. Seemingly of its own accord, my hand reached up slowly to her face. This time she didn't flinch away, as though she was frozen in shock watching my hand's progress. My fingertips grazed the side of her cheek to her jawline as my thumb swept water from her cheekbone. I'd moved forward and there was only an inch separating us. It felt like an outside force was drawing us together. Like it was out of either of our control.

"Please," I whispered. Absolute desperation threaded through that one word. Her lips parted as she stared up into my eyes. I thought for a moment we were going to kiss. We both swayed towards each other a fraction, but then Yaz blinked. A frown marred her forehead as she seemed to come back to herself. Both her hands went up to my chest and she pushed away from me, hard. As she moved back, I was left standing with my hand raised, just air now where her face had been.

"Don't you *dare* touch me. Ever again."

Her words were so cold, so final, I almost shivered there in the rain. I took a step away and held both my hands up in surrender. "Okay, I'm sorry. *Really* sorry. I just... please just let me help you pack up. That's all."

She stared at me with a mutinous expression, water running down her face and slicking her hair to her head. One sail chose that moment to flip over and pull the board with it. She glanced that way and then around at all the sails still to pack away and her shoulders dropped in defeat. "Fine," she clipped, back to ignoring me as she bent over to roll up the sail at her feet. I saw her roll her shoulder again and resisted the urge to order her under the canopy and let me finish all of this. At that point, I doubted I could order her to do anything. It took a good half hour before all the sails and boards were stowed away. Yaz clearly wasn't tall enough to reach the highest racks. I could hear her muttering about "sexist bloody storage systems" as I dragged the final board into the shed.

"Let me," I said, as I came up behind her and reached for the board before lifting it easily up there. My arm brushed against hers briefly before she leapt away as if I'd burned her skin.

"Right, well, thanks again," she said, not making eye contact as she stowed the last of the sails. "I'll just–" I moved quickly to stand in her way, careful not to get too far into her space.

"Yaz, please, can I talk to you just for a minute?" My voice had a pleading quality that I don't think I'd ever heard myself use before. Then again, I'd never been quite so desperate.

"We've said everything we need to say." Her voice was dull, and she was still avoiding eye contact. "I don't know what you're playing at, but there's nothing to atone for here. We both enjoyed what happened. The end. You're free to go off and find your suitable life partner – one who ticks all your boxes and not one you have to settle for."

"That's not what I want, Midge." Couldn't she see the misery written all over me? The dark circles under my eyes because I couldn't sleep without dreaming of her, the terror in my voice that she might be slipping through my fingers. "All I want is you. All I can think about is you."

"You'll get over it." She flicked her hand out dismissively and went to step around me, but I moved with her.

"I won't *get over it*. Didn't you feel it too?" Disbelief and desperation were back in my voice. "I've never felt like that with anyone in my life. I feel like I can't breathe when I'm not near you. Like I'm underwater and can't get to the surface. Even being near you with you hating me like this makes me feel more alive than I've felt for the last two weeks."

Her eyes widened during my speech and her mouth fell slightly open. She blinked up at me and a droplet of water fell from one of her lashes onto her cheekbone. I resisted the urge to move any closer, instinctively knowing I had to let her come to me. Her pupils dilated as her eyes took on that glazed look I recognised. Slowly, very slowly, her hand came up to my chest where she laid it flat over my heart, which felt like it was beating out of my chest.

"Heath," she whispered on an exhale, her other hand going up to my neck as she swayed towards me.

"Yes," I whispered back, my breath mingling with hers just before her lips meet mine. It was a light brush at first and I thought I had everything under control, but then she went up onto her tiptoes, her tongue swept into my mouth and that was it. Control was a thing of the past. My arms clamped around her, pulling her body into mine as I deepened the kiss. We backed up slowly until she was against the kayaks on the side wall of the shed. Her hand slipped around my back and under my t-shirt. Desperate to feel her skin, I reached up to the back of her neck to find the zip on her wetsuit. But at the sound of the Velcro and then the zip opening, she froze. After a moment, her lips broke away from mine and she tore away from me. Immediately, I stepped back, even though it felt like my heart was being ripped from my body.

"What am I doing?" Yaz whispered as she glanced around the shed a little wildly. She reached behind herself to do up the zip, but her hands were shaking and she kept fumbling with it. I took a step towards her, but she held up her hand to ward me off. "Stay back," she choked out, her eyes filling with tears.

"It's okay," I said, trying to keep my voice steady, calm. "Just... let me help you." I approached her slowly, and she sighed in resignation, sweeping her hair to the side so I could get to the zip and pull it up. I secured the Velcro over it for good measure, then spun around to grab her Dry Robe that was on the floor next to the kayaks. She let me help her into that and even zip her up to under her neck. Her mouth was in a tight line and she was avoiding eye contact. Once the zip was up to under her chin and none of her wetsuit clad body other than her lower legs were on show, I took a step back and cleared my throat.

"Midge, can we just spend some time together? Just talking. We can't ignore this thing between us. What just happened proved that."

"All *this* proves is that we need to stay away from each other." Her voice grew more distant and I could feel her withdrawing. That desperation gripped me again.

"Please, Midge." My voice was hoarse now. "I'm begging you. Please, just give me a chance."

Her gaze softened, and one of her hands lifted a couple of inches towards me. Just for a moment, I thought I might have broken through. But then she blanked her expression again and her hand dropped to her side. "You don't understand how much this could cost me. You've never understood." Her eyes raised to meet mine now, lit with determination. "You've hurt me, Heath. You've let me down. Not just now, but over the last few years. You're not the man I thought you were. I won't risk getting more involved with you. I'm not going down that rabbit hole. Now, all I'm asking is that you respect that and stay away from me." I opened my mouth to speak, but she swept out of there before I could get the words out, and for the first time since I was a child, I felt totally and utterly lost.

Chapter 14

I couldn't breathe in there

YAZ

Don't get me wrong – I love my mum and dad. But the last thing I needed right now was to have lunch with them. After the last encounter with Heath, I felt like I'd been turned inside out. My emotions were all over the place. Even the open water, which always settled my mind, didn't seem to cut it at the moment. The wind had been fantastic over the last week. I'd pulled off some jumps and lifts with my kitesurfer that topped anything I'd done before. Bodhi was getting more and more excited about the sponsorship offers we were getting. I mean the free kit and exposure for the business was great, and if I did decide to agree to Brazil it would be a perfect side hustle. But for me, all this felt like selling out. And the sponsors didn't just want to film the kiting, they even wanted to interview me. They said I was perfect for the brand. It was all just so corporate. But I was allowing myself to be swept along with it because I didn't seem to have the mental energy to decide whether it was right for me or not. All of that energy seemed to be engaged in squashing memories of Heath's lips on mine. His words floated through my head at the weirdest times.

I've never felt like that with anyone in my life.

That was what I heard as I was flying through the air yesterday, at least ten feet up – the highest I'd ever managed to get above the water.

I feel like I can't breathe when I'm not near you.

After I landed, my vision blurred and I almost lost control of the kite. It took a moment for me to realise that not all the wet on my cheeks was from sea water.

So, although I loved my parents, I wasn't really in the right state of mind to deal with them. My mum and dad required a certain level of mental resilience. They loved me, but they didn't really respect me or my life choices.

My mum had grown up in Yorkshire. Her childhood was relatively tough, and then her marriage to her first husband (Max's dad – a hard, cruel man who ran his farm and his home with an iron fist) was even tougher. She and Max lived with him for the first ten years of Max's life before she'd finally had enough and left. She met my father after she'd moved down south to get away from Max's dad.

My father is, by contrast, a gentle man, quiet and caring. He's a local GP. Mum is a science teacher and Max an architect. All of them are professionals. They all have serious jobs and live serious lives. I, on the other hand, was never academic at school. University didn't appeal to me; really anything that might take me away from the sea didn't appeal to me. And my family have never been able to understand what they consider to be my aimless path in life.

Maybe it's because Mum and Max both had hard, uncompromising existences before they moved away from Yorkshire, so they see my freer lifestyle as frivolous. I had long ago given up trying to explain what I was doing and what motivated me.

They just didn't understand. Their eyes glazed over if I started talking about spirituality, reiki, yoga, the healing powers of the sea... anything I really cared about. They were just serious people, and I... wasn't. But surely there's room for all sorts? We don't all have to be serious professionals.

It wasn't that they were deliberately trying to be hurtful when we were together – it was just all those tiny little digs, those small comments that acted like paper cuts to my self-esteem. I usually meditated by the sea before I saw my parents so that I felt centred, so that I could react to things calmly, accept that they didn't understand and not let them get to me. But right now, meditation simply wasn't an option. I couldn't clear my mind of Heath's voice, no matter how hard I tried. And if I gave my subconscious any leeway at all, I was back there underneath him, feeling him all around me, my body more alive than it had ever felt in my life. So no, there was no chance of my achieving a Zen state and being centred today. I would just have to make it through a family get together with no prep work. At least Mia would be there. Thank God for Mia. Family meals were way more tolerable with her around.

As I approached the massive door to Max's house, I heard a loud thud from behind it, followed by Roger's frenzied barking and whining. I didn't have time to see who had opened the door before sixty kilograms of over excited Alsatian knocked me off my feet. I laughed and hugged him around his thick, furry neck as he proceeded to lick my entire face with his paws on my shoulders.

"Come on, buddy," I said as I pushed him so I could kiss his head and ruffle his ears. "No tongue before nine." A hand was held out to me and a shiver went up my spine. I followed the hand up the muscled forearm and my throat closed over when I realised who was standing there. "Heath." I said his name on an exhale. It felt like all the wind had been knocked out of me. "What are you doing here?"

"Your mum and dad invited me and Verity. I haven't seen them in ages." His hand was still outstretched to me, but I ignored it and pushed myself up instead. He lowered his voice as I regained my feet. "I can leave if it makes you uncomfortable."

"Don't bother, Mum and Dad would be crushed. They always thought you were the bee's knees. They'd probably much rather have you here than me, to be honest."

"Midge, that's not true. They've missed you. They said you've been busy the last couple of family meet ups."

I rolled my eyes. "Whatever," I muttered under my breath. I would not waste time explaining why interactions with my parents were best kept to a minimum. Last time we were all together, Heath had agreed with them when they'd indulged their habit of *affectionate teasing,* which was basically crapping all over my life choices and calling me a waste of space. I had no idea why it should come as any surprise to him that I might want to limit my exposure to that sort of self-esteem bashing.

"I mean it, Yaz. If you want me to leave, I will." Heath's voice was still lowered. He touched my arm as I passed him, but I flinched away and darted in through the door.

"Stay," I said over my shoulder. "You'll just disappoint Mum and Dad if you go."

Before he could say anything else, I had opened the door at the end of the corridor and was in the huge double-height, open-plan living space. Light poured in through the wall of glass that stretched up to the second story, and fell onto Mum, Dad and Verity all sitting at the kitchen island. Opposite were Max and Mia, who was cooking while she smiled at my parents.

"Yaz!" Mia dropped the wooden spoon she was using to stir

the pasta sauce and jogged around the island to give me a hug. I smiled and hugged her back, her bump was starting to really hinder hugs now which I found exciting. Mia was one of my favourite people. I was so glad my brother had found her. She'd come a long way. Spontaneous affection did not used to come naturally to her after long years of abuse from her ex-husband. But that was changing now thanks to my brother and, according to Mia, thanks to me too (spontaneous affection was definitely one of my strong points). "I haven't seen you in ages. Where have you been hiding?"

I laughed. "I've not been hiding." That wasn't strictly true. To a certain extent, I had been avoiding Max and Mia in an attempt to avoid Heath at all costs. It wasn't fair to Mia, but my self-preservation instincts had kicked in. "I'm just busy right now with everything."

"Hey stranger," said Verity, she looked effortlessly glamourous as always – her hair swept up in casual bun, beautiful face perfectly made-up, four-inch heels on her feet. I don't think I'd ever seen Verity in flats. Her only concession to today being a supposedly relaxed Sunday was the fact she was wearing jeans. She gave me her standard two kisses and a hug. As she pulled back I noticed some dark circles under her eyes despite the make-up. I opened my mouth to ask her if she was okay but Mum cut off what I was going to say.

"The wind's been good, has it, love?" Mum said, as she stood from her stool. Verity released me so I could move to hug Mum and then Dad.

"Well, it's not just that. I've–"

"Max sent us this latest video, sweetheart," Dad said as he gave me a squeeze, then set me back to frown down at me. "It all looked *very* dangerous. Your mother and I were a bit shocked."

"These television crews will encourage you to do all sorts,

love," Mum put in. "I'm not surprised that they just want to get your pretty face on camera, but I'm sure they could sell swimsuits without you doing all that stuff out on the water."

"I know what I'm doing," I said with a forced smile. Mum looked at my father who sighed.

"Maybe you think you do, but you're taking too many risks—"

"Listen, let's eat, shall we?" Mia, ever the peacemaker, interrupted. Mum opened her mouth to speak again, but Max, who'd come up behind me to ruffle my hair, moved to Mum and steered her towards the table. Thankfully the conversation moved onto Max and Verity's new environmentally friendly affordable housing project. They'd been back on *Better Homes* last month. Mum was nearly bursting with pride.

"It's the talk of the Women's Institute," she said. "That Carole Taylor is always banging on about her human rights lawyer daughter, and here my son is housing the nation and saving the environment." She beamed at Max and he shifted uncomfortably in his chair. "And I was so proud of you too, Verity, love. And we heard about that huge campus building for the London School of Economics. Max tells me you're the driver behind that project." Verity flinched at the mention of the campus building that the business was pitching for in central London. She returned my mum's warm smile but it didn't meet her eyes. To be honest she'd seemed distracted all meal, and had hardly touched her food.

"Well, the chap behind that one's a right piece of work to be honest, Mum," Max muttered, eyeing Verity carefully. "Might be better we have nowt to do with him, arrogant tosser."

Verity looked down at her lap. Her face had drained of all colour now.

"Oh dear," Mum said, reaching over to rub Verity's shoulder. "Don't you put up with any nonsense, love. Plenty of other projects."

"Thanks, Fern," Verity said after clearing her throat. "But don't worry – I can deal with idiot billionaires."

"Of course you can. Best negotiator there ever was. Nobody's a match for my Verity. Billionaire or no," Mum said proudly. Verity gave her another weak smile. "And you, Mia, so brave what you did – speaking out like that."

Mia had recently spoken at a conference about her experiences with domestic violence.

"It was nothing," Mia said in a quiet voice, shrugging a little.

"Don't say that, Mia," I said, my tone so fervent that she glanced up at me with her eyebrows raised. "That was so brave and so important. What you did will help change lives. Don't play it down."

"Okay. Okay, honey." She reached over the table and squeezed my hand, a small smile on her lips but also a frown line between her eyebrows. I nodded, then realised the entire table was looking at me after my outburst. Maybe I'd come on a little strong, but I couldn't stand Mia putting herself and her achievements down like this. It wasn't only the work she was doing for domestic abuse charities, she was also the tech wizard at my brother's company and without her a lot of his projects wouldn't have been able to go ahead.

"So, Heath," Dad said after an uncomfortable silence. "How is everything in the emergency department? One of my patients spoke very highly of you the other day."

And so we moved on to Heath's achievements. I pushed my pasta around my plate, appetite a thing of the past. It appeared everyone around the table was either saving lives, housing people in need while saving the environment, or advocating for domestic abuse victims. I felt like an outsider within my own family. It wasn't only because of their worthy endeavours, it was the fact that their lives hadn't been easy. Mum, Max and Mia had been through so much. I'd had a cosseted childhood and had only ever lived a cushy existence ever since. Listening to them made me feel like a worthless, spoiled brat. My mood sank even further.

"Yazmin, are you going to eat that?" I looked up at Mum's sharp tone. "It's just you've lost weight. Those clothes you insist on wearing are hanging off you. It's bad enough that they're fraying and tattered, but they should at least fit properly."

"Mam," Max said in a warning tone.

"What? Isn't anyone else going to say anything? She's skin and bone – it's clear that she's not been taking care of herself." She turned back to me. "You shouldn't just spend all your time on the water and fiddling about with crystals, young lady. You need to eat healthily and take care of yourself as well, you know."

"Fern, I don't think–" Dad said, but Mum interrupted.

"Somebody's got to say it, Aubrey. She needs to take some responsibility for herself. Are you listening, Yazmin?"

"Sure," I muttered at my plate. "Whatever you say, Mum." My gaze went to the huge glass front of the house. I could see the wind picking up outside – the branches of the trees were moving. I wondered how long I had to sit here and put up with this. Once I could get away to the sea, then all this would disappear. I wouldn't have to worry about not feeling good enough. I wouldn't have to think about anything at all.

"I don't know if you are aware, but Yaz is actually a qualified windsurfing and yoga instructor and a certified reiki practitioner."

My head whipped around from the window to focus on Heath and my mouth fell open.

"What?" Mum asked, disbelief clear in her tone.

"Are those certificates you bought over the internet, love?" Dad asked with a chuckle, and I felt the familiar humiliation slash through me. Bloody Heath bringing up my stupid, irrelevant qualifications. I was sitting at a table with professionals who held medical, architectural and computing degrees. Was he trying to embarrass me?

"No, actually those qualifications involve a huge amount of work. And I understand she did it all while working full time." Heath's voice was laced with a fair amount of irritation now. I didn't know what he was trying to achieve, but if he thought my parents were going to be impressed with my off-beat 'qualifications', he was sorely mistaken.

"Oh well, that's great, love," Dad said.

"Yes... er, well done," Mum put in.

I'm sure they didn't mean it to happen, but their words just came across as patronising.

"Reiki?" Mum said. "That's poking around at people's feet, isn't it?"

There was a tense silence for a moment. I could have punched Heath. Dad broke the silence with a chuckle.

"Full time work you say, Heath? That's a new one as far as Yaz is concerned." He chuckled again. We were back on familiar ground now. "When you're not filling in on reception for Max, I thought you just dabbled in a bit of yoga, waved your crystals at people, then did your tricks on the water to sell a few bikinis, love."

"That's not all—" Mia started her usual defence of me. It was sweet of her, but it made no actual difference to be honest. But, to everyone's surprise, Heath cut her off.

"Yaz is a professional windsurfer and kitesurfer. She gets sponsorship because of the high standard she's reached. That's why she can sell the kit she uses – not just because she looks good in a bikini."

"We know she's good at all that, but... well, it's not exactly a career."

"Except it *is* a career. She's a business owner. Have you ever been to her well-being centre on the harbour?"

Everyone sat and stared at Heath. My mum's head was tilted to the side and her eyes were narrowed. Mum would always be the first person to guess that something was going on when I was a teenager. You couldn't hide things from Fern Hardcastle – she was too perceptive.

"Is that the little studio you use for your yoga?" Dad asked. I sighed inwardly. I did not want to discuss this with him. Dad cleared his throat, clearly uncomfortable. "Well, I'm sorry, sweetpea," he said. "You know we mean nothing by it when we tease you about your stuff. And we didn't know how hard you've been working."

"You should have said something," Mum told me, switching her piercing gaze from Heath to me.

I let out a hollow laugh and pushed my plate away. "What would be the point? I can't exactly compete with Max or any of you, can I? I'm well aware of how silly my... my *life* sounds in comparison."

"Yaz, that's not fair," Max said, frowning across the table at me. "You can't be mad at us for treating you like a flake when you act like one."

A flake. Wearing surf clothes over a bikini and flip-flops, loving the ocean and the wind, and believing in alternative therapies made me a flake. None of them had ever understood me. None of them understood how competitive the water sports market was. None of them would ever consider a well-being centre to be a proper business, not in the way that Max's was. Everything that was important to me they just brushed off as a collection of hobbies that I would grow out of. They didn't get that the passion I had for the sea wasn't something you could grow out of. Whatever else happened in my life, I would never walk away from that. All they saw was flaky, direction-less, over indulged Yaz. I was sick of it.

"I haven't asked you for money since I turned eighteen," I said to my parents, then turned to Max. "Can you say the same?"

"But... Max was in full-time education, Yazmin," Dad replied defensively.

"And architecture is a long degree course," Mum put in.

"Seven years," I said. "It's seven years."

"Well... er, yes it is," Dad went on, "but –"

"We always made it clear," interrupted Mum firmly, "that we would support either of you for as long as you were in full-time education."

"That was your way of trying to control me! Of trying to make me go to uni when you knew that wasn't what I wanted."

"You had the opportunity for a further education," Dad said, his face turning red as this old wound was opened up. "And you wasted it because you wanted to prat about on the water and with this well-being nonsense. You should have focused more on your schooling so you could get some decent qualifications."

Prat about on the water. Well-being nonsense. That's what they thought of me – that I just couldn't be bothered to put the work in at uni. Unfamiliar rage swept through me and I pushed my chair back violently from the table to stand. Everyone's eyes went wide, but I wasn't finished yet.

"I couldn't breathe in there, Dad!" I shouted, and it felt good – so, so good to finally get this off my chest. I'd been burying these feelings for years, but since I'd slept with Heath everything felt so much more raw. "I hated school. Hated being shut in. Every day felt like I was being suffocated slowly. I couldn't do it anymore. It wasn't even a choice. Don't you think it would have been easier if I'd just caved and done some shitty degree so that you'd have paid my rent? I moved out of your house with sixty quid in my bank account after I'd paid a deposit on that flat. I ate Pot Noodles and toast for six months to make ends meet. But it meant I could be on the water and I knew that's where I *had* to be.

"Do you think the kit I use is cheap? I get it for free now. I have sponsorship, but I had to work my way up to get this far. I might love windsurfing, but that doesn't mean it isn't a hard road to make a career out of. Dislocated shoulders, shredding myself on the reefs, head injuries – that's all part of the job. Not to mention the training I still have to do to stay in shape. How much stamina and upper body strength do you think it takes to do what I do? I do an hour of cardio, an hour of weights and an hour of yoga every single day. Why do you even think I started yoga? I need the strength, the flexibility and the focus it gives me. So no, I don't just *prat about on the water*. And the well-being centre helps people. There is value in this stuff you call *alternative crap*. It changes people's lives. What I do means something to me. I'm driven when it comes to my work, single-minded."

My voice dropped to a low whisper then, so that I could keep the tears that I could feel building at bay. "I know you're not proud of me. You've made that abundantly clear over the years, but don't *ever* call me directionless. I know exactly where I'm going. I have since I was twelve years old." With that, I spun on my heel and ran full pelt for the door.

Chapter 15

You're never going to do that again

YAZ

I stood on the ledge looking out over the water and felt my heart rate slow down. Always, *always* if I could make it to the sea I knew I would feel better. It was a clear day, no wind, no waves. The water was as still as a pond and so clear I could almost see the seabed from up here. Closing my eyes, I took in a deep breath through my mouth, letting it out through my nose. I couldn't believe how badly I had lost control in there. I never confronted my parents like that. But since all of this stuff with Heath had kicked off, it was like a fire had been lit inside me, and I didn't want to tolerate being put down anymore.

I felt another surge of anger and opened my eyes again to focus on the horizon. Bloody Heath, stirring things up. There was no point confronting my family. All it did was create conflict. So what if they still just assumed I was a flake? That was how my family operated: Max was the professional, responsible one; and I was the no-hoper. There really wasn't any point challenging that. I was glad that I'd left before Mum and Dad could reply. What I'd told them felt like it had been wrenched from somewhere deep in my psyche, and I just didn't think I could take them trying to placate me or, more likely, minimise what I'd said. Mum in particular had a knack of turning things around to make me feel small. I'd felt sure that she would manage that again. So, running out of there had been the best option. Luckily I hadn't bothered to chain my bike up so I could just jump straight on and take the path from the side of Max's house down to the clifftop. By the time I'd heard Heath shouting my name, I was already out of sight of the drive.

I shook my head to clear it. Enough thinking about opinions that I couldn't change. I'd spent way too much emotional energy already on that now. I reached down and pulled my t-shirt over my head, undid the button of my shorts and shimmied them down my legs. Stepping to the edge, I took one last deep breath before I launched myself into the air. As the wind rushed past my ears I thought I heard my name again, but then everything disappeared as I broke the surface of the water and felt the delicious cold envelop me. This is where my mind could really be clear. Here in the water was where I always found my soul.

I swam down, the water so clear that I could see the rocks and shells on the sea floor. Then I let myself drift a few feet below the surface, using my hands to stop myself from floating up. I could see the rock and reef below, fish and seaweed floating past, and slowly I felt my head clear – a deep sense of well-being washed over me. I'd long since trained myself to hold my breath for extended periods of time, almost as though I could meditate under the water. It involved moving as little as possible to conserve oxygen use in my muscles. I turned and pulled once through the water to swim down again, but as I was gliding along I heard a muted splash above me. Before I could turn to see what was happening, I was grabbed around the waist from behind by what felt like a band of steel and pulled upwards. I struggled but the band just tightened further until I was wrenched through the surface of the water. I blinked to clear my eyes of the salt water, spluttering as I continued to fight against the steel band around me.

"Jesus Christ," Heath's waterlogged voice sounded in my ear and I tried to turn to look at him, but he pinned me in place against his chest and began to swim. I realised he must be attempting to drag me in a lifesaver rescue hold to the shore. The direction he was headed in was littered with sharp coral that would shred us both to pieces. We needed to swim around the headland to the small inlet and the beach there. But Heath didn't know the coastline like me, and he clearly thought he was saving my life. I needed to disabuse him of this notion quickly if I was going to make sure he didn't get hurt and I didn't add to my already unsightly collection of scars.

"Heath!" I shouted. "Stop! Listen to me!" His arm loosened, and I managed to twist around so that I was facing him. His eyes were wild as they searched my face and he still kept a hold of me as if I would sink under the water at any moment, which was ridiculous seeing as I wasn't the one still wearing all my clothes. And although I knew he was a strong swimmer, it simply wasn't possible that he was a better one than me. "I'm fine. You can let go."

"You weren't fine." He sounded traumatised. "I watched you go under and you didn't come up. I thought that—"

"I free dive all the time. I know what I'm doing."

"You scared the shit out of me."

"Let's get on dry land, alright?"

"That's what I was trying to do." Heath started heaving me back in the direction of the coral again.

"Heath, stop! You're dragging us over to the rocks. We can't get out that way. You need to let me go and then follow me."

He started to shake his head, and I needed him to listen to me. So, I lifted my hand and rested it on the side of his face. "Trust me. Okay?"

His jaw clenched, but he managed a small nod, then his arm loosened so I could separate from him.

"We have to swim around the headland. There's a small inlet on the other side. Follow me. Swim exactly where I swim. I know where the rocks and reef are." Heath gave me another nod and I turned and started to swim away. I kept glancing back to make sure he was keeping up with my front crawl. Despite his clothes he managed to stay close. When we made it to the inlet, I was tempted to offer him my hand to help pull him onto dry land – the man looked exhausted – but I didn't think his pride could take any further hits. So I sat on the sand and watched him haul himself out. Instead of collapsing on the sand he walked directly out of the sea to me, his shirt moulded to his wide chest. The inlet we were in was deserted and shielded from the rest of the beach by the dunes on one side and the cliff face on the other.

"You've still got your shoes on, you weirdo," I said, glancing at his feet. "You should have taken them off. It's dangerous to swim with your feet restricted. And the leather will be ruined now." He dropped to his knees in front of where I was sitting, way too far into my personal space, and took my face in his hands, tilting it this way and that and then lifting my arms and finally looking over my legs and feet.

"You're not hurt," he said on an exhale, and filled with such a huge amount of relief that I frowned. His hands came back up to my face and slid either side of my jaw again. "Jesus Christ," he said again, his voice ragged as he searched my expression. "Don't ever do that to me again." Then he kissed me.

As his mouth met mine, that sense of relief swept over me

again. It was as though keeping our bodies apart from each other caused unacknowledged physical pain. One of my hands pushed up into his hair as I returned the kiss, craving this contact with him that had been haunting my fevered dreams for two weeks. But then voices from above us jolted my brain back into a semi-functioning state and I froze. It took a moment to realise that they were coming from the cliff path. I pushed at his huge shoulders and he immediately pulled back. Once his weight had left me, I wasted no time in leaping up to my feet and he followed suit. The voices faded away as the people passed by. Heath and I stared at each other and I felt my hands clench into fists by my sides. Just as I opened my mouth to ask him what the bloody hell he thought he was doing here, he beat me to it.

"Never do anything as dangerous as that ever again." Gone was the fear and concern, then desire from before. Heath was now clearly furious. My eyebrows shot up into my hairline and my mouth dropped open.

"Me? *I* wasn't the one sea swimming in all my bloody clothes and trying to get us both cut to shreds on the rocks. What on earth have *I* done that's dangerous?"

Heath ran both his hands through his wet hair and looked up at the sky for a moment before his eyes came back to mine. That haunted expression was back in them and his voice was also back to being ragged and tinged with disbelief. "You jumped off a cliff–"

"Pfft. It was a few feet up and–"

"It was a bloody *cliff!*"

"Well, you jumped off it too!"

"Only because I saw you disappear under the water and not resurface. I thought..." he trailed off and his face darkened again at the remembered pain. When he spoke, it was it just above a whisper. "I thought you were gone, Midge. I thought I'd lost you. Jesus, when you didn't come up, I couldn't... I didn't..." To my absolute and everlasting shock, his voice broke at the end. It was the unshed tears and his broken expression as he described me disappearing under the water that made me move to him.

"Hey, I'm okay, Heath. I promise," I said, my tone much softer as I took a step forward and reached for his hand. Once my fingers touched his, he enclosed my hand in a tight grip and pulled me towards him with a jerk against his chest. His arms wrapped themselves around me and squeezed me in a tight hug. Heath's heart was hammering in his chest under my ear and he took a huge breath in while he continued to hold me tight. I tried to pull back a little to look at his face, but he kept me right where I was. "Honestly," I mumbled, "I do that all the time." His arms flexed a little at that statement and he let out a rush of air. "I know where all the rocks are. I know this whole coastline like the back of my hand."

"Why didn't you surface?"

"I... I can think more clearly down there. It helps me clear my mind, makes me feel at peace, I guess."

My head moved with his chest as it expanded with another deep breath. He loosened his grip so that he could look at my face, but kept me in the circle of his arms. "I know I don't deserve to tell you what to do."

"Er... I hate to tell you this, big man, but even if you *hadn't* been a prick to me, you *still* wouldn't be able to tell me what to do. I'm kind of a fan of free will."

"Right, I understand that, but could I ask a favour? Even though I don't deserve it?"

"Depends what the favour is."

"Please, never do that again."

I frowned. "I just explained to you I knew what I was doing. You're the one who was in danger wearing all your clothes and those stupid shoes. I'm a strong swimmer and I know this coastline."

"Nobody should ever jump off a cliff–"

"It wasn't a–" His arms tightened for a moment to cut me off.

"Nobody should jump off a cliff into the water to free dive, not surfacing for longer than should be humanly possible on their own. Especially without anyone even knowing where they were."

I rolled my eyes. "It's fine. I–"

"Anything can happen, Yaz. You're the one that knows the sea so well, so you know that I'm telling the truth. The sea is unpredictable. You know someone should spot you when you free dive."

"Heath, you're being ridic– "

"I thought I'd lost you." There was that broken tone again. The pain that flitted across his expression was so stark I drew in a sharp breath in shock. "I don't even want to contemplate a world without you in it. I *won't*."

The ravaged quality of his voice and the residual wet in his eyes got to me then. Warmth bloomed in my chest as I stared up at him. That was why I whispered, "Okay," and why when the relief flooded his face, I allowed him to lean forward and rest his forehead on mine as he closed his eyes.

"I know you don't want me anymore," he said softly. "That what happened before was just our bodies' reactions. And I know I haven't earned this, but can I just hold you now? Just for a moment."

"Okay," I whispered again as he pulled me against his chest and rested his chin on top of my head. My arms went automatically around his back and I gave him a gentle squeeze as if to reassure him I was still here, that I was alive. Standing there in his arms, I felt something in my chest unfold. Some of the armour I'd built up around my heart when it came to him began to show the smallest chink.

Then he had to go and speak again.

"I'm so glad you've agreed you're never going to do that again."

He could hold me if that's what he needed. But if he thought he could tell me what to do, he had another thing coming. Being on my own since the age of eighteen with no parental support had made me fiercely independent. I relied on and only answered to myself. That was one of the reasons why none of my boyfriends had lasted very long (the other reason was my drawing endless and pointless comparisons between them and Heath – such was my obsession). I simply couldn't bear being restricted or having anything less than complete freedom. Therefore, at these words, I tensed and pulled back.

"Don't tell me what to do, Heath." I shoved away from him fully as the rest of the afternoon came flooding back. "And don't wade in with my parents for me. I can fight my own battles." I was striding towards the cliff steps now with Heath following, his shoes making sloshing noises as he went. Had I not been so angry I would have laughed.

"Yaz wait. Oh, fuck it." I glanced over my shoulder to see him toeing off his shoes (something he should have bloody well done before he jumped into the water in the first place) and leaving them on the steps so he could jog after me. I picked up my pace.

"Aren't you going to get those?" I flung back at him. "I'm sure all that Italian leather can't have come cheap." His shoes probably cost more than my clothing budget for an entire year, maybe even my entire adult life as most of my clothes I nabbed in sponsorship deals, anyway.

"It was exactly because you *weren't* fighting your own battles that I waded in with your folks."

We were at the top of the steps now. I decided it was beneath my dignity to run from him, so I walked to my bike and clothes. Once I made it there, I grabbed my shorts and shimmied them up over my legs before doing up the button fly.

"There is no point arguing with my parents or with Max. They have a fixed opinion when it comes to how I fit in with the family narrative. You can't change that."

Heath's eyes were fixed on my hands at my fly. Two flags of colour bloomed high on his cheekbones before he swallowed and cleared his throat, his gaze lifting from my midriff with visible effort.

"But you can change the narrative," he said fiercely. "It doesn't have to be fixed." He took a step towards me and his tone softened. "They should know how amazing you are at what you do. How dedicated you are to it, how much discipline it requires."

I blinked. Heath thought that about me? I felt that chink in my armour widen again as I stared at his open expression.

"It doesn't matter how good I am or how hard I work. They just don't consider my job to be a profession. And a few instructor qualifications won't impress anyone in my family."

"You don't know that, Midge. You–"

"It hurts me," I said through a closed throat and Heath shut his mouth. "Their attitude hurts me and it's worse if I try to convince them to take me seriously. I have tried that before and honestly it's much, *much* worse than just laughing along as they take the piss. When I put myself out there and they dismiss me, I can literally feel my self-worth sliding away. And I *need* to believe in myself – to believe that I deserve to be filmed and sponsored, that I deserve to have clients for the well-being centre, that I deserve to be paid astronomical amounts by rich adults to teach the sport I love so that I have enough to subsidize teaching the kids. I don't need my family to erode my self-worth any more than they already have. They love me in their way. It's enough."

"I misjudged you as well, Midge, but I changed my mind once I had all the information. You're not letting them have all the information."

I reached down and grabbed my t-shirt before chucking it over my head and pulling it down. "You didn't misjudge me, Heath. You took against me long before you started putting me down for my life choices. I don't know what I did to upset you so much all those years ago, but it wasn't about misjudging me." I grabbed my bike and swung my leg over it. Heath positioned himself in front of me with his hands resting on my handlebars in the middle. "Get off my bike."

"I just think that—"

"When I was a kid, you were my hero. I loved it when you defended me to my parents who were already despairing about my lack of academic prowess. That's why it hurt so badly when you turned on me, Heath. And that's why I can't forgive you and why I can't deal with you sticking up for me again with my parents. That's not who you are to me anymore. Now, *get off my bike*."

He took his hands away and stepped to the side immediately, looking like I'd slapped him. I pressed my lips together and kicked off from the ground to fly away down the path.

Unfortunately, I wasn't back in the sea. I couldn't properly clear my mind. So, I was unable to shake the image of Heath's tortured expression as he talked about losing me.

Chapter 16

That's why he needs you

YAZ

"Verity?" I said softly, and she looked up from her position, leaning over one of the office desks. Her eyes were a little wild, her usually perfect make-up smudged, and for some reason she only had one of her stilettos on. "Er... babe, are you okay?"

"I–I... I can't..." Her chest was rising and falling rapidly and her face was almost unnaturally pale. I flew across the office space to her side and laid my hand on her back.

"You can't what, love?" I said, rubbing small circles on her back. I could feel her trembling beneath my hand.

"I can't b–b–breathe," she choked out. I frowned as I fished my phone out of my back pocket. "I'll call an ambulance."

"No!" she shouted, grabbing my hand to pull my phone down from my ear. "No ambulance." She shook her head fiercely.

"But V, if you can't breathe then–"

"Panic," she managed to get out in between her gasping breaths. "Panic attack." Her pale face was now flooded with

137

colour. I lowered my hand slowly, with hers still clutched around it.

"Okay," I said slowly.

"Scared," Verity whispered on an exhale, her eyes filling with tears. I blinked. The Verity I knew hadn't ever shown any sign of actual weakness. But anxiety and panic attacks I could deal with.

"Right," I said, putting my phone down and taking both Verity's hands in mine. "We're going to sit down now, V. Okay? You with me?"

She nodded, her wild eyes fixed on mine and her chest still rising and falling rapidly. I tugged her down to the nearest chair and squatted in front of her so that our eyes were level. "Look at me, honey." She stared straight at me as I took one of her hands and laid it on the centre of my chest. "Can you feel my heartbeat?" She nodded. "Right, okay. Can you feel my breathing? Feel my chest moving?" Another nod. "I want you to breathe with me, V. You're safe here. You need to slow your breathing down. Close your eyes for me." V's breathing was evening out now as her eyelids fluttered shut. "Can you picture somewhere you feel safe?" She nodded. "Imagine you're there now." The tension in her expression began to fade as I spoke and I could feel her heartbeat slow beneath my hand. "Stay there in the safe space and breathe with me, okay? There is nothing but this moment. Let go of everything else." After another minute, her shoulders relaxed, then slowly she blinked her eyes open. She stared at me before breaking eye contact to look down at the floor and pulling her hand back from my chest.

"Christ," she whispered. "Yaz, I–" She was pulling away, so I took both of her hands in mine to prevent her retreat. "I don't know what to say. You must think–"

"I think you had a panic attack. They're scary and they can

happen to anyone. Do you... I mean, has this happened before?"

She shook her head at first and then glanced at me before nodding slowly. "Not for years, though. Not since—"

"Not since what?"

Verity stared at me for a moment before looking back down at the floor. "It's ancient history, childhood stuff. Best left in the past. There's just been some... er, reminders recently. That's all."

"Does Heath know?"

Her eyes flew to mine, and she squeezed both my hands. "You *can't* tell him," she said urgently. "Promise me, Yaz. Please, don't say anything to Heath."

I frowned. "But he's your brother. And if it's childhood stuff rearing again, doesn't that involve him too?"

"No," her tone was sharp now, back to the old no-nonsense Verity I knew. "No, he's not getting sucked into this. Not again." Before I could ask her to explain, she'd rolled the chair back and pushed up onto her feet. "Heath deserves to be free of this now," she whispered as she toed on her shoes and smoothed down her hair. There were some papers on the desk in front of her which she hastily gathered up before I could read anything on them.

"Okay, well, you know you can talk to me, don't you, V?" I said, moving forward to her and laying my hand on her arm. "I know you think Crazy Yaz can't deal with heavy shizzle, but I promise I'm *all* about the heavy stuff." I smiled. "And you don't have to have the amethyst worry stone, the lavender diffuser or the reiki therapy... but you might regret it."

Verity looked up at me then with a smile of her own. Over the years she'd made it very clear that she was allergic to anything even vaguely alternative. Once when she'd complained of a migraine at the office, I'd brought her a lapis lazuli crystal and a diffuser instead of the paracetamol she had asked for. I may not have read the room quite right at the time seeing as she was meeting with a group of high-profile property developers who'd come down from London. She threw the crystal at my head after they'd left. ("We'll never get the job now, you lunatic," she'd yelled. "Not when they think we're a bunch of crazy bloody hippies!")

Then there was the time I'd set off the fire alarm before an important presentation when I decided to cleanse the office of negative energy by burning some sage and wafting it through the space. I may have slightly underestimated the amount of smoke sage can give off. The office stank for a good week after that. On the plus side, some tasty fireman turned up. Although it turned out V was not in the mood to be set up with a fireman that day, however tasty he was. She threw the rose quartz crystal I slipped into her pocket to enhance her sex life at my head as well – which was short-sighted, seeing as if anyone needed that crystal it was Verity. Sexual repression was her middle name.

Verity laid her hand over mine and gave it a squeeze.

"You know, darling," Verity said. "Maybe I'll take you up on some of that."

I beamed at her, but she rolled her eyes.

"Nobody pokes at my feet, though," she added. "What are you doing here on a Saturday, anyway?" She eyed the rolled-up yoga mats I'd gathered and then looked back at me with her eyebrows raised.

"Oh," I said, glancing at the mats, then back at her, offering her a weak smile. Weak smiles seemed to be the only kind I could muster nowadays, which was probably for the best – both Max and Verity had accused me many times of being relentlessly cheerful. Once I'd lugged these mats down to the van, there would be no evidence of my office invasion. I'd already cleared out the essential oil diffusers and the odd crystal I'd left about the place. It was back to its fully sanitized, bleak glory. "I've finally taken the hint and will be getting out of your hair." I said this through a smile, thinking Verity would be relieved. She'd been almost as annoyed with my frequent impromptu office visits and yoga sessions as Max. But she didn't smile back, instead she frowned and moved to block my path to the mats.

"What you mean you won't be coming in anymore?"

"Er... well, that's kind of self-explanatory, no?"

"But you're part of the office."

My mouth fell open in surprise before I quickly snapped it shut. I said my next words carefully, mindful that I didn't want to upset a post-panic attack Verity but aware that I needed to tell the truth about how I felt. "Verity, I'm not part of the office. You and Max have made it very clear that I'm more of an annoyance than anything else."

"But... but you can't just walk out. Surely that's–?"

"You don't pay me anymore, V," I said softly, and she blinked at me. "I'm not your employee now. I only took the reception job for a few hours a week to help the office atmosphere after the move from London. Everyone was so wound up then, Max's stress levels were hitting the roof and he was mouthing off at all the baby architects... I just wanted to provide some light relief and chill things out a little. It humanised Max to have his little sister come in and do yoga on the office floor and take the piss out of him. But I stopped my reception hours ages ago. Didn't you notice that I only ever did the yoga and alternative therapies here now? I told Janice to take me off the payroll six months ago."

"Oh... well, that's a shame."

My eyebrows went up.

"Really?"

"Yes, of course it is," Verity snapped. "You've been great for staff retention. I acknowledge that."

"You do?" It was my turn to frown now. "Verity, when you're not laughing at me, you're actually *telling* me to leave. I don't know how you think that translates to me being an integral part of the office."

"You're like my little sister," she explained, and I blinked in shock. "I take the piss, but that's what you do with little sisters. It doesn't mean I don't value you."

"I'm not your sister, Verity," I said, and watched as her expression flashed from anger to hurt. I didn't want to hurt Verity, but I was tired of letting everyone walk all over me. "You might tease your little sister, yes, but at the end of the day, you should respect her – not dismiss her every chance you get. Maybe you would even try to support her, try to take her side once in a while. And I'm not needed in this office anymore. Max has Mia now. He's not the grumpy arsehole he used to be."

"You're wrong." Verity took a step towards me, her eyes filled with determination. "We *do* need you. The office, me, and especially Max."

I held her gaze and tilted my chin up. "I'm sorry, V, but *I* don't need to be here anymore. I love you and Max. I love the office, but I have to start prioritising myself."

"Heath needs you as well."

I had moved towards the door again, but that statement stopped me in my tracks.

"What are you talking about?" I asked, a cold feeling skating up my spine. Did Heath tell Verity about what happened between us? I thought we agreed not to say anything to anyone, including our families.

"We're twins, Yaz." Verity's voice had softened, but her expression remained intense. "He can't keep things from me.

Not really. I see the way he looks at you, the way he's looked at you for years. But at that meal last week, the way he was reacting to you... I–I've never seen Heath behave like that, never seen that level of intensity from him. I don't know exactly what's gone on, but I know my brother."

"I don't–"

"And I know you're in love with him."

"Y-you...I don't understand what you're saying." My throat had closed over, giving my voice a strained quality. Verity stared hard at me.

"You've been in love with Heath since you were a child."

"Verity, I–"

My words broke off as she came right up to me and took both my hands in hers, bringing them up between us. "I want my brother to be happy," she said, her voice cracked and to my complete shock her eyes had misted over. Verity rarely cried. She and Heath were very much of the stiff upper lip brigade, posh people-wise. "I've always wanted him to be happy. Until now, I wasn't sure if he was capable of it."

Not capable? What did Verity mean by *that*? I opened my mouth to speak, but she gripped my hands tighter and carried on.

"Our childhood..." she broke off and looked away for a moment. "I don't want to get into it now, but it made us both... guarded. We don't trust people easily. Heath has been looking for something that he *thinks* he needs, when what he actually needs is staring him in the face."

"Verity, Heath doesn't need me. I'm the exact opposite of his ideal woman."

"Pfft," she threw out dismissively. "None of those 'ideal' women he's serially monogamised over the years has done anything for him. It always fizzles out, however many boxes they tick on his stupid list."

"I'm not talking to you about this, V." I tried to make my voice as firm but kind as possible. "The fact Heath *has* a list in the first place just shows how poorly suited we are."

Verity groaned. "You don't understand. He just wants things ordered. Organised. He needs his life that way. With you it's complicated: he can't put you in a box, can't predict what you might do – and that scares him. Heath and I are planners for a reason. We don't like chaos. We don't like being out of control. But then there's *good chaos*, not the type we had when we..." She broke off and closed her eyes for a moment. "When he's with you, he's not in control. He's not focused on his orderly life and what he wants out of it. When he's with you, you're all he sees. He's free. He lights up. I want that for him. I don't want him living an ordered life just because he thinks it's safe. That's why you can't give up on him. That's why he needs you."

I gave Verity's hands a squeeze and then gently pulled mine from her grip before taking a step back.

"You're right," I said, my voice still a little rough. "I've loved Heath since childhood. Not like a crush, but with my whole heart, almost painfully. In my mind, he could walk on water, slay dragons – he was superhuman. It wasn't just how handsome and charming he was, it was his kindness, his strength of character."

"So you put him on a pedestal. Maybe it's good now he's knocked off it. You can move forward as equals."

"It's not just that he's come off the pedestal. You've seen how he's treated me the last few years. He's not the man I thought he was. That kindness and strength of character aren't ever there now when it comes to me." I bent down to pick up a stray yoga mat so that I could break eye contact with Verity. Any more of her pleading expression and I thought I might break down. As I straightened, I looked at her again and my voice dropped to a whisper. "I don't love him anymore."

She stepped aside to let me pass her, looking as though she'd been slapped.

"It does mean a lot to me that you consider me your little sister, V," I added. "But being everyone's slightly incapable little sister is getting old. I need to get on with my life in the way that I want to live it."

"Right," Verity muttered. "I see."

I managed a small smile for her as I was leaving. The look on her face was still a determined one. I wasn't sure what that meant for me, but it was unlikely to be anything good.

That night lying in bed, Verity's words about Heath and about their childhood came back to me.

I've always wanted him to be happy. Up until now, I wasn't sure if he was capable of it.

Our childhood... it's made us both... guarded. We don't trust people easily.

All I knew about Heath and Verity's upbringing was how very privileged it was. Their family home was practically a castle, for goodness' sake. Their dad was a lord. They had been to the best schools in the country – their cut-glass accents and connections were testament to that. But then, other small disturbing facts filtered into my memory as I lay in bed, staring up at the ceiling.

I remembered Heath once telling my nephew, "By your age I'd been living at school for three years, mate – least you can do is turn up at yours for a poxy six hours each day." Teddy had been ten at the time and played truant on occasion – most likely in an attempt to get his mum's attention, which was, unfortunately, a lost cause. Thankfully after Max's ex moved away, we became Teddy's family and that was that. So, Heath must have gone to boarding school at seven years old. Who sends their kid away at seven? Then I remembered a scar I'd once seen on Verity's forearm. When I'd asked her about it years ago she'd shrugged and said she burnt it trying to cook fish fingers as a child, and that at aged five she should have stuck to sandwiches. But why was she trying to cook at all when she was only five? Why wasn't there anyone there to stop her?

I went to sleep with an image of a beautiful seven-year-old Heath on his first day at boarding school.

Chapter 17

Something is wrong with Heath

YAZ

"Mia, what's up?"

"I've come to take you to Sandbaggers practice."

I stepped off my windsurfer as I glided it onto the shore. Mia was standing by the water's edge with her hands on her hips and a determined expression on her face. I sighed. Whilst I was glad that Mia had come out of herself, this newfound bossiness was inconvenient when it interfered with my avoidance strategies. Turning away from Mia, I pulled my rigging up onto the beach.

"Mia, Max won't even let you play at the moment, and I've got another client in half an hour, so– "

"Something is wrong with Heath and Verity," she said, cutting off my lame, half true excuse. I hadn't been to Sandbaggers practice for the last four weeks now. Originally just to avoid Heath, but then after the run in with my family, I'd added Max onto the list as well. I felt bad about Mia – by avoiding Max I inevitably ended up avoiding her – but I'd decided to protect *myself* first and foremost.

"What do you mean?" I dropped the sail and turned fully towards Mia. Her expression was still determined, but it was edged with concern as well.

"I don't *know*, that's the point." She gave a helpless shrug, her hands falling from her hips. "Verity called in sick at the beginning of the week."

"What?" I knew Verity had never taken a sick day in her life, especially not since working with Max. She was the client-facing partner. Max was not so good with people to say the least. Mia winced.

"It wasn't pretty. Max nearly lost us the eco village client. I had to do some serious smoothing over after that meeting – managed to cut him off before he told the client exactly where to shove his lightwell. But we're still on the project... just."

"V would never leave Max to deal with an important meeting like that."

"What was even more weird was that she wasn't answering her phone. Max rang Heath in the end, and he said she's fine and to "give her a couple of days". But Max didn't think he sounded right either. So he went over there, and Heath looked terrible. Max got pushy about what was going on and Heath shouted at him."

"Heath never shouts."

"Exactly. Something's happened. Max and I are worried. Heath rang to apologise. Max asked if he was coming to training and he said of course he was, like nothing's the matter, but he still sounded... off."

Verity's panic attack and her words had been bugging me for days now, and no matter how hard I tried I couldn't get Heath out of my mind. This obsession with him was like a sickness. Worse than all the years I pined for him as a teenager because now I had really concrete memories of how it felt to have his skin against mine, his breath on my face, his hands in my hair. It was as if there was a hole in my chest, a gaping wound left by the absence of him. The thought that something might be wrong with him or with Verity only intensified that ache.

"Fine. I'll come."

Mia smiled at me and then launched forward to give me a hug. As I squeezed her back, bump and all, I felt like a bit of a shit.

"I'm sorry I've been staying away from you as well, Mia," I said into the side of her head and she gave me another squeeze. "You feeling okay?"

"Second trimester's a breeze compared to the first. I'm fine. You've missed her kicking though."

"Her?" I gasped and Mia smiled.

"You know how impatient Max is. He had to find out. We had the scan last week."

I felt my eyes sting. "I'm going to have a niece?" I whispered then launched myself at Mia for another hug. Her stomach moved against me this time and I leapt back in surprise. "She kicked me! Oh no, she's going to be just as grumpy as her dad."

"God, I hope not," Mia said through her smile. "I can't handle two of them."

"Bloody hell, I really do feel out of the loop now. I'm sorry Mia."

"I know it wasn't me you wanted to avoid, and I understand why you're doing it. Max and Heath have both behaved like complete tossers." She took my hand and gave it a squeeze. "Remember though, I'm not just your brother's missus. We were friends first."

That was true. I was so hurt that I pushed away Mia as well without thinking. I vowed to do better, starting right now.

Mɪᴀ ᴡᴀsɴ'ᴛ ᴋɪᴅᴅɪɴɢ – Hᴇᴀᴛʜ ᴡᴀs ɴᴏᴛ ʜɪᴍsᴇʟꜰ. Tʜᴇʀᴇ were dark circles under his eyes, he clearly hadn't shaved for a good few days, and his reactions were completely off. Also, there was the fact that I'd been at the practice for at least twenty minutes and he'd yet to make proper eye contact. Max had, of course, been right up in my grill as soon as I arrived, asking why I wasn't responding to his texts, wanting to know when I could come over, when I was coming back to the office. He even managed a gruff "I'm sorry for being a dick" – a very out-of-character move, and although I attributed it in part to Mia, I could also see the genuine regret in his eyes. So, I'd agreed to come over that week so that he could make me his pasta. I did *not* agree to go back to the office.

But with Heath it was different, it was like he didn't even see me there. To be honest, he didn't seem like he was fully there himself. He was so distracted that he fumbled easy passes, made no attempt to sidestep anyone when he had the ball. It was weird – the man was a rugby machine. He left halfway through the game, but I felt like it would be too obvious to follow him.

Max and Mia convinced me to pop into the pub after practice. They were both still looking at me like I was an unexploded bomb, so I felt I had to humour them. I planned to go for one and then track down Heath. The hollow expression on his face was so weird that it had freaked me out. But it turned out that Heath was already at the pub when we arrived, slumped over the bar on a stool and nursing a pint. He looked up at me as I approached and blinked his red-rimmed eyes as if he wasn't sure whether I was real. My stomach hollowed out.

"Heath?" I said, as I drew up next to him. He looked so lost in that moment that I did the only thing I could do – I wrapped my arms around him and gave him a squeeze. At first, he did nothing. His arms remained limp by his side. But then he seemed to jerk to life, and they came up and around me in a vice-like grip as he shoved his face into my neck.

"Yaz," he breathed. "He's gone."

"Who's gone?" I tried to pull back a little so I could look at his face, but he kept me pinned against him.

"That bastard's gone, but I'll never be free of him."

"Heath." Verity's sharp voice broke into our huddle and Heath's arms loosened again. He drew back, and we both looked at her. Her eyes weren't red rimmed, she wasn't drunk, her outfit was immaculate as always – but the corner of her left eye was twitching and her mouth was held in a tight line. "There you are. Let's get out of here."

Heath turned back to me. I was still in the circle of his arms. He rested his forehead against mine and I could smell the alcohol on his breath. I racked my brain to think of another time I'd seen Heath drunk like this and couldn't recall any. He was always in control. Always. Almost unnaturally so – just like his sister.

"*She's* free of him," he said with his eyes closed and his forehead still resting on mine. His voice was slightly slurred. "Always been stronger than me, though. He respected that."

"Who are you talking about, love?" I asked in a soft voice, my lips only an inch from his. His eyes flickered open, and he drew back slightly to stare at me.

"Thank you." His words were heavy and laden with feeling. I frowned in confusion.

"Why are you thanking me?"

"He doesn't know what he's saying," Verity put in briskly. "Come on Heathcliff. Time to get you home."

He stiffened in my arms then, before pulling away fully and setting me back from him. His eyes had gone from warm to cold, his expression completely blank. "I'm not going home. *Home* can fuck off."

Verity moved between me and Heath and put her hands on his shoulders, giving him a small shake. "I'm not talking about *that* home. That was two decades ago, you numpty. I'm talking about *your* home here in Poole. Your nice house. Your nice *clean, warm* house."

His posture relaxed under her hands. He was back to looking lost again.

"Right," he said. "Of course."

She guided him up to standing and he wobbled for a moment before she ducked under his arm to stabilise him.

"Verity, what is going on?" I asked as I followed them through the pub.

"Verity? Heath? What are you guys doing?" Max came up on their other side and when Heath tripped over a low stool and lurched dangerously forward, Max stepped in front and stopped him hitting the deck.

"If you'd all mind your own business and get out of our way, I'm going to take my brother home."

Max frowned at Verity as he continued to support Heath's weight.

"V, you're not going to be able to get this great lump home without help. He'd be face down on Fergus' disgusting carpet if it wasn't for me."

Heath slurred out some sort of indistinguishable insult to Max then slapped one of his hands down in the centre of Max's chest.

"Yer my besssst friend, Maxy baby. You know that, you northern bastard?"

"Okay, okay mate," Max said in a soft voice, slapping Heath on the shoulder a couple of times – which was as close as Max came to giving hugs if you weren't his wife or his sister. "You're a bit of a git, but you're my best mate an' all."

"S'important."

"Er... yes it is," Max said carefully. "I think I might agree with your sister on this one though – time to get you home."

"I love your family."

"I love them too mate. But–"

"I love your sister."

"I know you do. We all love you as well so–"

"No, you don't understand. I *love* her."

Max froze in front of Heath and his eyes snapped to me. My mouth fell open, but I didn't know what to say. He looked back at Heath and narrowed his eyes.

"What the fu–?"

"Max," Verity's voice snapped through the tension. Everyone turned to her. Her breathing rate had increased, and I started to worry about another panic attack coming on. "Can we do this another time? I need to get him home. He's in no state to take on a protective brother at this point. Just–just *get out of my way!*"

The last part of that was practically screamed and silence descended on the pub. I stared at Verity, noticing her eye twitch was back in full force again, her breathing still rapid. Her mouth was so tight now there was a white ring around her lips. This was only the second time I'd ever seen her lose control of herself in any way before. I'd most definitely never heard her shout at anyone. The anger left Max's expression, morphing quickly into concern. Mia was next to him now, having rushed over on hearing Verity shout.

"Okay, V," Mia said in her soft voice. "Everything's going to be okay. Let's get you guys home, right?" Verity gave a stiff nod, her eyes facing forward. We all walked to the exit and somewhere along the way Heath took my hand in his. By this point he only seemed to be half conscious, but his large hand managed to find my much smaller one and he held fast in a firm grip. Even after everything I didn't have the heart to shake him off. When we got to Verity's car, she looked at our interlinked fingers and gave a deep sigh.

"Heath, let go of Yaz's hand."

He grunted and leaned against the car, but managed to keep hold of my hand.

"I can come with you," I offered.

She looked from Heath to me then gave me a short nod. Max helped get him into the car, then we drove to Heath's house with Max and Mia following behind. Heath fell asleep in the car and his hand relaxed its grip in mine, but I kept holding on. When we got to his house, he stirred only a little as Max hefted him out of the car and up the steps to his front door. Heath's house was a passive house. Max had designed it for him. Passive houses can be heated with only the body heat of the occupant. They are super insulated and very cleverly designed. Heath had a log burner though. I'd heard Max complain once that both Heath and Verity kept their houses "too bleeding hot" inside (Max was of the school of thought that you only really needed the heating on in January – maybe February – the rest of the year you should just put on another jumper).

Verity opened the door with her key then Max and I pulled Heath into the house behind her with Mia closing the door after us.

"Heath." At Verity's voice Heath's eyelids blinked open again and he looked around the living area before focusing on his sister.

"You're right," he whispered. "It *is* warm."

"Of course it's warm, Heathy," Verity said softly as she walked up to stand in front of him.

"And clean."

"*So* clean – you have a cleaner every day, remember?"

He nodded then let go of Max and me to fall forward into Verity in a drunken hug which took her back a step. Max hovered in anticipation of her not being able to take his weight.

"It *is* clean, isn't it," I heard Heath's muffled voice from where he'd shoved his face in Verity's neck.

"And you have nice things now," Verity said, her arms giving Heath a squeeze. It was as if she was soothing him. At her words I could see his body visibly relax. Why would he need to be reassured that he had a warm, clean house and nice things? None of this made sense. Heath and Verity had always been privileged. Hadn't they?

"Okay, time for bed," Verity said, still in that soothing voice. She started moving away with Heath. When Max went to help her, she shooed him away. "We're fine." She turned her head to look behind at all of us. "You guys can go home now. Thank you, but we'll be *fine*." Her tone was almost fierce, like *she* needed to be the one to look after her brother. Like outside help was unwelcome. Max let them go and they stumbled away. But we didn't leave. Mia, Max and I moved into the immaculate kitchen, made tea and we waited. When Verity emerged, she seemed annoyed that we were still there, but still took the outstretched tea from my hand (it would take a far more dire situation than this for Verity to decline tea).

"I thought I told you–"

"What is going on, V?" Max had crossed his arms over his chest and was wearing a stubborn expression.

"Nothing," Verity returned, holding her mug to her in a defensive gesture as she climbed up onto one of Heath's kitchen stools.

"Don't lie to me, Verity." Max's voice actually sounded hurt and Verity sighed. "Heath never gets drunk enough to lose control and you never call in sick to work. Ever. Something is going on with you two."

"It's just an... inconvenience." Verity took a sip of her tea and looked down at the granite surface. "We have to go up to Harrogate to sort out some things next week. It's going to be unpleasant. Heath's always been a bit more..." she trailed off and put her mug down to rub her temples. "Look it's nothing. Really."

"Why the fuck do you have to go to Harrogate?" Max seemed angry at the prospect of this which confused me. The twins had grown up in Harrogate. Part of the "posh north" as Max would say. They were the type of northerners who had no trace of an accent and lived in ancestral homes. A few hundred years ago Heath and Verity would have been the nobility and we would likely all have been working their land for them. "There's nothing for either of you up there," he said.

Mia was looking between Verity and Max in as much confusion as me. "What's in Harrogate?" she asked.

"My mother and my now dead father," Verity said in an emotionless voice. "We have to bury the old bastard next week."

Chapter 18

No big deal

HEATH

My head was pounding and my eyelids felt like they had been glued shut. Hangovers were not routine occurrences for me. Normally I had no desire to drink myself into oblivion. It was ironic that now was the time I chose to lose control. I took a deep breath in, allowing myself to be calmed by the scent of washing powder on my sheets. Everything in my home was clean – I made sure of it. But it wasn't just the scent of clean sheets I noticed. There was another light fragrance in the mix. That's when I realised that my hand was covering a much smaller one and my leg was thrown over a soft body in my bed. I blinked open my eyes and there she was. That beautiful face an inch from mine. I must have jerked in surprise as she stirred, and her eyelids blinked open. When confronted with her warm, brown-green eyes it took a moment before I could accept that this wasn't a dream. So many of my dreams were filled with her nowadays that it felt a little unreal.

"Hey," she said, her voice rough with sleep. "You okay?"

There was something in her tone that made me frown.

"You were pretty out of it last night," she explained.

"How did I–? I mean I don't remember... "

"We helped V get you home. Listen, Heath I'm so sorry about your–"

She broke off as I pulled away suddenly, putting a foot of distance between us. *That* was what was in her tone before. Pity. She was here out of pity.

She knew.

I sat up in bed and pulled my hands through my hair, covers falling to my waist and my chest on display. Yaz also sat up then moved to sit cross-legged on the bed facing me, a frown marring her forehead.

"Heath I–"

"Is that why you're here? You feel sorry for me?"

"No, I–"

"Because there's *nothing* to feel sorry about. Good fucking riddance to the old bastard."

Her mouth dropped open and then snapped shut. I'd shocked her. Good. Shock was better than pity.

"Okay," her tone was more cautious now. "Last night you seemed–"

"Shitfaced. I seemed shitfaced. You should probably forget anything I said last night. I don't make sense when I'm drunk."

"You don't drink."

I let out a bark of laughter. "There's a marching band stomping around in my head that would strongly disagree with you there."

"You know what I mean. You don't *normally* get drunk." She cocked her head to the side and narrowed her eyes. "I don't think you *are* okay. I think that–"

"Why do you even care?" I snapped. There was this ball of angry energy in the pit of my stomach. It had been building since I'd spoken to our family lawyer a week ago. The bastard was dead, but it *still* wasn't over. I still had to go back there. A wave of frustration washed over me and I felt like I couldn't get a deep enough breath in. "You've been avoiding me for weeks. You didn't care about me then. My dad carks it and you're—" I broke off as my throat started feeling too tight. Knifing out of bed, I sprang to my feet and lurched towards the window. I opened it wide and looked out at the sea, but still it felt like I couldn't quite take a deep enough breath. My vision started closing in on me and my fingers started to tingle. It was as if I was on a cliff edge with nothing to hold on to. Like I might get sucked back *there* again. I hadn't had flashbacks in years.

Then I felt the pressure of her warm hand on my back. For some reason it grounded me in the present, anchored me there.

"Heath," her voice was soft but firm enough to prompt me to turn and look at her. I stared down into those eyes, deep brown flecked with green, alive with concern, and my breathing slowed. Her eyes searched my face as one of her hands rested on my chest, the other swept down from my eyebrow over my cheekbone. She then lifted my hand to the centre of her chest, allowing me to feel her steady heartbeat and the rise and fall of her breathing. "That's it. Come back to me. I'm here." I allowed myself a blissful moment basking in all that was Yaz: her beauty this close was almost unreal. The soothing nature of her voice washed over me, and I felt the first small oasis of peace I'd had all week. But I knew that a moment was all I could really handle. So, I moved back and paced away to my chest of drawers, pulling on a t-shirt and then moving to shrug on a pair of jeans. Yaz was dressed already in her standard jeans and surf t-shirt. I didn't know if she'd slept that way or been up already. I couldn't remember much from last night apart from holding onto her hand... *that* I remembered. She'd been anchoring me then too. My head was really pounding now. A wave of nausea hit me and I flew into the bathroom, slamming the door behind me. Hopefully she'd take the hint and leave.

When I finally emerged, having had the unpleasant experience of re-experiencing yesterday's alcohol binge in reverse (there was no food – I hadn't eaten anything except breakfast the day before), Yaz wasn't in my bedroom. Relief and, if I'm honest, a whole lot of disappointment flooded through me, which was bizarre – I was in no state to deal with the intensity of my emotions for Yaz right then. But after I jogged downstairs in search of coffee, I found her at my kitchen island. As I approached, she gave me a small smile and pushed a large glass of thick purple liquid into one of my hands and two tablets into the other.

"I need caffeine, Yaz," I told her, placing the suspect glass down on the granite and eyeing the tablets. "And I'm not downing some sort of valerian root or whatever the bollocks this is."

"It's paracetamol," she replied, her lips twitched. "Some doctor you are. And this will rehydrate you better than your crappy coffee." She pushed the glass towards me, and I crossed my arms over my chest. That angry ball of energy was still there, making me stubborn and ungrateful for no reason. "Try it." Her voice was soft now. "For me."

I huffed but did uncross my arms to chuck back the tablets and down the purple stuff. It was surprisingly good. She smiled at me. The white of her teeth against her tanned skin with light pouring in from the floor-to-ceiling windows onto her golden curls made her seem almost ethereal. I blinked and took a step back to stop myself reaching for her. She frowned at the movement and her smile went down a notch. I needed to get her out. My mind was all over the place and I felt numb.

I had a feeling that I should have committed to the therapy Verity wanted me to have with her all those years ago. But I'd thought that if I just shoved it all down deep into the back of my mind, if I tried to forget, then I wouldn't have to deal with it. That bastard dying was raking it up all over again. As was the fact I had to go *there*. Why did V insist on going there for Christ's sake? My phone vibrated in my pocket with my sister's ring tone as if I'd summoned her to call. I broke eye contact with Yaz to answer it which I was glad of. She was making me *feel* way too much. I needed to stay numb.

"What?" I snapped into the phone.

"Just checking you're still alive."

"I'm fine, V."

"You weren't so fine last night." Verity's voice had dropped to a soft whisper. There was concern threaded through the words. She was worried. She was worried because, yet again, I was the weak one. It was different when we were children. Back then I had protected my sister, at least I'd tried to. But now... now she seemed to be the one who could process things, who could move on. *I* was the one she needed to protect, to worry about. And I hated it. I sighed as I slumped down into the nearest stool, my elbow hitting the granite and then my head going into my hand. I stared down at the floor and gripped the phone until I could feel it creak.

"Last night was... a blip," I said, lowering my voice and turning away from Yaz.

"You never drink, not like that. Not like..."

She trailed off but we both knew what she was going to say. Not like *them*. Never like them.

"You don't have to come back with me," Verity said again. She'd been telling me the same thing for the last week.

"You're going, so I'm going. If you ask me, we should just burn the place to the ground, but I know you feel you need to go, and I won't let you do it alone."

There was silence on the other end of the line. My hangover was kicking in with a vengeance now. I let my elbow slip down until my arm was flat on the granite and my forehead resting on it.

"Okay," she whispered finally. "Okay, Heathy."

"Okay, V-May." She disconnected and I lay the phone on the counter, not bothering to raise my head from my arm. My head was throbbing again. After a long moment, I felt a soft touch to my back and I stiffened. Why did Yaz have to be here now? Why did she have to see me like this? I'd already fucked up so much with this woman. Now was not the right time to start sorting that shit out. I couldn't even sort my own head out, let alone try to resolve things with Yaz.

"Here's your caffeine," she said as she pushed the cup in front of me.

"Thanks," I muttered at the floor. I felt her move closer, her arm wrapping around my back as her body moved into mine.

"We're all there for you and V, if you'll let us be," her mouth was so close now that I could feel her soft breath on my ear. "You and Verity hold too much to yourselves. Too many secrets. You both need to let your friends in." I allowed myself a moment to soak in the feel of her against me, allow her soft scent to fill my nostrils, then I took a deep breath in and gathered my self-control, before pushing up and away from the granite counter and from her. Both my hands went into my hair and I took a few steps back.

"Verity and I will deal with this on our own, like we always have. That's what works for us."

"But it's *not* working for you, is it? You can't say that after last night. I've never seen you like this Heath. If you could just tell us what—"

I let out a hollow laugh, cutting her off. "Trust me, you don't want to know *any* of this stuff. V and I will go and sort it. I just... I can't deal with you at the moment, Yaz."

A flash of hurt flitted through her expression before she cleared it. I was fucking this up. But how could I possibly explain everything to Yaz? Her family were so far removed from ours. How could I explain to someone who loved her own dad so completely, the mixture of relief and boiling anger I felt when mine died? I needed to be careful with Yaz now if I had any chance with her in the future.

I tried again. "That came out wrong... I'm just... everything is just so messed up in my head. I don't want to lash out at you, and I will. I'm not a good person to be around at the moment. And I've buggered up everything with you so much. I don't want to make things worse."

Yaz's expression softened and she moved closer until we were inches apart.

"Showing you're vulnerable is not buggering up." Then she stepped right into my space, laid her head on my chest and wrapped her arms around my middle in a hug. Until that moment, until I felt her arms around me, I hadn't realised how much stress I was carrying. As I wrapped my arms around her in return, it was like the tension fell away. My life started to look manageable again. I felt centred, calm almost – a miracle considering how ramped up I'd become since the news last week. The faint feeling of nausea receded. I let myself revel in it for longer than I probably should, breathing in the light, shampoo smell of her hair but then I straightened up and set her away from me before clearing my throat.

"Right, well thanks for the hangover cure. I can feel it kicking in already." That last comment was, to my shock, not an actual lie – I did feel a hell of a lot better, physically at least.

"You're not going to let me in, are you?" There was no heat in her voice, just resignation.

"It's all fine, honestly. V and I will just go and sort out a load of boring shit up north and then it'll be done. No big deal."

The lie fell easily from my lips. The only problem was that my bloody voice shook just slightly with those last three words. Yaz caught it, of course – Yaz caught everything – and her eyes narrowed a little before she gave me a small smile.

"No big deal," she said softly, her eyes holding mine as she moved forward and reached out to squeeze my hand.

Chapter 19

They were thin, love

YAZ

No big deal, my arse. I could feel the pain radiating from Heath, could see the wariness in his expression. I didn't know what the twins were hiding about their parents, but theirs was not a normal reaction to learning your father had passed away. Something was very wrong. When I thought back on it, I realised it was odd that Heath and Verity *never* mentioned their parents. They always changed the subject whenever home or anything about their childhood came up. And despite having used their family's many properties over the years, neither Max nor I had ever encountered any of their family members. Heath and Verity had spent countless holidays and Sunday lunches with our family – wasn't it odd that none of us had ever met their parents? And why, after the twins had spent so much time with my family, didn't their parents offer to have Max over to stay? Curiosity won over my desire to avoid my mother, and I found myself at my parents' house the next morning.

"Hey, Mum."

To my shock, Mum's eyes filled with tears, and she grabbed me in a tight hug – an uncharacteristically touchy-feely manoeuvre for her.

Before I could even return the hug, she'd pulled back and framed my face with both her hands.

"I'm sorry," she said, a tear spilling over onto her cheek.

"Mum, I–"

"We *are* proud of you, love," I heard Dad's voice say and looked over my mum's shoulder to see he'd come up behind her. Mum released my face, and I was pulled into a tight hug with my dad. When he pulled back, I could see that his eyes were a little bright as well. Mum shuffled us all inside and Dad tucked me into his side with his arm around my shoulder as he led me through to the kitchen. It was like he was worried I would turn tail and make a run for it at any moment. That level of insecurity from them made me feel bad for ignoring them for the last few weeks and for hauling them over the coals at Max's house. I hated to see my folks upset – if this is what an overdose of honesty got me, I wished I'd continued with half-truths.

Dad went on. "We didn't realise how serious you were about all this well-being and water sports stuff."

"Aubrey!" Mum cut in sharply and Dad held up his hand to her.

"I know, I know. I don't mean to sound dismissive. We always thought that it was just you mucking around with some essential oils, a few crystals, and on the water. We didn't know how important it was to you and we certainly didn't realise how much effort you'd put into building your business up."

"Dad, it's fine. I–"

"We're ashamed that we've never visited your studio," Mum said. "It took Heath pointing out the disparity in how we treat you and Max to make us see how wrong we've been."

"We watched you teaching the kids on the water last week, love," Dad put in. "You were amazing out there."

"And we've seen those videos you've done for sponsorship," said Mum. "Heath shared them with us. You're really talented."

My mouth fell open in shock. "You watched me on the water?"

"Why didn't you ever show us yourself, love?" Mum asked. Her voice was soft, but there was accusation and hurt in her tone.

"Or tell us how the business was going," Dad put in. "How did you even start it up with no funds? You've employees and everything. It's extraordinary."

I took a deep breath in and let it out through my nose. My dad put the kettle on – his solution to any type of emotional conversation.

"Honestly, I really didn't think you would be interested."

"How can you say that?" Dad put in, crossing his arms over his chest. "Of course we're interested in what you do. If we'd have known that–"

"I'm sorry, Dad, but it wouldn't have made any difference. To you guys, yoga, alternative therapies and windsurfing were all just examples of me mucking about to avoid real life. You would never have considered them to be a career – you think all that stuff just holds me back." I shrugged. "I'm sorry, I don't mean it to sound like I'm accusing you. I'm only stating the facts. Any time I bring up anything to do with the water or well-being, you shut me down. I learned not to talk about it years ago."

"Oh sweetheart." Dad looked like my words had caused him physical pain and I felt guilty all over again.

"It's fine," I said, reaching over the kitchen table and laying my hand over his. "I get it, okay? You guys want the best for me. In your mind, that means higher education and a profession."

"All we ever really wanted was for you to be happy," Mum said, looking just as miserable as Dad.

"I know that as well. And I know that you both felt the only way to achieve that was for me to have job security. But that way, it just... it just isn't right for me. I love what I do, and I need the sea. It's like my oxygen."

"I can see that now," my dad said softly, shifting his hand so that he could squeeze my fingers.

"Are you going to return my calls now?" Mum asked in a small voice. I'd never heard her sound less like herself.

"Of course, Mum." I reached over to her with my other hand and gripped her hand in mine. "I love you guys." I looked between both my parents' faces. "I just needed some space for a bit so that–"

"It's not just the last month though," Mum said, her voice rising a little. "You've been distant for *years*. I realise why now, and we promise our attitudes will change. We won't go back to how we were before. I didn't know how much it was hurting you. You're always so... stoic, really. I don't know why we've never seen that. You're the stoic, the steady one, and Max is more turbulent and highly strung. I think we thought that if we kept pushing, you would eventually change your mind. We didn't really see that we were the ones pushing you away."

"Okay, no more distance then. Alright, Mum?"

"Yes, right." Mum sniffed and gave my hand another squeeze. "Your father meant what he said – we *are* proud of you. It's just we value education, and it's hard to..." she broke off and clamped her mouth shut in a visible effort to censor her-self. "I'll try, okay?"

"Right, tea." Dad said, letting go of my hand to bustle over to the kettle. Clearly the man had reached his deep and meaningful conversation limit for the day.

"Listen, I came here to talk to you guys about something else as well," I said. "It's about Heath."

"Oh yes," Mum took a cup of tea from Dad and they exchanged a knowing look. "What about him, love?" She tried to maintain an innocent tone, but I could tell that they knew something was up between Heath and me, and that she was fiercely curious – it had probably been more than obvious the last time I saw them. Running off like an overdramatic heroine in a romance novel wouldn't have helped matters.

"It's about Verity as well. About their parents."

That surprised Mum. Her eyebrows went up as she put her tea back down on the table. "Their parents?"

"Well, yes. Their dad died last week and I... well, they're both acting weird."

"Oh no, I didn't realise their father died. Weird in what way?"

"Just... weird. Off."

"Well, they've just lost their dad, love, so..."

"It's not grief. Or at least not grief like I've ever seen it. It's twisted and... I'm worried about them. I just wanted to know if you knew anything. Heath and Verity were here for so many holidays when they were at boarding school with Max. I'm wondering why Max never went to theirs."

Mum lowered her cup slowly to the table and looked down at its surface for a moment, as Dad straightened his glasses.

"Max going there – that was out of the question," Dad finally said.

"But why?"

"I wouldn't have allowed the dog to stay with those people," Mum said, looking at my father and then at me. "You won't remember – you were only four or five at the time – but that first summer holiday there was a reason we took the twins home with us. Nobody showed up to collect them."

"What? But–"

"The twins were a lifeline for Max at school – we knew that. They helped him fit in – those places can be a bit snobby, and Max's accent was very thick when he started there, plus he was a scholarship kid. He got some stick that first term until the twins took him under their wing. Your father and I were very grateful to them. So when we went to pick up Max for the holidays and the twins' folks didn't show, we waited with them. Eventually Heath and Verity gave us their parents' mobile numbers, but they went straight to voicemail. I asked the twins if they definitely had the right phone numbers but they just shrugged. They said they hadn't spoken to their parents all term. The schools were a bit more blasé back then. They just wanted the kids to be picked up. Heath and Verity had lied to them and said that they were getting the train, but they didn't have money for the fare."

I blinked and shook my head slowly. My cosseted upbringing with over-involved parents made what Mum was telling me almost incomprehensible.

"I finally spoke to their mum about a week into the holidays *after* we'd taken them both home with us. She was... I don't even have the words to describe that woman."

"Why? What did she say?"

"She laughed. When I told her that term had finished, and the kids were with me, she laughed. She wasn't embarrassed or worried about them, just told me she'd always been 'Bloody useless with dates' and that she hoped the kids hadn't been 'little shits like they always are'. Her voice was slurred, and I could hear people in the background like there was some sort of party going on. At one point she put her hand over the receiver I think to muffle it and shouted that 'We've really ballsed up

170

now, Giles – Heath and Verity are staying with a bunch of townies'. There was loads of laughter in reaction to that statement. I didn't know what to say. Dad ran them back up there eventually because your gran was coming to stay, and we needed the spare room."

"I felt horrible leaving them there, to be honest," Dad said, grimacing at the memory. "That vast house was freezing and felt like a mausoleum. Their mum ushered us in, very obviously hungover with bloodshot eyes and stinking of booze. When we got to the kitchen, there was mess everywhere – empty bottles, cigarette butts, it was chaos. She offered me a tea before I went, but then realised the only liquid they had in the house was vodka in the freezer. Heath and Verity looked mortified. I didn't know what to say. Heath's mum she... she made me feel very uncomfortable."

Dad blushed, and my mouth fell open in shock. "Bloody hell, Dad, did she make a pass at you or something?"

"Well, I–I–I..." He straightened a tie that he wasn't wearing and swallowed as he glanced at Mum, whose mouth was pressed together in a thin line.

"That woman was a complete liability," Mum cut in. "Don't look so shocked, young lady. Your father is a handsome man."

I squashed the small giggle that rose in my throat. Dad was tomato red now. Even twenty years ago he'd been a balding, bespectacled, sweater-vest-wearing, elbow patches type of man. Not exactly the type of chap women proposition on a regular basis.

"I felt it best to get out of there as soon as I could. The kids had our number – I told them they were free to ring us if there were any problems. Heath was adamant I should go. He seemed so acutely embarrassed of his mother that I thought it best I leave. After all, they were both fourteen." He shrugged. "I've always regretted it if I'm honest."

"So that's why they spent most of the other holidays with us?"

Mum nodded. "There was that one summer when their father came to collect them from school. He was very charming. Despite the obvious level of neglect of the twins, the staff at the school still seemed to be totally in awe of their parents. Glamourous types, not like your dad and me, and super posh. Aristocracy or some such. Lord and Lady Markham. They own half of Cumbria if you'd believe it – family money. People are impressed by that sort of thing you see. Anyway, the dad took them home that summer and we didn't see them again until the start of the next term. But..." Mum paused, and her expression clouded with anger for a moment before she cleared it. "Well, we made sure that *never* happened again."

"Why?"

"They were thin, love," Dad said quietly. "They didn't look right. Heath didn't smile when he saw us. The light had left that boy's eyes. It–it wasn't right."

I felt my face drain of colour and sat back in my chair. I'd always presumed that Heath and Verity's life was infused with privilege, that they'd had everything they wanted. As adults, they had access to properties all over the globe, endless funds to take our whole family away. I thought they just did that because they could, because it was pocket change to them. But I was beginning to see just how important my family must have been to them back then. I didn't want to consider why a summer with their own family as children left them worryingly thin, why the light in Heath's eyes had been dulled. It made my chest ache just thinking about it. But one thing was for sure – they were *not* going to go back to that place without Hardcastle support. Not if I could help it.

Chapter 20

When it came to humans

HEATH

I scowled at V and gripped the steering wheel a little tighter. Fern Hardcastle and Mia waved at me from the back of Yaz's van, whilst Aubrey and Max gave me vaguely apologetic expressions from the front next to a smiling Yaz. She was wearing the most bizarre outfit of dungarees, a barely there vest top, a bandana securing her mass of blond curls on top of her head, and of course the flip flops that rarely left her feet (apparently Yaz's feet need "freedom from the oppression of shoes" or some such nonsense).

"Are you responsible for this?" I asked my sister through gritted teeth as I pulled away from the drive. The ancient van moved after us, emitting a plume of toxic smoke. For someone who purported to care so much about the environment, Yaz's van was an environmental disaster. How it passed its last MOT was a mystery. I could imagine the mechanic at the local garage falling into a Yaz-induced trance (not an unusual occurrence for men in her presence) and signing off a dangerous vehicle without having full control of his mental faculties. Apparently she needed the van for the business now and it was more eco-conscious to keep that heap of junk going than to buy brand new. I suspected it had more to do with Yaz being too damn proud to accept any help with financing a new van than anything. She was so *stubborn*. Following V and me on this grim journey was further evidence of that.

"They said they wanted to come and pay their last respects," V replied. "What was I supposed to do? Tell them to sod off?"

"The funeral's not until Monday. We're clearing the house out tomorrow. We don't need them to– "

Verity laid her hand on my arm and gave it a small squeeze to silence me. We'd always been able to communicate without words from when we were small. I knew she was telling me to accept the help, that we *needed* the help. I swallowed and glanced in the rearview mirror. Aubrey had a gigantic map opened out and was grappling with it in the front seat. Max grabbed it out of his hand and pointed at the phone that was programmed with satnav on the dashboard. Yaz was grinning throughout this exchange but batted her dad's hand away when he started poking at the screen with a frown on his face. I stole a couple more glances back at them over the next half hour. The map versus satnav debate seemed to be ongoing, despite the fact they didn't need either, seeing as we were going in convoy, and V and I knew exactly how to get there.

Once when I looked back again, I glanced at Yaz and she rolled her eyes at me – communicating that her dad was barmy but that she loved him. Sharing that joke with me. I felt some of the tension in my shoulders drain away. Maybe Verity was right. Maybe I *did* need them there. But down in the pit of my stomach I just didn't want anybody to *see*. Deep down I was still the embarrassed child, ashamed of my parents, and fiercely hoping nobody found out the truth about how they lived, how *we* had lived.

Some kids hate boarding school. Verity and I bloody loved it. God bless the posh schools of the UK for taking kids from the age of seven. Regular meals, clean sheets – such luxuries were a novelty to us. Other seven-year-old kids were crying at night during the first term – missing home, missing their parents. We thought they were crazy. We couldn't understand it back then. It wasn't until we realised how different our home life was from other peoples' that we began to understand.

"Do you think *she'll* be there?" I whispered, but I knew that V had heard me when I saw her shoulders go up and her arms move to go around her middle, so she was hugging herself.

"I hope not," she whispered back, and we left it at that.

"Right, well I–" Fern broke off for a moment, obviously searching for the right thing to say under the circumstances.

It was five hours later and all the Hardcastles, Verity and I were standing in the vast kitchen of the main house. It shouldn't have been a shock, but still I couldn't quite wrap my head around the state of it. Every surface was covered in bottles, old plates, cigarettes. Black rubbish bags were overflowing next to the almost buried kitchen table. The only space cleared on the wood surface was for a couple of rotting dead pheasants, with a gun (very likely loaded) sitting next to them.

Fern cleared her throat. "Let's find a kettle, shall we? Tea will make everything clearer."

"I very much doubt there'll be a usable kettle, any tea bags or mugs, and since the fridge hasn't worked in over two decades, there definitely won't be any milk," I said in a tight voice.

"Ah," Fern replied, and we all fell silent again. A soft hand closed around my fingers, and I glanced down at Yaz. Beautiful Yaz in this horror show of a house, looking at me with her heart in her eyes was almost too much to take. Then the barking started. Roger, Max's Alsatian, who'd made the trip with the Hardcastles in the van, was going nuts. He shot from Max's side, barking all the way as he raced to the kitchen table. After a few more seconds of barking he stopped, but kept his attention fixed on the floor under the table. That was when we heard it, this awful, terrified, low whimpering sound. Mia was the first to approach the table, with Max hot on her heels, trying to hold her back. But she shrugged him off to duck down next to Roger under the table and we heard her shocked gasp accompanied by more whimpering. She started making soft, encouraging noises. Roger started whining and eventually a small brown and white (well, what must have been white before it was caked in old mud) spaniel emerged. It was limping and so thin you could see its ribcage under its fur. It skirted around Mia and instead went to Roger. The two dogs touched noses, and then after a bout of sniffing, the little dog's tail gave a half-hearted wag before it backed away under the table again.

Suddenly the room felt too hot. It was autumn, the bloody house had no heating (never had, even before the old bastard died) but I was sweating. A lump had lodged itself in my throat and however much I swallowed, I couldn't seem to clear it. My legs felt weird, like they were in danger of not holding me up, and I staggered back. Everyone's attention went from the dog under the table to me. I felt cornered. This kitchen, this house, everything was too much. It was like my brain was overloading, and the sight of that pathetic dog tipped me over the edge.

"I–I can't stay here," I heard myself saying in a raspy voice I didn't recognise. "I'm sorry, V."

The bloody hallway was so massive and so full of crap that I thought I wouldn't make it, but I managed to get outside and slammed the front door behind me, hoping that would slam shut the door to my memories as well. But nothing could do that. Much as I'd like to just forget, I knew I never would. This wave of realisation was accompanied by an unstoppable one of nausea, and I lost the coffee and the Wagon Wheel that Verity had forced on me earlier that morning into the overgrown rose bushes.

I knew she was there before I felt her warm hand on my back. That feeling of well-being punctuated through the nausea and pain, and my vision started to focus again. Both my hands were supporting my weight on the wall while my head hung between them as she stroked my back, murmuring reas-surances like, "It's all going to be okay. You'll get through this. We're all here for you."

But the one that cut through my panic attack the most was the simple statement, "I won't leave you."

When I pushed away from the wall, her hand fell away and she gave me some space but held out a bottle of water. I took it and used the water to swill my mouth out and spit before drinking down a small sip.

"I think that Wagon Wheel must have been dodgy or some-thing," I muttered, feeling my cheeks heat, which was almost unheard of for me.

Those green-brown eyes looked up at me and she nodded. "Yes, I've heard you can get the odd dodgy one. That's why I stick to Curly Wurlies."

And so, despite all this shit and filth and pain, despite feeling more fucked up than I had in decades, and despite the acute embarrassment of this entire situation – despite *all* that, I smiled.

Chapter 21

Burn it to the ground

YAZ

The drive up north had taken nearly six hours. During that time we'd all decided to pool our knowledge of the Markham family. Apart from what my parents had already told me, all Max knew was that the twins hated their parents and hated coming back to this place. The Markhams were one of those seriously ancient aristocratic families, suffused with history, money and land (which generated even more money). Apparently there's a bridge in Yorkshire where people have to pay money to the Markham family in order to cross it.

Although neither of the twins ever mentioned their parents, Heath and Verity did talk fondly about their grandparents. Unfortunately both sets had died. Mum reminded me of something from years ago, back when we'd gone to pick up Max and the twins for the summer. When we arrived Verity was crying, which was really unusual – they were both normally so happy to see us – but Heath was in a rage. I remembered vividly what he had said that day, mostly because of the swearing – something I hadn't heard much of aged only seven. In fact, it may have been the first time I'd ever heard the f-word out loud, and it was all the more shocking because Heath was always so charming, always saying the right thing in the right way – but not then.

"That fucking bitch!" he'd shouted as Verity collapsed into his side sobbing, and he'd put his arm around her to hold her up. "We deserved to know what was going on."

"Granny," Verity had whimpered as Heath turned her into his chest and told the teacher who'd been speaking to him to *fuck off*. In my seven-year-old mind, saying the f-word to a teacher was the height of recklessness. I couldn't quite believe it. Dad ushered me away before I could hear any more while Mum and Max went to comfort the twins.

"Didn't they go to her funeral?" I asked Mum after she'd jogged my memory of that day. I was sitting in between Mum and Mia in the back. I glanced at Mum and she pressed her lips together, shaking her head. When she spoke, her voice was tight with anger.

"The parents let a teacher tell them. A *teacher*. Didn't even come in person to do it themselves. And those poor children – they never got to say goodbye to their grandmother. From what Verity told me they'd been very close to her. She'd died halfway through the term and the funeral happened without them."

"Oh no," Mia whispered. "Why wouldn't their parents tell them?"

"Those animals were only interested in themselves," Dad put in, his voice gruff and his hands gripping the steering wheel a little tighter. "'No point interrupting their schooling' was the excuse the teachers came up with for them."

"Of the two of them it was Heath that worried me most," Mum said as she stared out of the window. "Verity cried, she let me hug her, she talked about her granny – apparently she had purple-tinted hair, and made them little meringues which she carried about in her handbag. Heath didn't cry at all. He stuck close to his sister, made sure she was okay, made sure she ate, slept on the floor next to her bed – until I found him and set up a cot bed instead. But after that angry outburst on the first day, he was back to his old self – charming, polite, as if nothing was wrong. But I could tell he wasn't right. When he thought nobody was looking, his smile would drop and he'd stare off into nothing, clenching his fists so tight his knuckles would turn white. The poor love."

When we had arrived at the Markham estate that morning I knew instantly that I *hated* it. Before we even made it to the front door, we'd had to suffer the spooky, half-mile-long drive-way. The house itself only came into view after we'd almost given up on it. Then, from around massive hedges, a huge stone monstrosity appeared. It looked like something out of a bad Gothic novel, not a childhood home.

"V told me that her father had let the gardeners carry on, but that the old bugger hadn't let anyone into the house in years." Max had said as we approached the house. "Who knows what state it's in."

"Where's their mum?" I asked from the backseat.

"Spain, I think V said. She wasn't sure though – it sounded as if that was where V *hoped* she was. I don't think there was much love lost there either."

Now, standing next to Heath outside this monster of a house, after he'd just vomited from the anxiety of having to return here, I was also glad his mum wasn't here – the thought of either of Heath's parents made me feel murderous. Heath's face was ashen, and his eyes still looked a little wild, but that small smile he forced out eased some of the tightening in my chest. I looked down at Heath's hands now and, sure enough, just like mum described from when he was a child, they were bunched into tight fists. His brief smile emboldened me to cover the fist nearest to me with my smaller hand. He tightened it for a moment before I felt the muscles relax under my touch and he let his fingers unfurl. I moved my hand, so we were palm to palm, and threaded my fingers through his. He hesitated before giving my hand an almost painful squeeze, like I was some sort of lifeline he had to hold on to. He shook his head, then gave me another weak smile.

"How do you like the family pile then?" he asked after clearing his throat. I tugged him away from the wall and the house. I could almost feel the tension rolling off him the further from the front door we got.

"I hate it with a vengeance, and I think you should burn it to the ground."

Heath's eyebrows went up and he let out a small, surprised laugh.

"Okay, say how you really feel."

I smiled up at him. "I will." There was a crunching on the gravel next to us and we both looked down to see the pathetic-looking dog from earlier – its big eyes were staring up at Heath, and it gave a small whimper. Keeping hold of Heath's hand, I reached down and held out my hand, letting it come to me. After it sniffed my fingers for a moment, it let me stroke its head, but when Heath crouched down it whimpered and flinched away from him.

"She'll be one of Dad's hunting dogs. Looks like a working cocker bitch."

"Why didn't anyone tell you there was a dog here?"

"She must have been hiding when the groundkeeper came in. Probably did a lot of that – hiding, I mean." He pulled his hand away from the dog, as she was clearly scared of him, and sighed. "You know, the RSPCA came once to take away all my dad's dogs. Someone reported him. I loved those dogs. They slept in the shed next to our room. V and I watched as they took them away. V was crying, but I was glad – I loved those dogs enough to be glad that they were getting away." He let out a hollow laugh. "It's funny, isn't it? Mum and Dad weren't deemed good enough to look after some dogs, but when it came to humans..."

He trailed off, and I felt my throat constrict.

"I don't think it's funny," I told him, my voice rough with emotion.

"No, I guess it's not," he whispered, staring off into the garden. I could feel the tears building and a lump forming in my throat. Images of Heath and Verity as small children watching their dogs getting taken away whilst they were left behind assaulted me. I shoved my face into Heath's chest, and I let myself cry into his shirt, uncurling my hand from his to wrap my arm around his back. He paused for a moment, taking a deep shuddering breath in and then wrapped me in his arms.

"Jesus, Midge," he said into my hair at the top of my head. "I didn't mean to upset you, love. I'm sorry."

"Don't you apologise to me," I snapped as best I could, with my voice muffled in his chest and tears streaming down my face. "And I'll cry if I want."

He sighed. "Don't pity me, Yaz. I'm fully grown now – not a child anymore."

"It's not about pity. I'm angry. These are angry tears."

"There's no point being angry. He's dead now, and Mum may as well be."

I didn't press him to ask what that comment meant. There was no sign of his mother at the house. Mum and Dad had told me that the Markhams had divorced when the twins were teenagers. I'd seen pictures of his mum. She was very beautiful.

Her father had owned a drug company, making her one of the mega-rich. She'd then married Heath's dad, giving her a title on top of her vast wealth. But maybe being stuck out here in this mausoleum of a building was too constrictive for someone like her. After the divorce she apparently travelled the world, hanging out with the rich and famous.

Looking back, I realised I had seen her before in person during one of the times we stayed in a Markham family property in the south of France. I must have been about ten at the time. It was the middle of the night when I heard a crash downstairs, then wild laughter which woke me up. When I crept out into the corridor to look through the bannisters, I saw Heath crouched over a woman who was sprawled on the floor, a broken lamp lying next to her.

"Felicity, what are you doing here?" Heath said. His voice sounded funny – not soft and kind like it was normally. It sounded hard and annoyed, even angry. Her dress was shiny and tight, she was so *so* thin and wore bright red lipstick. She was one of the most glamorous people I'd ever seen.

"Heathy Beefy," she sing-songed in a slurred voice. "How ever did you get so big, darling?" Heath put his arm around her back and hauled her up. She wobbled on her feet. "My boy, all grown up. Let's have a drink. Where's your sister? Verity!"

"Shh! It's two in the morning. Verity's sleeping and so is everyone else."

"Psht, I can shout if I want in my own house."

"Actually, it's *my* house now. Or had you forgotten?"

There was that wild laughter again – she teetered to the side with the force of it, throwing her head back with her sandy blonde hair flying down her back in glamorous waves.

"Fuck you," she spat when she had recovered from her laughing fit. "You always were a jumped-up little prick. Not so little now, but the same fun-sponge attitude. You and your sister, sucking all the joy out of my life like leeches. Now bring me some fucking champagne, *leech*." She veered to the side to get around Heath but ended up falling at the foot of the stairs in a crumpled heap. Heath moved fast then, grabbing her by the back of her dress and hauling her to her feet.

"You can sleep it off here, but you're out in the morning. And keep this shit with you." He shoved her handbag at her. "There're kids here, for Christ's sake."

Her beautiful face went pale for a moment before she retched. Heath wasn't fast enough to step out of the way, and she threw up all over him. He looked absolutely furious as he hauled her off down the hallway to one of the spare rooms, her laughter echoing around the large space as she went. I'd run back to my bedroom when I heard Heath's footsteps again – not wanting him to know I'd seen his mum (even at that age I was savvy enough to realise that Heath wouldn't have wanted witnesses to that exchange). Mum woke me early the next morning. We weren't due to leave till the following day, but she packed up and we were out of the door before even eating any breakfast. The spare room door remained shut, and as we were leaving everyone kept eyeing it like it was an unexploded bomb. There was no sign of the broken lamp or vomit in the hallway, and Heath was back to being normal Heath again. When Verity got up, he ushered her out of the house as quickly as possible. We took Verity to the airport, leaving a grim-faced Heath standing in the villa's doorway with his arms crossed over his chest. When he met us at the airport later on, nobody asked him anything. Mum just reached out to give his hand a quick squeeze, asked him if he'd eaten breakfast, and then gave him a slightly squashed cheese sandwich from her handbag, which he was too polite to refuse.

A little whimper from the dog and some movement from the front door pulled me back into the present.

"I think she needs feeding," I said, pulling back a little to look up at Heath's face. "Let's all go get lunch somewhere. We can make a plan and feed the dogs. I don't think there'll be much edible in there."

"There never really was," Heath muttered, giving my hand a squeeze as we walked back to the others.

Chapter 22

You don't even fit on the bed

YAZ

We went to the village pub for lunch and sat outside with the dogs. Winnie (her name was on the collar she was wearing) was given a bowl of Roger's food and I fed Max's sausage to both the dogs under the table, much to his disgust. I couldn't exactly feed them my mushroom risotto, though – what did the tightwad expect? Heath and Verity were quiet at lunch, although there seemed to be some sort of unspoken twin conversation going on between them which we weren't party to. The way they sometimes communicated was a little spooky. Dad gave Heath a couple of pats on the back and bought him a pint – I wouldn't have thought that was the best cure for throwing up on the side of your family home, but in my dad's book a pint of beer could solve just about anything. Mum fussed over them both, asking how we could help with the funeral arrangements – apparently the funeral directors had it covered. I did my usual thing when the atmosphere was heavy – goofing around to try and lighten it.

"Oh wow. This is bad, really bad, Max," I said in an ominous voice as I examined his palm. He and Verity were discussing the LSE bid, and I'd offered to read his palm to let him know if they were going to get it. Weirdly, my brother actually believed in this stuff, even though it was the one element of my alternative repertoire that was completely made up for his benefit. I'd predicted correctly about a bad construction firm once and now he was hooked.

"What?" he asked in a panicked voice. "Is that shit Yurgen going to get it again?"

"No, no. You'll get the job, it's just..." I trailed off and he leaned forward in his chair towards me. "What?"

"This line here. See it?"

"Yes?" Everyone was leaning forward to get a look at Max's palm now.

"Well, it's *really* deep and long. I'm afraid it means that you're a full numpty."

"What?"

"A numpty. A few pennies short of a pound. This is the numpty line."

He snatched his hand away and scowled at me as the whole table started laughing, including the previously sombre twins. "You are *so* annoying," Max snapped, then turned to Mum. "Mam, tell her she's not to tease me when I'm worried about a bid."

"Darling, it's not my fault if you're a gullible numpty," Mum said, and I gave a sombre nod.

"The numpty line doesn't lie, Max. I hate to tell you this, but I've known for a while."

"Yeah, mate," Heath put in through a smile. "We all have."

Driving back though I could feel Heath's mood darken, see the tension return to his shoulders. Both he and Verity looked pale and were uncharacteristically quiet when we returned to the house. Winnie, who, after the sausage, trusted me enough to pick her up, whimpered in my arms – even the dog didn't want to go back in there.

A wave of frustration swept over me. This wasn't fair. There was real trauma here in this house. The twins shouldn't have to go through this. That's why, after we'd exited the vehicles and started walking back to the front door, I stopped in my tracks on the drive, grabbing Heath's arm to bring him to a stop as well.

"Right, this is nutballs," I snapped. Everyone else drew to a halt to look at me.

"What's nutballs?" Mia asked.

"You two," I pointed at Heath and Verity, "have more money than God, right?" Apparently the twins had inherited nearly all of their grandparents' money in trust funds that they accessed at eighteen. I could understand why the grandparents might want to bypass their own children.

Verity rolled her eyes and Heath cracked a small smile.

"Right," Heath said when I raised my eyebrows.

"Well, I refuse to let you both go back inside that hell hole, it's not fit for a manky badger. There are plenty of companies that will deal with all this crap. Get someone in to strip the house bare. There's nothing in there that you need."

"There might be valuable things, love," Dad said. I shook my head.

"Maybe there are, maybe there aren't, but the fact remains that Heath and Verity don't *need* any more money. I doubt they'd even want any money associated with that house, those... people." I refused to call them parents. Nothing I'd seen or heard about them so far qualified them for that title.

"We don't want the money," Verity's voice cut through my anger and I jerked in surprise – she hadn't really spoken since we arrived. "Not for ourselves anyway."

"V and I have donated the house to a charity that runs retreats for underprivileged kids. The stuff inside we're collecting to sell and donate the proceeds to them as well. If we don't go through it, then we might not get as much money."

I took a few steps forward, gently handed Winnie to Mia and turned to Heath before taking his hand and giving it a squeeze.

"You're not going back into that fucking house ever again," I said, my voice soft but firm.

"Yaz–" Verity started, but I cut her off.

"Neither of you are, right? *We* can check there's nothing the house clearers are going to nick. We – the Hardcastles – will be going back in. You two will not be." I gave Heath's hand another squeeze and he closed his fingers around mine, which I took as an encouraging sign.

"We need to–" Heath said but stopped when Verity laid her hand on his other arm.

"Let's just go to the shed, Heathy. Anything we cared about would be there. I doubt they ever bothered to clear it out."

"Verity I–"

"Let them help," she whispered.

Heath scanned his sister's face. Another unspoken conversation passed between them before he sighed and gave a brief nod.

"Okay, so whilst you lot were arguing over the bill as usual, I looked up numbers for firms to do this shizzle – in fact, I *might* have already booked one to come today..." I trailed off as a large van followed by a skip started rumbling up the driveway. Perfect timing.

Heath blinked and everyone's mouths dropped open in shock. "I... er–"

"Christ, Midge," Max said. "Since when were you so bloody organised?"

I just rolled my eyes – not keen to point out that I'd been running my own business since I was a teenager. We could get into that later.

~

HEATH

I pulled out the tattered box from under the small bed and then straightened up before sitting down heavily on the mattress, which squeaked and protested under my weight. A few springs dug into my arse, and I thanked God I no longer had to sleep on this torture device.

"I can't stay in here," Verity whispered, and I looked up from the box to her. Composed as always, she sat opposite me on her own thin, squeaky nightmare of a mattress. Her hands were clutching our grandmother's brooch in her lap and her knuckles were white. "This is all I need to take. I thought..." she trailed off and closed her eyes slowly. "I thought coming back here would help, but you were right – we should just leave it in the past where it belongs."

I shook my head. "I'm not sure it's as easy as that."

"But you said–"

"I know what I said, but maybe you were right. Maybe we had to come back one last time. We owe it to Granny to bury her son."

She gave me a small, sad smile, pinned the brooch to her jumper and then stood. "Granny wouldn't want us back here either." She gave my shoulder a squeeze. "And she hated her son as much as we did."

The floorboards creaked under V's feet as she left, taking me back thirty years. I brushed the dust off the top of the box and lifted the lid. A smaller, much skinnier version of myself looked back at me. I was standing next to Max in our class photo – his face grumpy and mine smiling, same as all our photos. Max arrived at that school feeling out of place, and I arrived just ridiculously grateful to be somewhere I could eat regularly, wear clean clothes and sleep in a bed with a decent mattress. I chucked the box on the floor and lay down on the bed with my feet still on the ground on the side and closed my eyes.

"Heath?"

Yaz's soft voice filtered into my subconscious, and I frowned. I'd been dreaming that I was back living in the shed, sleeping on that bed with springs digging into my back. I shivered, remembering the cold that had felt like it was burrowing its way into my bones, despite the large number of coats and jumpers Verity and I would pile on top of ourselves. I felt the bed dip next to me and a warm body press against the length on mine. A small hand closed around my fingers that were lying on my chest and gave them a squeeze. It was like a wave of calm and relief crashed over me, just from having her near – as if an unacknowledged pain had lifted.

"You've been in here a while," she said into my chest as I shifted to put my arm around her and pull her into me further. "We were getting a bit worried."

"I must have drifted off," I said, my voice hoarse. "I haven't been getting much sleep lately."

"I bet." There was a long pause. I stared up at the cobwebs on the wooden ceiling as the breeze that rattled through the slate blew them this way and that.

"Heath, why are we in a shed?" Yaz asked, and I let out a surprised bark of laughter.

"You lot must all think we're totally insane. I'm sorry, sometimes Verity and I forget that... We forget other people don't just *know*. That we can't communicate with the outside world the way we do with each other."

"I know you do," Yaz said, acknowledging the weird twin-ness but not sounding annoyed by it. Other women had been. My last proper girlfriend hadn't really wanted to be around Verity at all – one of the reasons it didn't work out, but not the only one. Another reason was pressed to my side, talking softly in my ear. "But we'd like to understand too."

I sighed, my chest with Yaz rising with my breath coming in. "This is our room."

"What?" Yaz shifted so that she was up on her side and could see my face. She was frowning in confusion. "Like a den or something?"

I shook my head. "No, *not* like a den. Like where we lived."

A swift intake of breath was the only sign that I'd shocked her – that and the swirling depths of anger highlighting the green flecks in her brown eyes.

"What *the fuck* do you mean by that?" she snapped. It was strange, but Yaz's anger seemed to be abating and quelling my own – it was like a wave of cool water putting out a fire, healing something deep inside me that I hadn't acknowledged was broken. It was partly because Yaz always seemed so serene, so at peace. 'Zen' would be her way of putting it. She let the world do its thing and she did hers. So, her righteous indignation at my neglectful childhood was somehow like a soothing balm to my own.

"I mean, this is where V and I slept. This was our room."

"What about the goddamn bloody *mansion* right next door?"

I shrugged. "There was an incident at one of their parties: they had a lot of parties. I... I didn't think it was safe for us to stay in the house anymore."

"What kind of incident?" Yaz asked, her tone careful and concerned.

"Some bloke crashed into our room while we were sleeping,

stinking of booze and smoke. He grabbed the duvet off Verity's bed so I hit him over the head with a hockey stick. He backhanded me but I managed somehow to keep hold of that hockey stick and when the bloke came at Verity again, I smashed it at his crotch. He went down then, howling, and we ran out of the bedroom, down the stairs and out of the back door. The party was still going on. We were scared, my eye was swelling shut and we just wanted to hide. But it started to rain so we went into the shed where my father kept his pack of beagles. There was an area for equipment separate to the dogs and we hunkered down in there. The next day I decided that was where we were going to live. We lugged mattresses down there from the house. Nobody noticed. Mum and Dad were passed out."

"Please, please tell me that your parents called the police the next day," Yaz's voice was trembling with rage now. I was starting to regret saying too much about what went on. My childhood memories are a lot to take. I didn't want to put that on Yaz and I really didn't want her pity.

I shrugged. "That's not the way my parents operated."

"And they let you move into the shed?" her voice had risen in disbelief.

"My father didn't want us under his feet and Felicity just wanted to get pissed with her friends. Having a couple of kids around took the fun out of the kind of parties she wanted to throw."

I shivered as a memory of another of my mother's parties flashed through my brain. V and I had been hungry. We'd been shooed out of the kitchen earlier with a sandwich, but that had been at lunchtime and it was late evening. We didn't have any cash, and this was before I'd managed to snag one of mum's credit cards; to top it off, the village shop was over four miles away. There'd been music coming from the main house, which was a sure indicator that we should not go in, but Verity had a cold – and even aged nine I knew you should eat when you were sick. So I snuck into the kitchen through the side door to grab something from the fridge.

That was the last time I ever tried to go into the house during a party.

No nine-year-old should see his pissed-up mother kissing a stranger against the kitchen counter with his hand up her skirt. Not to mention the fact that two other strangers were going at it on the kitchen table, and the whole place stank of booze and cigarettes. At the time I understood the empty bottles of alcohol – it was only later that I realised what the lines of white powder meant. By the next day Verity was properly sick. I managed to steal Felicity's mobile out from her nightstand, after negotiating an array of hungover party goers who were either passed out on the floor or wandering bleary-eyed through the house. I called Granny and she came to get us. It was a two-hour round trip, and she was seventy and not in the best of health, but there was no other alternative. She cried when she saw us in the shed, then went into the house to scream at Felicity. Father was away on a shooting trip, or a sailing trip... it was always one or the other. We spent the rest of the summer at Granny's house. I loved it there. It was warm, and the cupboards were full of meringues. Verity had to have some antibiotics for a chest infection, and her chest has never been quite the same since. To this day, she needs inhalers and always develops a cough in winter. I felt this particular memory was best kept to myself seeing as Yaz was now practically vibrating with fury.

She was looking around us at the dilapidated shed now – old gardening equipment in the corner, the remnants of a few peeling posters that V and I had put on the walls to try and make it seem more like a proper room. "You don't even fit on the bed," she said when her gaze fell on the rotting wood frame we were lying on.

"Well, I did when I was little. But yes, from about the age of fourteen my feet had to hang over the end."

"Heath, what age were you when that incident happened? When you started sleeping in this shed?" Her voice sounded strained, as if she was having to force the words out whilst maintaining her composure. When I looked up at her face, I could see the green sparking in her eyes and her nostrils flaring.

"It doesn't matter now," I said, trying to soothe her mounting anger. One of my hands went up to her face – my thumb trying to smooth out her frown before my fingers went into her hair and the side of her face, pushing the soft mass of curls back behind her shoulder.

"How old were you, Heath?"

I sighed. "I think we were about six or seven."

"There are no radiators in here."

"We used to have an old fan heater. There's power." I pointed to the solitary light bulb swinging over our heads.

I heard and felt her take a deep breath in, letting it out slowly, before she sat up on the bed and swung her legs over the side. When she spoke again, her voice was tight. "Do you need anything from here?"

I pushed up to sitting as well, opened the shoebox to retrieve the school photo, then threw the box on the floor.

"No."

Yaz nodded, stood, grabbed my hand to pull me up too, and then made her way to the exit, tugging me along behind her. When she opened the door, Winnie was sitting there waiting for her. Yaz bent down and scooped her up in her arms. Winnie gave her jaw a couple of licks and then settled into her chest. She kept hold of my hand and we walked out of the shed together. When we were out and on the lawn, Yaz handed

Winnie to me then turned back towards the shed. Once she'd marched over there her leg flew up high so that her foot struck the door square in the centre, causing it to slam back into the doorway so hard it almost came off its hinges. Without looking back she came to me, took Winnie from my arms and walked back to her family holding my hand, with a dog tucked under her other arm as if nothing had happened. There was a loud creak behind us. I looked back to see the door actually give up the ghost and fall off its hinges completely, crashing down onto the ground.

"Right, that is *enough*. We're getting out of here," Yaz snapped. "We're all booked into the pub for tonight so let's go." Everyone nodded in agreement, and I realised that somehow Yaz had become the de facto leader of this whole expedition. As much of a bastard I'd been to her in the past, she'd still stepped up when I needed her. *She* was looking after *me*. Sure, Verity had given that a go before, but this was the first time I'd really let anyone else do it.

To have this from Yaz, who for so long I'd considered just that bit flaky, was completely unexpected. I felt a renewed sense of shame about how I'd judged and dismissed her for so many years. In my mind, people were either reliable or unreliable. Reliability and dependability were incredibly important to me. My parents fell so squarely in the unreliable camp that I was biased against anyone I thought might share the same tendencies, anyone who might let me down. In a lot of ways I was still that thirteen-year-old child whose parents didn't pick him up from school one summer. I still felt that rejection, like I didn't matter enough, and I was wary of anyone who might make me feel like that again. But I should have known. Of course, Yaz wasn't unreliable. It was obvious in the way she cared for her family and her neighbour, in how hard she worked for her business, how dedicated she was to being the best at her sport. She was the complete opposite of everything my parents were, and I'd been too fucking blind and stupid to see it.

I just had to hope I wasn't too late, or she'd slip through my fingers like the water she loved so much.

Chapter 23

Shame on you

YAZ

The funeral was exactly as depressing as I expected, but what I hadn't expected was the number of people who turned out for it – or how obnoxiously upper class they would all be. Of course I knew Heath and Verity were posh – their accents, the way they carried themselves, the fact they had trust funds and properties all over the world. But these people were next-level British aristocracy at its finest: pearls, tweed, red trousers (weird choice at a funeral, but whatever). Some ultra-posh bloke whom the vicar introduced as Lord Davenport gave the eulogy, which comprised a couple of fox-hunting stories and an anecdote about Eton. Nothing about the man's children or his family. Nothing real or of any substance. Heath and Verity didn't say anything. They both just sat through it with blank expressions, no hint of emotion.

But the worst was yet to come. At the end of the service, just as everyone was filing out (a few grumbling about the lack of a wake – apparently even if you were totally loaded, you still wanted a free drink if at all possible) the church doors opened

199

and a thin, blonde woman stumbled in. We had been sitting at the front so were bringing up the rear of the crowd when she elbowed her way over to us. The woman stopped in front of us, staring up at Heath. I could smell the alcohol from a few feet away.

"Darling," she slurred. "You got s'big. When'd ya get s'big?"

"Felicity," Heath clipped. Verity froze next to him, but their mother didn't even acknowledge her. It was a little freaky as she also looked not much older than either of her children, but in a weird her-face-doesn't-move way rather than natural youth. She did manage what looked to be an unhappy expression at Heath's use of her name.

"How many times do I have to remind you, darling, I'm your *mother*."

"Funny, but as I recall, you conveniently forgot that very fact when I actually needed a mother."

A younger man came up next to the woman and took her arm when she stumbled slightly to the side. He looked about Heath's age. He seemed pleasant enough – very white teeth.

"Hi there, I'm Gilbert."

The twins ignored Gilbert. I gave him a weak smile – he looked like he might be in over his head. Felicity broke the awkward silence.

"I spoke to Crawley and he–"

"There's nothing for you in the will," Heath rapped this out through gritted teeth and Felicity's eyes flashed.

"That fucking bastard," she spat, then took an unsteady step towards Heath before she grabbed onto the front of his jacket. A wave of pure rage swept through me as I watched him recoil from her alcohol infused breath. "He owed me. *You* owe me." She turned to face Verity. It was the first time she'd even acknowledged that her daughter was standing there. "You fucking leeches, ageing me before my time. You and your–"

That was when I lost it. I can count on one hand the number of times in my life I've lost my temper. One of the reasons my family had been so shocked when I had a go at them the other week was because it's just not in my nature to be anything but chill. But in that moment, after everything I'd seen and heard that day, after lying in that miserable shed with Heath and hearing that he'd slept there since he was six-fuck-ing-years old after his parents had failed to protect him and his sister in the worst way, I was almost incandescent with rage.

"Get your filthy hands off him right fucking now," I snapped, yanking her back by the neck of her dress with one hand and wrenching her fingers from Heath's lapel with the other. Then I gave her a firm push. She flew backwards into Gilbert, whose smile had dropped. In fact, he looked like he wanted to find the nearest exit.

"Who the bloody hell are you?" she slurred at me as she straightened.

"More to the point. Who the fuck are *you?*" I snapped back. "Because you are certainly *not* Heath and Verity's mother. A mother doesn't let her six-year-old kids sleep in the goddamn shed. She doesn't let them get hurt. A mother doesn't neglect them to the extent that even the sight of their childhood home makes them physically unwell. All that privilege and wealth, all the advantages you were given, and you couldn't even be bothered to take care of your own children."

"I looked after my–"

"Shame on you." The anger vibrating through my voice now was totally foreign to me, but it has the desired effect of snapping this woman's mouth shut. "Shame on you for what you've done. I hope it haunts you for the rest of your miserable, lonely life." She opened her mouth to speak, but I moved into her personal space before she could get the words out. "Don't *ever* come anywhere near Heath or Verity again."

"You can't tell me what to do, you little gutter rat. My son—"

"He's not your son," Mum said, stepping up beside me. "And Verity's not your daughter. You haven't earnt that right."

"I—"

"You stay away from those kids," Dad put in from behind my mum. The fact Heath and Verity were well into their thirties was by the by. "If you think that there isn't enough evidence in that mausoleum of a house to convict you on multiple counts of drug dealing and child neglect, you're very wrong."

Her face went pale, and she took a step back.

"I know Grandpa and Granny cut you off, but there's no money for you here either, Mother," Verity said. Her voice was soft and held no anger, just resignation and a little sadness. "We'll never give you any of the money. So there'll be no point speaking to us again anyway. You may as well leave."

"You always were a self-righteous little bitch," Felicity spat. She gave the twins one last look of contempt then spun around to stumble back up the aisle of the church. Her stunned toyboy took a moment to collect himself. He opened his mouth and looked as though he wanted to apologise to us, but then closed it again, his face flushing red with embarrassment before he turned away to leave. As he caught up with Felicity she made a grab for his arm to steady herself, but he shook her off and power-walked out of the church – obviously very keen to get as far away from her as possible. In fact, when we made it out of the church we found Felicity standing in an empty parking space, watching as her boyfriend's car sped out of the church car park. My last image of her was in the rear-view mirror as we were driving away, throwing her designer handbag on the ground and swearing at the retreating vehicles. If her face could have moved, I'm sure her expression would have been furious.

We drove straight from the funeral back to the motorway to leave for home, having packed up and finalised everything with the removal people earlier. All the arrangements could now be done remotely via the agent I'd found. Heath and Verity never needed to go there again. Somehow the car situation had rearranged. I was now next to Heath in the front of his car with Winnie on my lap, and Verity had gone with my family in the van with Dad driving. As we drove away from the church, I took Heath's hand in mine to give it a squeeze and he just kept hold of it. We drove for the next hour like that – in silence, with him holding onto my hand on his lap. When we stopped for petrol, I took Winnie off into the bushes at the side of the service station. Verity followed me out there. I turned to smile at her, but she didn't return it. She just kept coming at me until she collided with me and dragged me into a tight hug. It was the least Verity-type behaviour I had ever experienced. To be honest, I was too shocked to speak.

"Thank you," she whispered in my ear, then pulled back and walked away.

Another half hour on the road later, Heath finally broke the silence.

"I'm sorry," he said, staring ahead at the road. He hadn't taken my hand hostage again, but was instead intermittently stroking Winnie's head. We were trying to get Winnie used to Heath, since he was adamant that she was coming to live with him.

"What are you sorry for?"

"For underestimating you."

"I don't understand."

He cleared his throat and shifted in his seat, clearly uncom-fortable. "I thought that..." he trailed off, and I watched his throat move as he swallowed. "I tend to categorise people."

"Okay," I said slowly.

"At first, I categorised you as a child, because you were one – obviously. A child who I thought was cute, and who I knew was kind-hearted, spirited, adventurous, great fun. Then you became a teenager and I..." he cleared his throat again. "You were so beautiful. I've never been into younger women, but you at sixteen – it was insane how beautiful you were. It made me uncomfortable, especially as you were Max's little sister. Your family meant so much to me. So, then I tried to avoid you as much as possible."

"Ah." I had been hurt at the time. I thought that Heath had just lost interest in our family. The idea that he found me attractive had never crossed my mind.

"Then you were an adult, and I was so drawn to you it felt almost beyond my control. I've never been keen on not being in control."

"I've noticed."

"You've got to understand, I had so little control as a child. When I could finally be the one calling the shots, I wanted everything to be on my terms, to be ordered how I needed it to be. I should have had counselling like Verity, but I told her I didn't want to dredge it all up. That I was fine. I believed I'd be fine – if only I could control everything around me, make sure there weren't any unpredictable elements in my life. I thought I would have it all sorted. I have a list. Did I ever tell you that?" He let out a dry laugh. "A list of criteria... for my ideal woman: educated, preferably with a profession, attractive but not *too* beautiful – not beautiful enough to addle my mind – prompt, reliable, predictable, hard-working, organised, teetotal, able to cook, showing low-expressed emotion, and not keen on staying out late."

"Wow, your ideal woman sounds *super* fun."

Heath flicked a glance at me and flashed me a small smile

before looking back at the road. "I know it sounds crazy, but I..."

"You didn't want to end up with someone like your mother. Someone who would let you down." He pressed his lips together and then nodded slowly.

"So, you categorised me into the unreliable, uneducated and totally unsuitable category by the time I left my teens behind. You viewed me as unworthy."

Heath's jaw clenched so tight that a muscle ticked in his cheek. "It wasn't just the list. It was how wild you were. Beautiful and wild. You hated the confinement of school – everyone could see that. You took risks on the water, which I didn't understand. All I saw was you out there in the sea, flying through the air, doing incredibly dangerous stunts. I didn't see how much training and dedication you put in, or how safety conscious you were. All your alternative therapy stuff I thought was just nonsense. I didn't see how you were shaping it into your career. Or how much you were helping people. If I'm honest, I didn't *want* to see. I was so drawn to you it was terrifying. I noticed the way you looked at me – I knew that if I wanted you I could have you, and deep down I knew that if I let myself have you I would get so lost I'd be out of control... again. I'd be at the mercy of someone like..."

"Someone like your mother," I finished for him in a dull voice. Had he really compared me to that monster?

He groaned. "No, Yaz. I don't mean it like that. I knew you were nothing like her. Maybe I didn't realise how hard you worked or how dedicated and responsible you were, but I *did* know how kind and how loving you were. It was just... the strength of my feelings scared me, and I didn't trust you, not enough."

Silence filled the car. As I looked out of the window, I could feel my eyes stinging and my vision blurred. I sniffed and then felt Heath's hand over mine where it was resting in Winnie's fur.

"I'm sorry, Yaz. Please give me another chance."

"So now your list doesn't matter to you?"

"That list was always just a bunch of bullshit to make sure I never really *lived*. I know that now. I know that I'll never find what I've found with you. I trust you now – more than I've trusted anyone in my life. I want to feel out of control with you, because I know you'd never let me down."

I turned my hand over in his and gave it a squeeze. One of my tears spilled over and fell down my cheek. He glanced at me as we pulled up to a traffic light and I gave him a watery smile.

"I'm in love with you, Heath." He sucked in a sharp breath, and the hope in his face nearly cracked my resolve. "I've been in love with you since I was eleven years old. But I'm sorry, *I* don't trust *you*. Knowing what I know now, I can understand *why* you might have been wary of me, but I never deserved the way you treated me." Heath turned to me with a devastated expression. My gaze flicked out of the window, then back to him as we pulled up to a stop on the kerb. I'd been so focused on our conversation that I hadn't even noticed that we'd arrived at my flat. "You've got to understand. I thought you were every-thing when I was little. You were my hero. Then you were... you were so *mean*. To me. It was so shocking and upsetting that I still have nightmares about it." His face was really pale now, and I felt terrible for delivering this blow after everything he'd been through this weekend. But I had to be honest with him and I just didn't think I could get past this. "That's why I can't trust you again. Why I can't allow myself to. But I *am* here for you, just like you were always there for me when I was little."

"You don't trust me *now*," he said. "I can work with that. Trust can be earned."

I turned away from his determined expression to look out of

the window. The truth was that he'd let me down so very badly that I really wasn't convinced there was a way back from it. The strength of my feelings for him made it worse in a way – made me more exposed. I might have been a risk-taker by nature, but this was a step too far.

"I'm sorry about what you had to go through this weekend. You know we're all here for you and V. We love you both. Your parents were evil and cruel – note I've put your mum in the past tense as well, because that's where she belongs." I leaned over and kissed him on the cheek, squeezed his arm and then turned to get out of the car, blinking back tears as I laid Winnie carefully down on the passenger seat. I made it to the front door, swiped my face to remove a rogue tear, then turned to watch Heath drive away. He was focused on the road ahead, that fierce determination still on his face.

Chapter 24

We miss you

Y<small>AZ</small>

"I had to turn them away," Dee told me. "He didn't even bother to cancel the class."

"What? B–but he promised he'd–"

"Yaz, honestly, you were away for three days and he really didn't do much of anything that I could see. The only class he ran was for the advanced adults and even with that, you had to do all the clean-up when you got back. Just like you're having to do now."

I carried on rolling up the sail I was busy with. Dee was right. There was equipment everywhere, and this was becoming a regular thing with Bodhi. But what really upset me was the fact that he'd bailed on the kids while I was away last week. I knew he didn't approve of the academy side of the business – he'd dropped enough hints to that effect – but to let them all down like that. I bit my lip as I looked up at Dee.

"Okay, it's not ideal. But–"

"You deserve better, Yaz."

I looked away from her. The problem was that I struggled

208

to believe I did deserve better. Bodhi was a decent water sports instructor, but more importantly he looked after the finances and I really couldn't manage that side of things. Yes, I could ask for some help from my family. But that would mean admitting that I couldn't manage on my own – it would reinforce all of their beliefs that education was key to success. The trouble was that, regardless of how long I'd spent at school, I would never be good with numbers. They just didn't make any sense to me, however hard I tried. Maths just never made sense to me. I'd only just scrapped past in my GCSE and that had been on the second sitting. Bodhi had a great head for numbers so I thought we'd make a good team. The only problem was that he didn't seem to be too forthcoming when it came to explaining the books to me, or keeping me updated on how we were doing financially. He said it would take too long, and that I was better out on the water. But I was starting to get a bit worried. Bodhi had bought himself a new set of wing foiling equipment with company money and yet told me we couldn't afford any more small learner sails for the kids, which we desperately needed as the class was growing. But when I'd asked to look at all the spreadsheets, which he'd produced without hesitation, I just couldn't make head nor tail of them. He'd noticed my confused, defeated expression and just shaken my head from side to side using my ponytail (a move which was starting to really piss me off) and told me not to worry about it, that it was all in hand.

"I'll talk to him about letting the kids down," I muttered. "But you don't understand, Dee. I need him to be involved in the business."

Dee crouched down next to me and laid her hands over mine to stop me from fiddling with the sail ties. "You're exhausted, honey," she said softly. "You're running yourself into the ground making money for that prick and not seeing any of the rewards yourself. When was the last time you bought any new clothes that weren't gifted in sponsorship deals? When's the last time you did anything for yourself at all?"

"Yes, Yaz." My head snapped around at the sound of Heath's deep voice from the door of the shed. "When was that?" Dee and I straightened from our crouched positions over the sail and my hands went to my hips.

"What are you doing here?" I asked.

"We're friends now, aren't we?" Heath said with a shrug, and I narrowed my eyes at him. "Can't friends drop by to bring other friends lunch?"

Dee was looking at Heath with her head tilted to the side, her gaze assessing. I'd explained everything that happened with the funeral and some of the background about Heath and Verity's family. She'd commented that it explained a lot, but still didn't excuse his repeated shitty behaviour.

He pulled two bags from behind his back and gave us one each. "Don't worry, not an animal product in sight."

I hesitated but Dee shot forward to snatch one of bags out of his hand. "Thanks, big guy," she said, beaming at him, the traitor. Dee had skipped lunch to help me out, and the woman could work up a savage hunger. It seemed that she was prepared to forgive shitty behaviour if food was involved.

I gave Heath a small smile. "Thanks," I said as I took the other bag from his outstretched hand. He returned my smile before shoving both his hands into his pockets and taking a step back, as if holding himself back from touching me. My chest felt tight. I wished things were different – that Heath hadn't let me down too many times for me to trust him, that I didn't feel like I had so much to prove to him and my family, that I didn't feel I had to do all this on my own. But I was still smarting from Heath's rejection and my family's constant belittling. I couldn't move past it. Not yet.

"You didn't answer Dee's question," Heath went on. "When *was* the last time you did something for yourself?"

My smile dropped as I paused to scowl at Dee before putting my sandwich bag up on one of the shelves and squatting back down to continue rolling up the sail.

"You work too hard, you know," Heath said.

"He's right," Dee put in around a mouth full of sandwich. "I've been saying the same for weeks."

"Heath, you can hardly talk," I snapped, my movements becoming jerky as I packed down the next sail. "You're an emergency department doctor. You work crazy hours."

"I have days off, Yaz," Heath said softly. "I can still make time to see the people I care about, to have some fun."

"Who says I don't have fun?"

Heath squatted down in front of me so that I would be forced to look at him. "Your mum got a lot of things wrong that day at Max's, but she was right about one thing. You have lost weight. And you look tired, love. You're not the usual Yaz."

"What? Flaky, crazy, and idiotic Yaz, you mean?" I said, scowling at Heath now.

"How about chill, funny, quick to laugh, had-time-to-go-to-the-pub, Yaz? How about the Yaz who wasn't underweight and didn't have shadows under her eyes?"

Heath started folding up one of the other sails and I snatched it out of his hands and threw it to the side. Dee paused in her sandwich eating, her eyes going wide. Heath kept eye contact with me but straightened up from the ground with his hands held up, palm facing forward, as if to surrender.

"I'm fine," I spat out. "I don't need you interfering."

He crossed his arms over his chest. "You didn't ask *my* permission when you interfered in my life last week."

I broke eye contact to look to the side. He had a point, but I wasn't willing to concede anything. I took a deep breath in and let it out slowly.

"Things will improve. I'm building up the business."

"Could you let us help?" he asked. "Max and V already run a business. And I know..." He cleared his throat and lowered his voice a little. "I know numbers were always a bit... er... tricky for you. We could–"

"No," I snapped, my face now feeling too hot. Familiar shame washed over me. Incapable, ridiculous Yaz. They all still think I'm a joke.

Heath held up his hands again as I forced myself to swallow past the lump that had formed in my throat. "Everything is under control," I said in a tight voice that didn't sound like my own.

This wasn't the first offer of help I'd had over the last month. Max and my parents had gone from writing me off as the black sheep of the family to being right up in my grill. Now Mum and Dad visited the surf school, came down to the yoga studio, watched me windsurfing for a promotional video. They'd even approached me numerous times with financial offers, all of which I'd declined. Last week they'd tentatively asked if I needed help with balancing the books. They tried to be subtle about it, but I could tell they were worried.

Maybe I should have accepted my family's help, given that my trust in Bodhi was waning, but a fierce independent streak was now hard-wired into my psyche, and I couldn't come back from that. Accepting their money or help would be a sign of defeat, of weakness. I had come this far without their help or encouragement (active discouragement would actually be more accurate) and I wasn't going to go back now.

"Yaz," Dee said tentatively, her sandwich now forgotten. "Maybe it wouldn't be a bad idea to–"

"I said no!" I slashed my hand through the air and accidentally knocked a mast over, which clattered onto the concrete.

"Right, okay," Dee said. "Chill your beans. No need to take it out on the rigging."

Heath squatted down to lift the mast back up and leant it against the wall. More heat flooded my face as I looked down at the ground, one of my hands going up to rub the back of my neck.

"I'm sorry, Yaz," he said as he backed away again like I was a wild animal he was afraid of spooking. "I didn't mean to imply that you weren't on top of everything. I just worry about you. We all do. And we miss you."

I sighed. "I know you guys mean well. I just..." I didn't know how to explain it. All I knew was that I had to prove myself, and I had to do it on my own.

"You'll still come this weekend though, right?" Heath asked. "To the gala? You don't have to follow the dress code. If you wanted to tip up in flip-flops, nobody would care. Everyone's going to be there."

Of course, he'd expect me to turn up to a black-tie dinner in flip-flops, despite the fact that I had actually worn dresses before for Max and Verity's award ceremonies. Okay, so they hadn't exactly been conservative choices, but it wasn't as though I'd turned up in my beach gear. I decided then and there that yes, I was going to the bloody gala – but not as typical ridiculous Yaz.

Verity owed me one anyway.

Chapter 25

Crazy man

YAZ

"Right, let's get this show on the road," I said as I pushed open the front door to Max and Mia's house and strode into their house with Verity following closely behind. "The sooner I can get these heels off and into the bin, the better."

I was trying to shove my phone into a stupid tiny bag made for elves as I walked into the kitchen, and once I'd snapped it shut I looked up to see Max, Mia, Heath and Teddy standing around the island staring at me. They all looked like they'd been smacked across the face with a wet fish. Teddy actually dropped a cup, sending it clattering onto the granite surface and swearing as the tea slopped over onto his hand.

"Bloody hell, Midge," Max was the first to break the silence, and his voice was laced with shock. "You look... different."

I rolled my eyes. My brother probably thought that 'different' constituted high praise indeed. Truth was, I hadn't even had much of a chance to look in the mirror. Verity had arrived at my flat two hours ago armed with a dress, these torture devices I currently had strapped to my feet, and a whole suit-case full of make-up.

"Doesn't she just," said Verity, moving around me to come up beside her brother and elbow him sharply in his side. His mouth snapped shut, and he cleared his throat.

"Yaz... I–"

I tilted my head to the side in confusion as I watched him scramble for words. Heath was always so confident and charming – he always had the right compliment ready for the right situation. The fact he couldn't muster up one now was a bit disappointing. And I'd never seen him lost for words.

He tried again. "You look... I don't even know–"

"Crikey, Auntie Midge, you look proper mint," Teddy exclaimed.

I smiled at Teddy. At least the teenager in the room could string a sentence together.

"Thanks Ted. I'd like to say the same, but I reckon that t-shirt has seen better days."

Teddy was home for the summer holidays from university, and when he wasn't at his temporary job in Max's office, he was in full slovenly teenager mode. Everyone else, however, was dressed up – the men in black tie and the women in long ball gown style arrangements.

"V, you look mint as well, mind," Teddy added. "It's just I'm used to seeing you and Mia all trussed up in this stuff. It's rare Auntie Midge gets caught in a skirt."

"Don't make it weird, man-child," I said, shifting uncom-fortably on my feet and not liking this level of scrutiny. What the hell had Verity done to me? I felt like I'd grown a second head.

"I think we'd better get going," Mia said, as always being perceptive enough to notice my discomfort and doing some-thing to alleviate it. "I'm driving, obviously." One of her hands dropped to her bump self-consciously, and I moved to her with a wide smile on my face, pulling her in for a hug when I rounded the island. It was getting exciting now. Only four weeks to go. To say I was pleased for her and my brother was an understatement. Max was made to be a dad. He'd always been such a wonderful father figure to Teddy, even when Teddy's mum deserted them both for London. I was thrilled he would be able to have the opportunity again, but this time with someone who I knew would stick with him every second of the way.

"You are one hot mama-to-be," I said as I gave her and my future niece a squeeze. I wasn't lying. Mia looked totally stunning. But then she always did for this sort of thing. At every award ceremony she'd been to with Max over the last year, her appearance had been flawless. But I knew that, like me, she didn't enjoy having to dress up, didn't like being on show. Before she met my brother, Mia had been in an abusive marriage, and a lot of importance was put on the proviso that she look perfect at all times. Being 'trussed up' brought back painful memories for her, but she did it for my brother because she loved him, and she knew that even if she wore a bin bag, Max wouldn't bat an eye. My brother might be a gruff, grumpy northerner, but he loved his wife and wanted her happy. "But you don't have to drive just because you're preggers. We could—"

"I'm driving," Max said.

"Honey, it's fine," Mia put in. "You can have a beer and then—"

"Are you drinking?" Max asked.

"No but—"

"Then why am I drinking? Anyway, you hate driving late. Let's all stop staring at my sister and get out of here."

"Heath?" Verity asked, waving her hand in front of his face.

"Have you had a stroke? We need to go. This is your deal. They're not going to care if *we're* late. You're the one speaking."

Heath shook his head as if to clear it, glanced at me again before visibly swallowing as his gaze swept from the top of my head to my shoes / instruments of Satan. Tonight was 'his show', as Verity put it. It was a gala dinner in aid of the children's retreat that Heath and Verity were helping to build at the site of their parents' former house. Heath would be speaking about the difference that the retreat would make to young people's lives in order to drum up some on-the-night donations. Most of his colleagues from the hospital would be there, as would his local friends along with many of the twins' insanely posh friends. I'd considered trying to get out of it (I craved Heath too much to have to suffer through seeing him in black tie – the few times I'd seen him wearing it before the oestrogen rush nearly killed me) but after he visited me at the harbour, pulled the friend card out again and implied I wasn't capable of dressing posh, I couldn't say no. From his expression just now, he clearly had not expected me to follow the dress code to the letter.

"Have fun now, kids!" Teddy called after us as we all made our way to the front door. Both the dogs blocked our way with Winnie darting in front of me so fast I almost went over on these stupid stilts. Just as I was pitching forward, a strong arm wrapped around my back, with another going to my hand to steady me. It had been over a month since he'd touched me and it was like lighting a fuse. Like my body had been asleep and was only now sparking back to life. I looked up into those clear blue eyes, and for a moment it was as if time stood still. Everything else faded away.

"Want to get your bloody hands off my sister, mate?" Max's voice cut through my Heath-induced trance, and we both flinched away from each other as if we'd received an electric shock.

"She fell, Max," Heath snapped, giving Winnie's head a rub and then belly rub when she dropped to her back (it was safe to say that Winnie had warmed up to Heath in a big way over the last month) and then moving her out of the way.

"A likely story," Max muttered as he fell back between me and Heath, putting his hand to my lower back and guiding me out of the door like I was still his ten-year-old little sister.

This new, attentive version of Max would regularly drop into my flat to check I was okay. He even came over to fix my washing machine after I'd mentioned it in passing to Mia. And he'd turned ultra-protective – hence the back-off vibes to Heath.

I sighed and followed Verity out of the door. She was looking back at her brother with a small smile on her face.

Chapter 26

I know how to handle myself

HEATH

I pulled at my shirt collar and cleared my throat as I followed Yaz out of the door. What the fuck has my sister done now? I'm not sure what I'd expected Yaz to wear, but I certainly hadn't thought she would allow Verity to dress her in a full-length, silvery blue, backless gown with matching four-inch heel stilettos. Somehow V had not only managed to get Yaz into the outfit, but she'd even convinced her to wear make-up with smoky eyes and pale lips. Yaz's unenhanced beauty was difficult to deal with and garnered a fair amount of attention – this Yaz was off the charts. And what had I done when she walked in? I'd stood there with my mouth open like a goldfish out of water and then stuttered a couple of nonsensical words. Complimenting women was my forte, for Christ's sake! Where was all my hard-won charm when I needed it? Couldn't I have managed to tell her she looked beautiful? The trouble was that beautiful didn't even cover it. When she'd walked into that room, it was like all the oxygen was sucked out. She was all I could see, and my mind went blank. I stewed over it in the car, not concentrating on the conversation around me – Verity was sitting in between me and Yaz, with Mia and Max in the front. I gave myself a pep talk, chastised myself for dropping the ball with the one woman I really wanted to impress, and then decided to do something about it.

"You look beautiful," I blurted out, rather louder than I had intended, into the car. There was silence for a beat.

"Er... thanks, man," Max said. "But I was only asking about your grouting. Awkward."

I sighed and scrubbed my hands down my face. I needed to get it together. This was ridiculous. V squeezed my hand. When I looked down at her, she was smiling a very smug smile – she'd done this to me deliberately.

Things only went downhill from there. When I'd guilt-tripped Yaz into coming tonight, I had not anticipated the consequences. I hadn't realised just how much attention she would attract. I'd forgotten that day in the emergency department when she came in with Bryn.

"Who is *that*, mate?" asked Tim, one of the ED nurses, staring across the room at Yaz, who had kicked off her shoes and dragged Mia onto the dance floor. Yaz's dancing was, and always had been... unusual. It was slightly off the beat, she used a lot of sweeping arm movements, the occasional leap across the floor, lots of spinning – she'd even been known to put in the odd forward roll. It was like some sort of weird, inept modern ballet on steroids. And it was so... so *Yaz*. She didn't care what she looked like out there – she was totally free. Mia was looking rather more self-conscious until Yaz swept her up and started carefully twirling her around, pushing everyone else out of their way so that Mia would feel safe to dance, even if heavily pregnant. Mia's face went from mortified at Yaz's antics to bright red before she started giggling when Yaz grabbed Verity from the side of the dance floor and dipped her almost to the ground. My sister rarely danced and she certainly never let anyone dip her. Yaz had the element of surprise on her side though and before long Verity was giggling as well. More than anyone else I had ever met, Yaz knew how to have a good time, and how to sweep everyone else along with her

"Jesus Christ," Ruben the orthopaedic consultant piped up. "Whoever she is, I would walk through hellfire to drink her bath water. Wait–" He squinted over at Yaz for a moment. "Isn't she that bird from the other day? Came into the ED. She yours, Heath?"

"I don't think it's appropriate to objectify women," I said in the most condescending tone I could muster. "I'm sure Liz and Penny don't appreciate it."

Liz snorted. "Don't worry about us, Heath. I hear much worse on a daily basis working with these meatheads."

"And she does look beautiful," Penny put in, elbowing me in the ribs and nodding encouragingly towards Yaz. It was almost insulting how over me she was. "I think gay or straight, male or female, it would be impossible not to comment on how insanely attractive that woman is. I reckon I'd drink her bath-water too, and I usually like my lovers big, hairy and very, very male."

"You didn't answer the question, Heath," Ruben said. "She yours or not?"

"Now *that* I object to," Liz said, frowning at Ruben. "You don't own a person, you sexist pig. It's not possible for her to be his, even if they're together."

"It *is* possible," I muttered, my eyes still fixed on Yaz. She was twirling Verity now. They both had a near miss with a server carrying a tray of champagne glasses. Yaz paused to apologise profusely to him. To be honest, he looked more likely to drop the tray in the face of Yaz's expressive apology than he had when she'd nearly crashed into him. He shook his head, a star-struck look in his eyes, and I could see him saying "It's fine". After some more apologies, Yaz dazzled him with a bright smile before she spun away. It took a good few seconds for the poor man to recover from the encounter. He blinked down at his tray as if he'd forgotten it was even there before he moved away again into the crowd.

"Ugh," Liz huffed out. "Don't you start. I thought you were more evolved than that, Heath. What about the objectification of women?"

"I didn't say *I* owned *her*. If anything, it's the other way around."

I didn't wait for a reply or bother to look at their shocked expressions. I just walked towards Yaz. But by the time I made it to the dance floor she was walking away to the bar arm-in-arm with Mia and Verity. A couple of my old schoolmates blocked my path, and it was too tricky to shake them off, especially given the amount they'd pledged in the auction earlier. When I finally managed to get away, it took me ages to track her down.

She was tucked in a corner with Josh, who appeared to be pouring his heart out to her and looked on the verge of tears. Yaz had her head tipped to the side, all her attention on him, as if she was able to look down into his soul. She'd met the guy twice and appeared to be getting further with him than I had in six months of being his educational supervisor. Then he hugged her, and I felt like my head was going to explode. On my way over to them I had to remind myself that Josh was scared of me, that I didn't believe in physical violence as a way to solve my problems, *and* that it would probably be poor form to rip off Josh's arm from its socket just because it was wrapped around Yaz's mostly bare back.

"Josh," I gritted out as I drew level with them.

"Oh, hi, Dr Markham," he said, thankfully releasing Yaz to look up at me.

"I've told you to call me Heath," I said, my voice tight with the anger I was trying to suppress. I took a step closer to Yaz, positioning myself between her and Josh enough to force him to take a small step back. Despite this, he seemed oblivious to my rapidly deteriorating mood.

"Right, yes – that's what we were just talking about," he said, his eyes wide and earnest. "I've *got* to try and find that inner confidence so that I can believe I deserve to be on a first name basis with a man like you."

My eyebrows went up. "A man like *me*? What are you on about?"

"It's not just that you're my boss, it's this whole alpha vibe – it throws me off. Yaz was just telling me how to dig deep and believe in myself enough to hold my own." He took a deep breath in and then let it out slowly.

"Tell him, Josh," Yaz encouraged. "Remember: Superman pose. You are your own man." She put both of her hands on her hips and threw her shoulders back in the manner of a super-hero, and Josh followed her lead. It was enough for some humour to leak through my anger, and I found myself having to suppress a smile. When he turned back to me, his voice was clearer, with even a little of steel behind it – unheard of for Josh.

"Working in emergency medicine gives me massive anxiety."

I blinked. A conversation about Josh's career was not what I had envisaged when I made my way over here. But the man had a point.

"No shit."

"Exactly! You know how stressed I get. I hate it. I can't stand the unpredictability, the risk, the uncertainty, the level of patient contact."

He looked on the verge of tears. My anger fell away, and

Josh went from being a man who'd been touching the most important woman in the world to me, to being my trainee again. I put my hand on his shoulder and gave it a squeeze. "Hey, that's okay, Josh. It's not for everyone. Maybe you can–"

"I'm going to be a pathologist. There's no point doing something just because I want to be George Clooney. The ED just isn't for me."

"Josh, did you join that training scheme so you could be like George Clooney?"

He shrugged. "Maybe. And I thought it might push me to be... oh, I don't know – to be more like you."

"Like *me*?"

"Well, you or someone similar. Someone a bit more alpha. More confident. But Yaz thinks I should just be myself. She says that's good enough."

"Not just good enough, Josh," Yaz put in, stepping around me to lay her hand on his arm. "You're fan-bloody-tastic. You just have to believe in yourself."

Josh gave her a small smile. "That means such a lot to me. I just... I can't tell you how much..." his voice became too choked to continue, and he launched himself back at Yaz, who of course allowed herself to be hugged, *again*. Okay, so the man was having some sort of mental breakthrough, but did he have to do it with his paws all over Yaz?

"That's great, Josh," I said through my teeth, clapping him a little too hard on the back and then pulling him back from Yaz by the back of his coat, so that he was quite rapidly a good three feet away from her. He looked a little bewildered by the sudden extrication, but I gave his shoulder a couple of hard pats to distract him and forced a smile.

"I'm sorry if I've disappointed you," he said in a small voice, and I felt the anger drain away again, but did take the opportunity to block his path to another Yaz hug.

"Josh, you are a great registrar. To be honest, over-confidence is way more of a problem than under confidence in medicine. But Yaz is right – you've got to do what makes you happy. You've got another thirty years at least left of this crap – you don't want to be miserable for decades. You need to be in the right speciality for you."

"Thanks, Heath," Josh said, using my first name unprompted for the first time. He looked lighter somehow, as though a weight had been lifted from his shoulders.

"Go for what you want, Josh," Yaz said, widening her eyes at him for some reason and then jerking her head to the side. Josh looked over her shoulder and squared his shoulders.

"Right," he said, his voice full of the kind of determination I didn't think I'd ever heard from him before. "Bloody right I will."

With that, he walked straight through Yaz and me, not sparing either of us a second glance. When I clocked his direction of travel, I almost sprang forward to halt his progress. He was headed straight towards Mel, one of the pharmacists who worked in our department. I did not fancy his chances. But then after a couple of awkward moments where Mel gave him her polite but slightly forced smile, he said something to surprise a genuine laugh out of her, and the conversation seemed to flow from there. I was shocked. I would never have imagined he'd get up the courage to approach her.

While I was distracted by the miracle of a confident Josh, my arsehole colleagues had closed in on Yaz. Ruben had brought her a fresh glass of champagne and Tim stopped one of the servers so that Yaz could grab a canapé – when he realised Yaz couldn't eat any of them as they were all beef, Tim went off and found one of the few trays of mini quinoa crackers, presenting it to her like he'd hunted a buffalo for her, not just sourced some vegan snacks from the buffet table.

When they asked what she did, and she told them about the well-being centre and that she was a yoga and water sports instructor, their mouths collectively dropped open.

"So, you uh..." Ruben swallowed before continuing, "spend a fair amount of your working day in a wetsuit, then?"

Yaz laughed.

"Well, I don't swan off down the harbour like this, that's for sure."

"I might be interested in learning to–"

"Don't even think about it," I blurted out, my grip on my glass tightening until my knuckles were white.

"Heath," Yaz said in a warning tone, which I stupidly ignored.

"Hey, man," Ruben held his hands up in surrender, levelling a knowing smile in my direction, "I was just trying to get my watersports on. No need to go caveman on us."

"She's a *professional*. She only teaches adults who are already competent. You're about thirty years too old for her beginner classes. She also doesn't need some pervert staring at her chest in a wetsuit for hours on end."

"Heath!" Yaz's voice was furious now. "Will you lay off?"

Ruben was smirking – he seemed happy enough to have pushed me over the edge and lose my cool.

"Interesting," Tim said. "Never seen you even vaguely close to losing your shit. Must be something in the champagne."

"Fuck off," I muttered before I could stop myself, which only made their smiles grow wider.

"Come on, Ruben," Tim said, clearly not taking any offence at being told to fuck off. "Let's leave Heath to finish pissing around his area."

As those two pricks disappeared into the crowd, I turned towards a visibly furious Yaz.

"What on earth was that about?" she snapped.

"They were hitting on you," I said. "They can be real dick-heads and I didn't want them making you feel uncomfortable."

"Heath, men have been hitting on me since I was thirteen years old." I flinched at this unpleasant but not altogether surprising piece of news. "I know how to handle myself, and I know how to deal with men like that. They were perfectly harmless. In fact, I'm willing to bet the only reason they even started flirting was to bait you into a reaction, which they got in spades."

I scuffed my feet on the floor and looked down at my champagne glass. If I wasn't careful and didn't loosen my grip, I was going to snap the thin stem and look even more like a crazy man. I didn't know what to say without digging myself into a bigger hole with Yaz. The fact was that I ached for her with such longing, it was almost unbearable. That sense of acute yearning, coupled with everyone else bloody touching and flirting with her, was sending me over the edge. I had never really experienced real jealousy before. And it wasn't as if Yaz was even mine to feel jealous over – she'd made that very clear. I heard her sigh and felt her hand on my arm. It felt like her touch was burning through my suit jacket, branding my skin.

"Heath I–" she paused, then took in a deep breath, moving closer to me. I could smell her light perfume and the shampoo from her hair. "I can go if that's easier. I don't want to ruin tonight for you." I closed my eyes for a moment. When I opened them, they fixed on Yaz's beautiful green-brown ones, looking up at me with concern.

"Stay," I said. "I'm sorry. I don't know what's got into me. Please stay. It's funny, I thought... well, I thought you'd hate this sort of thing. I didn't imagine that you would..."

She smiled up at me, and for a moment; I forgot how to breathe. "You thought I'd turn up in my denim cut-offs and make an arse out of myself?"

"Yes–I mean, no. I didn't think that you–"

"I know exactly what you thought." Her smile had slipped now, and she took her hand off my arm, which felt cold at its loss. "Your opinion of me hasn't changed as much as you like to say it has. Not really. You don't think I belong in your world? Well, I know for a fact you wouldn't last five minutes in mine."

With that, she turned and left me standing there with my mouth open. How had that degenerated so quickly? For the rest of the evening, she made it very obvious how well she did fit in with all my colleagues.

I needed to stop making assumptions where Yaz was concerned.

And I also needed to prove her wrong. I could charm the pants off her world, no problem.

Chapter 27

Not into all this aggression

HEATH

I held my breath as she landed on the crest of a wave after pulling off an incredible front loop. The flash of white in her tanned face proved that the stunts I found anxiety-provoking to watch made her so happy it was visible from the shore. The drone buzzing overhead came a little lower, no doubt to focus on her face for a moment before she went into the next stunt.

"Jesus, Midge'll break her neck one of these days," Max muttered.

"She knows what she's doing," Mia said. "If you'd taken more of an interest in her 'buggering about on the water', then this wouldn't surprise you."

"Okay, okay! I'm a shite brother. You don't have to bang on about it."

"You're not a shite brother – you just continually underestimate her and it's annoying." Mia took Max's hand, and he moved in to whisper something into her ear. Huge, grumpy Max being told off by his much smaller and quieter wife was always entertaining, but I could do without the lovey dovey stuff at the moment. If you'd asked me two years ago if my best friend was capable of public displays of emotion, other than the gruff back slaps he bestows on his stepson, I would have given you a resounding *no*. But Mia was the best thing that ever happened to him. I only wished I listened to her sooner about Yaz and the way I had treated her.

"Whoop! Whoop! Go, Auntie Midge! You da man!" shouted Teddy, ignoring his dad and Mia, as was his latest policy when it came to their rogue PDAs.

"Teddy, darling," Verity said from my other side. "I don't think they need cheering on the video they're making. And Yaz is anything but a man."

"She kicks arse out there," he said, giving Verity a playful shove. "And she's so da man it's totally unhooked."

"I just hope she makes it back in one piece," I said under my breath and Verity elbowed me in the ribs.

"Hey, aren't you meant to be the ultimate in chilled today?" she asked. "With your new look and all."

I was dressed in board shorts and flip-flops, which was as close to *surfer dude* as I was ever likely to get. I ignored her and looked out to sea. Finally Yaz seemed to be heading inland. When she hit the surf, I jogged over to help her bring in her sail and board. To my extreme annoyance, I wasn't the only one ready to haul her stuff out. Bodhi was closer and had already unhooked her board from her sail before I could make it out over the breaking surf. The fucker winked at me as he walked past. Yaz looked surprised to see me as she waded out of the water. I made a gesture to take her sail, but she just raised one eyebrow and laughed. Both dogs were dancing around her feet as she made her surefooted way up the sand.

"Sorry, big man," she said. "But I've got this. Wind's too strong unless you're used to the sail." When I got up to the bank with her, she proceeded to sort out her windsurfer and all her other equipment with the same adept efficiency with which she'd handled the sail. And we were all left looking on as she and Bodhi loaded up the sails and boards from the day of teaching.

"What brings you all down here?" she asked. Now that she was on the floor rolling up her sail, both dogs were able to lick her face and nuzzle at her neck. She eventually had to pause her efforts to oblige them with head scratches, followed by full-on rolling around on the floor with them.

My chest seized at the surprise in her voice. How many award ceremonies of Max and Verity's had she been to? I could picture her now at *my* graduation from medical school and at all the minor victories along the way. We'd celebrated my consultant job when she was eighteen and that had been after I'd started avoiding her in. It didn't stop her turning out to support me, though.

"We wanted to see what all the fuss was about," Verity said into the awkward silence. "This one has been banging on about it for weeks."

Yaz darted me a surprised look, which made me feel even more of a shit. Of course, she didn't know how much I admired what she did on the water. I'd never bothered to tell her.

"I always knew you kicked butt out there, Auntie Midge," Teddy said, trying to control Roger and get him back on the lead so Yaz could pack everything up.

"Thanks, Ted," she said, smiling at him as she reached up to unzip the back of her wetsuit. I started forward to help her, but bloody Bodhi was there again before I could jump in front of him. He smirked at me as he swept Yaz's hair out of the way and took way too long to pull the zip down, standing so close his lips were practically touching her neck.

"Well, I hope they got some good shots. Helps with the promo for the centre, doesn't it, Bode?"

"And for Brazil," Bodhi said as Yaz started shimmying out of her wetsuit. "Don't forget about that."

Yaz bit her lip. "Bodhi, I've still not agreed to anything with – "

"You're going to Brazil?" Verity asked, her gaze sharp on Yaz.

"We'll kill it out there with guiding," Bodhi put in.

"It's just an idea," Yaz said softly to Verity. "I haven't committed to it. I just...I did think it might be a good change for me. Just for a few months." She's shed her wetsuit entirely now and the rash vest below was practically transparent, with her bikini leaving little to the imagination. But that was Yaz – totally at ease with her body. Happy to be covered in salt and sand as long as she was looking out on the sea and doing what she loved. "Listen, I've got to go and talk to these peeps now."

The film-makers were signalling her over for an interview and, in typical Yaz fashion, she simply shrugged on some cut-offs, left her salty curls to hang down her back, and didn't even check in a mirror before she jogged over to them. But not before Max had given her an uncharacteristic bear hug and told her how proud he was of her. My heart felt heavy as she had to clear her throat and blink away tears of surprise at her brother's gesture. Everyone else said their goodbyes as well, Teddy lifting her up off her feet and spinning her around in celebration.

"What are you going to do about that?" Verity asked me in a low voice as we watched Yaz walk away.

I shrugged. "What do you expect me to do, V?"

"Give her a reason to stay," she whispered before turning to leave with the others.

Bodhi and I were the only ones left watching her interview, just out of her earshot.

"Would have been a lot easier for me if she'd just shagged the director," Bodhi said in a casual tone as he leaned back and against his van and crossed his arms over his chest. I had been engrossed in watching one of Yaz's animated descriptions to the camera crew, using her whole body to demonstrate something she'd done on the water.

"You are such a piece of shit, you know that right?" I said through gritted teeth.

He shrugged. "She needs to know how to play the game, man. There are lots of hot chicks out there who can rip it up on the waves. If she wants more airtime then she's gotta loosen up. For a bird that pretends to be chill, she's pretty frigid."

I took a deep breath in through my nose and let it out slowly through my mouth. It wouldn't do my cause any good to punch Yaz's business partner in the face. I needed to bide my time so that I could tell my 'friend' later what this slimeball had been saying behind her back and have her actually believe me.

"Talk like that about her again and you'll be in my emergency department needing a pretty extensive trauma survey from my colleagues. Understand?"

He smirked. "Whatever. Yaz is non-violent, man. Don't think you're gonna get to her v-jay-jay that way." With that, he walked off in the direction of the volleyball court, where a group of Yaz's friends were gathered. They were an eclectic bunch – some surfer types, hippies in tie-dye, a couple sporting some pretty impressive dreadlocks. All were tanned, and a fair few were covered in tattoos. They all seemed at home on the beach with the same salt-encrusted barefoot look as Yaz, and they all had this beautiful, slightly wild quality to them – again, like Yaz. Even with my board shorts and flip-flops, I did not fit in with these people. I glanced at Yaz again. She was laughing into the camera – totally uninhibited, completely free, almost painfully beautiful. I needed to focus on what was important. I took a moment to calm down, then headed off in her direction. The interview had finished now and one producer was standing just a little too close to her. She flinched slightly when he reached up to brush from sand from her cheek. I quickened my pace.

"Hey, babe," I said, surprising myself – it was probably the first time the word 'babe' had ever passed my lips. Yaz turned to me and blinked. I came up next to her and took her hand. Her fingers clutched mine instantly in an almost desperate way, and I really had the urge to shake that slimeball of a producer. "You finished?" The snap in my tone caused the creepy producer bloke to take a step back, and I gave him an insincere smile.

"Um, I think so," she said. "Dex, you need anything else?"

Dex looked down at our entwined hands, then back up at Yaz, a flash of annoyance in his expression for a moment, before he cleared it and forced a smile.

"Sure," he said, in a rather forced, casual tone. "We'll just hang around and get a few shots with you and your mates, if you don't mind. Helps with the promo."

So that was how I ended up playing volleyball on the beach with Yaz's friends and a camera crew looking on. I'd like to say that Bodhi and I were mature enough to not let things degenerate, but before I knew it we were full-on *Top Gun*-ning that sitch. We may as well have covered our torsos with oil and worn the aviators. Luckily Yaz was on my team, and I rule at volleyball. So between us, we smashed Bodhi's side.

Other than Bodhi, Yaz's mates were all pretty decent people. Some were totally tied to the sea like Yaz, making their living on the water whether via water sports or diving – there was even a fisherman among the group – others were yoga teachers or alternative therapy practitioners. None were conventional, and all clearly loved Yaz. And from the conversations that went on around me it was also clear that Yaz was the friend many of them could rely on. She was the one who'd volunteered to pick up her mate's kids from school last week. She was the one who had taught a windsurfing class when her other mate had a cold. How I ever thought Yaz was unreliable, beggared belief, to be honest. The only fly in the ointment of Yaz's friends was Bodhi. Unfortunately he seemed very adept at hiding his arseholery from Yaz and all her mates, apart from Dee, that is. I'd caught Dee giving Bodhi some strong side-eye a couple of times now. Clearly she didn't fully buy into his act either. Dee and Yaz seemed close, and I knew Dee was essential to the well-being side of the business, but it seemed that Bodhi had wormed his way further into the actual running of it than anyone else involved.

"You think you'll manage to tap that?" Bodhi said under his breath as he sat down on the sand next to me. Yaz and some of the girls had gone out on paddleboards to do yoga out at sea, and there was just me, Bodhi and a handful of others left – but with the wind direction, I was the only one in earshot of Bodhi's comment.

"Are you seriously this much of a prick?" I answered, giving Bodhi a disgusted look, which just caused his smirk to ramp up a couple of notches.

"Come on, man," he said. "We both know you're not hanging out with this bunch of losers for the fun of it."

"I thought these people were your friends?" It was getting hard to keep my voice down. This water monkey was seriously winding me up.

He snorted and took another gulp of his beer. His eyes were glassy and red-rimmed now, and I wondered how much he'd had to drink and whether he was taking anything else with it. "I'm not one of these hippy fuckers. I can ride and I'm making cash out of it, but I don't buy into any of this bollocks. Yaz makes me money, end of."

"You are the worst business partner *ever*. Not to mention a despicable human being."

"Don't pretend to be all high and mighty. I've seen you treat her like shit before. Only reason you're here is because you want in there. Only reason I'm here is so I can take advantage of these fucking idiots and rake in the cash. Can't say I blame you – wouldn't mind tapping it myself if she wasn't such a frigid bitch."

My temper is something that I rarely lose outwardly. Seeing my parents out of control so much as a child had made me very cautious about expressed emotion. But listening to Bodhi, whom I'd just watched over the last four hours pretending to be super chilled and great mates with these people, openly admitting that he would rip them all off given half a chance and calling Yaz a frigid bitch, tipped me over the edge. My beer fell out of my hand onto the ground, and I launched myself at him. As I pinned him to the sand, he still had that fucking smirk on his face, as if he'd won whatever battle we were engaged in.

"Don't you ever talk about her like that!" I shouted as I shook him by the front of his t-shirt.

I felt a hand on my shoulder and shook it off, focusing still on Bodhi.

"Heath!" Yaz's voice broke through the red mist and I relaxed my grip on Bodhi. "Let him go. What are you doing?"

I pushed away from him, shoving him back into the sand in disgust. Bodhi's smirk had been replaced by a totally fake shocked look and he was rubbing his chest as he sat up as if I'd hurt him.

"For fuck's sake," I muttered under my breath as I saw Yaz bend over him, checking his chest and shoulders for injuries. "Yaz, I barely touched the bastard."

When she turned back to me, it was clear that she was furious.

"Bodhi is *completely* non-violent. You can't just come here and assault my friends, Heath."

"He's *not* your friend. You should have heard what he was saying about you. He's a bloody con man. Yaz, you've got to listen to me. I–"

"I gave you a chance here," she said in a low voice. When I glanced over her shoulder, Bodhi flashed me a triumphant smirk. It took all my self-control not to launch at him again. "Just because we're unconventional and we don't see the world like you doesn't mean we're all a dodgy bunch of weirdos."

"I'm not judging any of you guys." I swept my arm out towards Yaz and her friends. "It's *him* I have a problem with." I pointed at Bodhi, who was still rubbing his chest and looking fake-shocked.

"If you can't treat me and my friends with respect, then I think you'd better leave." Her eyes flashed and her hands went to her hips. There would be no explaining anything to her while she was still so angry. How had I buggered this up so royally? It was made even worse as it followed the fundraiser where Yaz had fitted in so well with all my friends and colleagues. Of the two of us, I was proving to be the liability, the one with the potential to embarrass. I felt a flash of anger and scowled across at Bodhi.

"This isn't over," I snarled at him. The bastard winked at me before rearranging his features into a confused expression and holding both his hands up.

"Yo, man. I'm not into all this aggression. You should try meditating. It can really balance out all that testosterone." A few of the others were nodding along with him. I was willing to bet that this dickhead had never meditated in his life. I did notice Dee looking at him through narrowed eyes though.

"Just go, Heath. I should never have let you stay anyway. This isn't your scene."

"Yaz, listen," I started toward her, but she took a step back. My shoulders dropped in defeat and I stopped in my tracks. If only I hadn't lost Yaz's trust in a hundred different ways then she might have believed me about Bodhi. As it was, I was going to have to concede defeat. This round, anyway.

Chapter 28

I want to be there for you

YAZ

"Bryn?" I rapped on the door again. Still no response. His hearing had deteriorated over the last year, but I had bought him one of those doorbells that echoed around the house like a foghorn a few months ago – even he couldn't ignore that unless he'd unplugged the bloody thing. After a couple more minutes alternating between rapping on the door and leaning on the doorbell, I opened the keysafe to get my key. When I let myself in I was met with awful silence, and a terrible feeling of foreboding ran through me.

I found him in the living room. He was sitting in the same chair I'd left him in that morning when I'd brought him down a cup of tea, but now was slumped over to the side.

"Bryn?" I dropped onto my knees in front of him and shook his shoulder. He stirred slightly, his eyelids flickered, but otherwise there was no response. That was when I noticed one side of his mouth was downturned and lax. I grabbed both his hands in mine. "Bryn, honey, squeeze my hands." One side gave a light squeeze, the other stayed completely limp.

"Okay, okay," I muttered, withdrawing one of my hands, which was shaking and using it to draw out my mobile from my back pocket.

My hands were still shaking as I stroked some of Bryn's hair back from his forehead two hours later. He looked so small on the hospital bed. How could anyone with as much presence and personality as Bryn look small? He was pale and his eyes were closed now. He had stirred briefly in the ambulance on the way here and tried to speak to me, but half of his face wasn't cooperating, and I couldn't decipher what he was trying to say. He did manage to squeeze my hand again with his good one when I told him I'd stay with him. There had been so much going on since we'd arrived in A&E that this was the first opportunity I'd had to really look at him. An oxygen mask covered his nose and mouth, and he was hooked up to all manner of wires and tubing. I felt a tear slip down my cheek and swiped it away before it could drop. There was no use me falling apart – I had to be strong for Bryn.

"Yaz?" I turned to see Heath standing at the end of the bed. Where had he come from and how long had he been standing there? "Are you alright?"

I was staggered by the amount of relief I felt on just seeing him and hearing his deep, steady voice. All I wanted to do was run the few steps to get to him and melt into his arms so he could tell me that everything was going to be okay. But I stiffened my spine and forced myself to stay where I was. He wasn't the one I should run to – he'd proved that more than once.

"I'm fine. It's Bryn I want to know about." After the initial flurry of activity and the CT scan, everyone seemed to have backed off now. Shouldn't they be shoving tubes down his throat and getting him up to an intensive care unit? "His breathing sounds funny. Doesn't he need–?"

"Midge, let's talk outside a minute, okay?" He'd moved to stand next to me now, and I felt his large, warm hand on my back.

"No, I need to stay with him. I don't–"

"Tim will stay with him a minute."

I noticed a nurse had come into the cubicle now, his kind smile directed at me. My brows drew together. "He needs someone with him he knows. I should–"

"Five minutes, Midge."

I gave Bryn's hair one last stroke and then huffed out a sigh. "Okay, five minutes," I conceded as I pulled back from the bed. Heath's hand stayed on my back as he guided me out of the cubicle and into the centre of the emergency department. I barely registered all the activity going on around us, or the series of orders Heath was giving out to his juniors as we went past, deftly handing over control of the department and not breaking his stride to steer me out of the double doors and into the corridor. We made it to his office, and he guided me to a seat while he perched on his desk. I frowned.

"I don't want to sit down, Heath. I need to get back to– "

"Please, Midge," his soft-spoken command broke through my determination. As I looked into his eyes and saw the concern there, I had another sick sense of foreboding. My legs felt stiff, but I forced myself to bend them enough to sit in the chair.

"Listen, Heath. You need to arrange some sort of intensive care for him or something. His breathing's all funny and he's so pale. I think he needs a ventilator or some sort of– "

"Yaz, I'm so sorry, but Bryn really isn't very well."

I threw my hands up and then slapped them down on the

arms of the stupid chair. "That's what I'm saying. He's *sick*. He needs to be sorted out. There must be some sort of–"

"He's had a massive stroke, Yaz," Heath continued in that same calm voice. "It's taken out a large percentage of his left hemisphere."

"Exactly! That's why he needs to be–"

"You did everything right. Okay? His daughter's very grateful that you were there."

"You've spoken to Margot?" I blinked up at him, and he gave a slow nod. "Shit, I completely forgot to ring her. She must be frantic. I can't–"

"Margot's fine. She's on her way down here, but with traffic, she doesn't think she'll make it for a couple of hours. Hopefully, she'll be here before..." He trailed off and then cleared his throat.

"Before what?"

"Bryn's very sick, Yaz."

Suddenly, his gaze felt too intense. I had to close my eyes to shut it out.

"B–but we've still got a Monopoly game on the go. He bought a hotel on Mayfair yesterday. I brought him a cup of tea this morning and he told me my leggings were offensive. He can't be..."

Heath pushed off the desk and crouched down in front of me. It was only after he'd framed my face with his hands, and swiped both of my cheeks with his thumbs, that I realised I was crying. He then reached into his pocket and pulled out a tissue for me, which I took and wiped my face with. Jesus, I needed to get it together so I could stick up for Bryn.

"He's had a large stroke and I don't think he's going to be able to recover from it."

"You don't know that," I said, my voice all choked up now, causing me to be even more frustrated. "People recover from strokes. He's a tough old bastard. You can't just write him off."

Heath shook his head slowly and then took both my hands. His felt so warm as they engulfed mine. "He's ninety-one, Midge."

"I know but—"

"He didn't want any heroics if something like this happened to him. He's got an advance directive to that effect. The last thing he wants is to be hooked up to machines with no quality of life. You know how independent he is. You know he wouldn't want that."

His face blurred in front of me now as the tears came thick and fast. A sob hitched in my throat, and I lost that strength I'd been clinging to with my fingernails. My body simply fell forward into Heath's. He caught me in his strong arms and pulled me into him, bringing us both up to standing. I continued to sob against his chest as he stroked my hair and spoke softly into my hair about how Bryn wouldn't want me to be sad, how everything was going to be okay, how I could stay with Bryn, how they'd make him comfortable. When my crying fit finally subsided, I felt embarrassment shoot through me at my loss of control and tried to pull back from Heath to put some space between us. He gave me one last squeeze then let me go. As his arms fell away I took a good step back, using the tissue he'd given me to continue swiping at my face.

"Okay," I said eventually, my voice hoarse from crying. "Thank you for explaining it to me." For someone who'd just spent the last few minutes sobbing into a man's chest, I sounded ridiculously formal. "I'd better get back to him." I swallowed the rest of my tears and squared my shoulders. Bryn needed me. Now was not the time to fall apart into some sort of weepy mess.

"I'll take you back to his cubicle." Again, that large hand

settled at the base of my spine, steadying me and my emotions, which I found both comforting and annoying.

"I can find my way there."

"I'll take you back to him, Yaz." His voice was soft still, but his tone was firm, with maybe a subtle undercurrent of annoyance. "You don't have to do every damn thing by yourself." The annoyance was unmistakable now. "Shit, sorry." He said after a beat, and then in a softer tone, "But I *want* to be there for you. I need to. I'd appreciate it if you could let me do that. Just this once."

I looked away from the pleading look in his eyes and gave a brief nod. He sighed and opened the door for me. His hand stayed on my back until I was back by Bryn's bedside. Before he left me, he leaned down and kissed my temple. I felt the warmth of that kiss all the way through to my bones.

The next three hours passed slowly. Bryn was moved to a side room which was much quieter, but within which my voice seemed to reverberate. I talked to him about our Monopoly games and how much of a cheat he was. About how the tight bastard hadn't had the boiler updated in over forty years and that the water pressure was total crap. I reassured him that Doris, his cat, would be looked after while he was sick. I even read him some of the *Daily Mail* as I knew the stubborn right-wing old coot would like it. I even threatened to read him the *Guardian*, half expecting him to sit up and tell me to *bugger off*. People came and went during that time, but it was Heath who brought me tea and a sandwich. When he came in, I was in a flat panic.

"His breathing's changed," I said as Heath came up behind me. I was holding Bryn's hand on the bed and staring down at the erratic movement of his chest. He would take a few breaths and then stop for a long period of time before another set of breaths. It was scaring me.

Heath pulled a chair over and sat it next to mine. Then he took my other hand in his and held it tight. "It's part of the process. Don't worry – we'd expect this type of breathing at this stage."

"Is his daughter going to make it before...?" I whispered.

There was a long pause. "I don't think so, no."

It was another hour before he stopped breathing altogether. Heath sat there with me the whole time, holding my hand.

"He's gone, isn't he?" I asked. Half an hour had passed since Bryn had taken a breath.

"Yes." Heath gave my hand a squeeze then stood up to do all the checks he had to do to confirm things. I stood by the bed, totally frozen in one spot. When he come back round to me, put both hands on my shoulders and turned me into him. I sobbed into his chest for the second time that day.

"I'm taking you home," he said.

"Heath, I–"

"You shouldn't be alone, Yaz."

I pulled back so I could look up at his face. "I don't think–"

"My shift finished two hours ago. I need to go home and you're coming with me. I can't bear to think of you going back to that house alone. Please come home with me. Just for tonight, let me look after you. You've done it for me so many times now."

And with that, the fight drained out of me. No, I didn't want to go home. Not yet. Not tonight. I sank back into Heath and nodded against his chest.

Chapter 29

Worthwhile

Y<small>AZ</small>

When we got to his car, Heath shoved the forgotten sandwich at me along with fresh takeaway tea, and kept glancing at me on the way to his place until I opened the packet. I told myself his fussing was annoying, but it was surprising how much better I felt by the time we arrived at his house after eating some food. He guided me inside and up to his spare bedroom. By that stage, it was gone midnight.

"How long was your shift today?" I asked as he chucked one of his t-shirts on the bed for me to wear.

"What? Oh, I started at seven for handover." He gave me a small smile and I could see the lines of exhaustion around his face and dark shadows under his eyes. One of his eyelids flickered, which I knew from old was a sign that he hadn't been sleeping enough. I frowned. Had he not been sleeping since his dad's funeral? Was everything still weighing on him? Since that incident with Bodhi at the beach, I hadn't seen him at all. Verity seemed okay. She'd actually relented and let me set up some essential oil diffusers in her cottage. On my last visit, she'd even accepted a calming crystal by her bedside and practised some breathing exercises with me. She wouldn't admit to having any more panic attacks, but then she *was* a typical evasive Markham. What if Heath was taking it worse than her? To compound that guilt, I also realised that I'd been the reason he'd just spent an extra two hours in the hospital, which would only have added to his exhaustion.

"Thanks for today," I said, moving to him to take his hand and give it a squeeze. He looked down at our linked hands for a moment, then back up at my face. We stared at each other long enough for me to watch his pupils dilate. It was hard to say who moved first. Maybe we moved at the same time – our bodies seemed to be in complete synchrony, and the current between us just snapped. Before I knew it my arms were around his neck, his hands spanning my back, and we were kissing. Everything after that was frantic, edged with desperation. Tearing off each other's clothes, we were both consumed by the same urgent need to be closer. The relief of coming together and of drowning out all the sadness and loss of the day was acute. I needed Heath, and he needed me, and there was nothing either of us could do about it. We fell asleep wrapped in each other, Heath's forgotten t-shirt lying on the floor next to the bed. I let myself float on the cloud of bliss and security in Heath's arms. Shoving my doubts to the back of my mind for now.

∽

HEATH

I knew I should sleep. It was frankly ridiculous not to sleep after such a long shift, and I did manage a few hours at first. But at six in the morning when I was woken by Yaz shifting against me, sleep was not at the top of my priority list. I felt better than I had in weeks. Holding Yaz in my arms was the most powerfully right experience I had ever had in my life. It was as though she was meant to be there and, now that she was, the universe was back in the proper order. I felt like I could breathe again without that hole punched in my chest. But in the back of my mind there was a niggle of worry – had I taken some sort of advantage of Yaz's state of mind yesterday? When she'd kissed me I was beyond all reasoning to that effect, but now in the cold light of day I wondered if I should have made myself wait so that I could talk to her before we started anything – make her understand how much she means to me, how much *this* would mean to me.

Just before eight, Yaz's eyes opened, and she blinked up at me from her position on my chest.

"Hi," she whispered, then to my immense relief she smiled a sleepy smile, which I returned, my arm around her shoulders giving her a squeeze.

"Hi," I whispered back. She glanced up at the sun streaming in through the window and frowned.

"Shit, what time is it?" She moved, pulling away from me at lightning speed and grabbing her phone. "Oh bugger! It's nearly eight. I've got a class at nine." She jumped out of bed and started pulling on her clothes. My body felt cold without her.

"Look, Midge, can't you just cancel it for today? I'm sure your clients will understand. You must be exhausted after yesterday." I followed her out of bed and grabbed some jeans from my cupboard. By the time I'd dragged them on, she was nearly fully dressed.

"I'm fine." She flashed me a brief, unconvincing smile and shoved her phone into her back pocket. "Work will keep my mind off it anyway."

I had a few other ideas for activities to keep her mind off it, and Yaz flitting out of my door the moment she woke up didn't fit into any of them.

"We need to talk about what happened last night."

"I know we do, Heath. And we will, I promise. Later."

I huffed, feeling annoyance bubble up to the surface. It was Saturday morning, and I wasn't on a shift. The woman I loved had woken up in my arms. As far as I was concerned this was perfect. I was in no way prepared to have it ripped away from me so soon. So, I spoke without thinking.

"Surely it doesn't matter that much if you give it a miss for once? It's not life or death."

Yaz stopped in her tracks and slowly turned to me. One look at her face, and I knew I'd said the wrong thing.

"So, if you had a shift in the emergency department now, you'd be happy just to chill your beans and not bother showing up?"

"It's hardly the same thing. It's not like you're..." I trailed off as I saw the colour rise in Yaz's face.

"Go on," she said in a low, dangerous voice. "Not like I'm what? Saving lives? Maybe, maybe not. I do teach water safety as well to the kids, so it depends on how you look at things. Maybe there are a few humans who haven't ended up in your life-saving department because of my efforts at prevention. But, Heath, what I do and how worthwhile it is according to *you* isn't the issue here. This is my livelihood. It's important to me. I had thought that you were coming to understand that, but judging by this conversation and the way you treated Bodhi the other night I'm starting to think you're just a really good liar."

Fuck, I'd done it again. How was I such an insensitive prick?

"No, no, I didn't mean it that way," I rushed to say, following her out into the corridor. "Of course what you do is worthwhile.

Look, you suffered a loss yesterday, so yes, actually in the same position I might well call in sick if I'd just lost someone close to me just the day before." She rolled her eyes before shoving her feet into her trainers. "Okay, okay, let me drive you."

"It's about two hundred yards. I think I can manage."

With that, she flung open my front door and stormed out. By the time I'd grabbed a t-shirt and my shoes, she was long gone.

Chapter 30

Not cool, bro

YAZ

"I'm sorry, but I just don't understand how we're not in profit?"

Bodhi shrugged. "It's a tough business. Big competition. And you waste your time on those kids – they're not exactly money spinners."

I turned back to the computer screen and kept scrolling through the business account. "What are these withdrawals, though?"

"Oh, that was just for those boards we ordered."

My eyebrows went up. "The boards? I chose them and they were way under this amount. Jesus, there are other withdrawals as well." I felt my eyes getting wider the further I scrolled back through the account. Even with my horrific maths skills I could see that Bodhi had been making withdrawals like this for three months now – ever since he told me he'd take over balancing the books so I could concentrate on the practical side of the business. The only reason I was checking up at all was because

I really needed that new kit for the kids now and he'd told me, again, the business couldn't afford it, which sounded odd seeing as we were busier than ever. I stood up from my chair and turned towards Bodhi so we were facing each other. He held my eyes for a moment, then looked away.

"There were loads of expenses that you have no clue about," he said defensively. "We needed all kinds of shit, and that electrician the other day was a right rip-off."

"My brother recommended that guy, and I know exactly how much he cost. It was nowhere near being a rip-off, and it's nowhere near the amount missing from this account. Oh God." I felt the colour drain from my face and swayed on my feet, feeling almost lightheaded for a moment. "That van outside. The brand new one that you've been driving. It's not a mate's like you said, is it?"

Bodhi's expression twisted and his chin lifted to a stubborn angle. "So what? I spent a *little* bit of our profits. I can't live on air and trundle around on a bloody bike and a clapped-out disaster of a van like you, can I?"

"B–but you always said money didn't matter to you. You agreed we should plough any profits back into the business. You're a minimalist, a free spirit – possessions just tie you down – that's what you told me. I–"

"Oh, for fuck's sake!" he snapped. "I spouted all that bullshit so you would bring me in as a partner to the business. Nobody thinks possessions are pointless, Yaz. That's a line. Okay?"

"Right. A line." My voice seemed far away now, like it wasn't quite my own. All my hard work and I'd still managed to mess this up. My parents were right. Heath was right. I was simply not clever enough, responsible enough, enough of anything really to run my own business. It was stupid to even try. All I'd done was line the pockets of this arsehole. He huffed in the background and scuffed his feet on the floor.

"Listen, we just need to bring in a lot more this month and then we can even everything out – afford the equipment."

"And the rent. You forgot about the rent." There was such a shortfall that I couldn't see us managing to cover it this month. Not unless I went to my parents or Max, which I would rather die than do in this circumstance.

"Listen, the rent won't matter if you agree to Brazil."

"Bodhi, if you think I will ever agree to go anywhere with you after this, you're delusional."

"Be honest!" he snapped. "You were never going to agree to it anyway. You just strung me along."

"No, no I don't suppose I was." As I spoke those words I realised that I was never really considering Brazil seriously. It had sounded like an easy way out for a while, like a way to escape, but it would never have been the right thing to do. I was too invested in the business. And, if I was honest with myself, I would miss my family. I would miss Heath. "But compared to you I'm as honest as the day is long. You've been lying to me from the beginning. How on earth are we getting out of this mess?"

"You'll just have to take that group out that I told you about."

"What group?"

"The stag party? That billionaire dude? They're willing to pay a huge amount as long as it's extreme water sports and as long as you..." he trailed off, then mumbled the rest into his hand.

"As long as I what?"

"As long as you wear a bikini."

"What are you on about?" I said, but a knot had already

formed in my stomach as Bodhi shifted uncomfortably again and rubbed the back of his neck.

"I may have sent them some images of you on the beach doing your thing. They were quite specific that they want you to lose the wetsuit."

"Like a–a–a stripper?" My voice was completely hollow now. I had sunk to rock bottom. Bodhi sighed.

"You're in a bikini all the time. What's the diff?" I opened my mouth to tell him exactly what *the diff* was, but he slapped an invoice into my hand before I could speak. The number on it was totally ridiculous. I closed my eyes for a moment, and took a deep breath in through my mouth, letting it out through my nose.

"If I do this, I'll give you a cut – and then you're *out*. No contesting. No claiming any part of the business."

"Wait a minute. You can't–"

"We haven't signed the partnership agreement yet Bodhi, and let's face it – I *am* the business. If I walk, you'll have nothing left. You'll be bankrupt by the end of the month."

His face flushed red and his mouth twisted. How had I ever thought he was attractive?

"Fine," he snapped, turning on his heel and storming out of the studio, but not without throwing a "fucking bitch" back at me as he left. I looked down at the invoice and sighed.

"WE'RE NOT TAKING THEM OUT." I CROSSED MY ARMS OVER my chest and set my mouth in a firm line.

I had been prepared to sacrifice some of my pride to take these guys on the water, but I was not prepared to compromise on safety. They were either still drunk or they'd taken something. I watched out of the window as one of them fell off the training rig we had set up for the kids, another was staring off into space, two others were rolling around on the floor and there was a guy throwing up into a bush to the side. Nice.

"They're fine," Bodhi replied. There was a crash as the rig toppled over, flattening the guy on it and two of his mates. Bodhi glanced over his shoulder at them, then shrugged as he turned back to me. "Okay, so maybe they're a wee bit sauced, but it's nothing a good blast on the water won't solve."

"Who *are* you?" I asked. It was a genuine question. This version of Bodhi was a complete stranger to me. I shook my head. "You know we can't take them out like this."

"What *I* know is that I'm not turning down that kind of money, just because you've gone all health and safety on me."

I scowled at him. "Two of them couldn't even hold the pen properly to sign the consent forms, and one actually drooled on the paper. I don't think I'm being overly cautious when I say that they are not fit to go out on the water."

He rolled his eyes and proceeded to shove his arms into his wetsuit. "Whatever. *I'll* take them out. You can stay here and meditate or whatever other pointless shit you wanna do. I'll go and earn some actual cash." He spun on his heel and charged out of the office towards the group of idiots mucking about with my training sail. How they'd managed to get their wetsuits on was anyone's guess. I slammed my hand down on the desk in frustration, then pushed up to follow him.

"Don't do this, Bodhi," I said through gritted teeth. My hand went to his shoulder but he shook me off, leaning down to pick up one of the boards.

"Right lads," he shouted. "Grab a board and we'll take them down to the water to get set up. Those of you who haven't done this before, take the massive boards on the right there. Kiters grab those kite bags. Experienced windsurfers – the smaller boards are up there. Let's get this show on the road!"

"Bodhi!" I hissed, following him as he made his way down to the water with two boards tucked under each arm. "Mixed ability? Kiting *and* windsurfing? This is madness. Even if they were sober it would be a bad idea. You don't know these people and the wind is gusty as shit today." As if to highlight my point, a massive blast of wind hit us both, causing my hair to fly out to the side and pushing the board across so hard that Bodhi nearly stumbled and had to pause to readjust his grip.

"Yo, little surfer chick." A heavy arm was slung over my shoulder, and I got a strong whiff of stale beer.

"Er... hi," I said, ducking down to extract myself from under his weight.

"What's with the wetsuit, babe?" he slurred, pitching to the side slightly when I ducked away and then straightening up with a lopsided grin. "Your boss here told us you'd be fully *Baywatch* for the day."

I pasted a smile on my face. "I'm sorry you were misinformed, but this man is not my boss and I've no intention of going 'fully *Baywatch*'. I'm afraid you guys won't be able to go out on the water today either."

"What are you on about, girlie?" Another bloke stumbled across to us over the sand. Bodhi kept ploughing on to the water, with some of the guys following. "We've paid to go out on the goddamn water." This guy was not in the slightly slurring, hungover, still-drunk category. He looked wired. His pupils were pinpoint, and the whites of his eyes were red. My guess would be a line of coke before he left this morning.

"Jesus Christ," I muttered under my breath, side eyeing Wired Guy before I ran to catch up with Bodhi again. He was busy laying the boards on the shoreline now. "Seriously, Bode." I tried to make my voice reasonable, make sure it didn't shake with the anger I was feeling now. "This is dangerous."

"Just fuck off then," he spat, not bothering to lower his

voice. There were a few sniggers from the pissed-up idiots who'd had the coordination needed to actually catch up with us. "I can take them out. You're not the only one that can do this shit, you know."

"I'm not going to let you," I said, squaring my shoulders as I stepped between him and the sail that he was about to attach to the board. "It's *my* business, Bodhi. My reputation. You're not taking this lot on the water." Another huge gust of wind blew my hair up from behind me as if to emphasise my point. I reached for the sail, but before I could grab the boom Bodhi's heavy hand landed in the centre of my chest and shoved me back. The impact was hard enough that I was thrown a few feet away landing on my back in the sand with the breath knocked out of me. Bodhi didn't even glance back at me. He was too busy rigging up the kit. A few of the guys shifted uncomfortably in the sand. One of them offered me his hand to get up.

"Hey," one of the slightly more subdued men said. "Not cool, bro."

"Maybe we should give this a miss," another one said, biting his lip and looking unsure.

"Come on, you pussies," Wired Guy shouted about the wind. "I've kited in much stronger shit than this. Let's get this show on the road." To my dismay, I saw he was dumping the kiting kit out of the bag. Kiting in this weather was not a good idea for anyone. The gusts could have you flying across the harbour – people had died that way. But in the hands of someone with impaired judgement and a God complex it was a recipe for disaster. Two more unsure guys backed off with their hands raised, muttering about how they'd give it a miss, and shooting me furtive, concerned glances. The vomiting guy had retreated as well to sit on the sand with his head between his knees. But there were still about five guys rigging up – two of them had beginner windsurfing boards, two of them were unravelling the kite surfing kits, and one was on a smaller wind-surfing board. In other words, a complete shitshow. I watched on, feeling totally helpless, knowing I couldn't physically stop them. After only a moment's hesitation, I grabbed my phone from its waterproof pouch around my neck and swallowed my pride.

Chapter 31

Do you trust me?

HEATH

"You working?" Max's gruff voice demanded.

"Well, good morning to you too, arsehole," I said. Winnie and I were sitting on my sofa feeling sorry for ourselves. She shared my love for Yaz, and I often felt like she was just humouring me by staying at my place, waiting for Yaz to walk through the door. At least she wasn't scared of me anymore. She even slept in my bed now.

"Right, you need to get your arse down to the beach, pronto. There's a problem with my sister."

I sat up to attention immediately. Winnie's ear pricked up and her head cocked to the side.

"What kind of problem?"

"I'm not too sure. That bloody tosser she works with had winded her, and she was still trying to catch her breath. Plus, the weather is insane down there, so I couldn't catch everything she was saying. But she needs help. I'm on my way, but you're closer. I know things have been weird with– "

"He did *what*?" I shouted, shoving on my shoes with my

259

phone shoved between my ear and my shoulder. "That *prick*. I'm going to kill him!"

"Not sure what's going on now, but he was trying to take out a load of pissed-up stag weekend lads. Yaz didn't think it's safe and tried to stop him. He shoved her back onto her arse."

"What the actual fuck?" I was racing out of the door now, Winnie hot on my heels. I didn't have time to stop her, so simply jumped in my car and let her jump in after me.

"She wanted me to come down there and help her stop them, but halfway through explaining, she started swearing and saying how she was going to have to get on the water herself," Max's voice was panicked now. "She put the phone down on me, and I can't get her back again. I'm on my way but you're closer."

"Shit!" I pulled out of my driveway and set off towards the harbour. Making it there in under two minutes, I jumped out of the car and ran down to the sand, closely followed by Winnie. I saw a couple of Yaz's mates on the shoreline looking out to sea and jogged over to them.

"Hey," I called, and Dee turned to me – her face was pale and her expression worried. Winnie was going nuts barking at the water.

"You know what's happening?"

"Some fucking idiots have gone out with Bodhi and totally overpowered kites. Yaz tried to stop them but they launched the kites before she could get us to help." She looked out to sea briefly and then her face paled further. "Christ!" she shouted. "What is he doing? Listen, I'm going to get on my rig."

Dee ran into the water to a windsurfer one of the others was holding for her. I followed the direction of her gaze and saw a man flying through the air towards the harbour wall. The gust of wind he was caught in then died, and he crashed back into the water. My heart dropped into my stomach when I saw the unmistakable silhouette of Yaz on her windsurfer in hot pursuit of the out-of-control maniac. That bloody idiot was going to get himself killed, and I didn't want Yaz anywhere near him when he did it. She swept around him to avoid the kite strings and then did an impressive jibe to double back. There was another gust of wind and the idiot's kite flew back up into the air, taking him with it. He needed to unhook via the safety release, but either he had no idea how to do that or his ego would not let him abandon the kite. The guy was in mid-air now and hurtling toward the harbour wall again. I swore under my breath, feeling completely helpless as I watched Yaz charge after him. At the last moment, she leapt from her windsurfer and onto the man's board.

That's when I started running. I had no plan, I only knew that I needed to get to Yaz. When I drew level with them on the shore, I started wading into the water fully clothed. A couple of Yaz's other friends flanked me, but we were too far to reach Yaz.

"Oh my God," one of them said, and I felt my heart almost stop beating. Both the man and Yaz were now on course to crash into the wall. Then suddenly the kite was free and sailing off into the air. Yaz had released the safety harness, and as soon as she had she shoved the man backwards, away from the wall. But the board's momentum was such that there was no way she could avoid hitting it herself. Her body slammed against the concrete then slid into the water. Luckily Dee's rig had already reached Yaz by the time she hit the water. Another windsurfer out there took care of the idiot Yaz'd saved, and Dee dived in after Yaz. When Dee pulled her out of the water and I could see Yaz coughing, I felt relief so acute it almost felt like I might black out. Dee stumbled and both she and Yaz fell back into the water, regaining their feet as I made it to them.

"Heath!" Yaz shouted over the wind. I took her from Dee's arms and held her up against my chest. It was a measure of how hurt she was that as soon as she was in my arms, she started sobbing.

"There's something wrong with her shoulder," Dee shouted. "And... oh fuck!" She looked down at her hands and her wetsuit. "Shit, there's blood. She's bleeding!"

"You're going to be fine," I told Yaz through gritted teeth as I carried her to the shore, Winnie barking at my feet.

"Call an ambulance!" I shouted at the assembled crowd on the sand as I put her down and started frantically searching for the source of the bleeding. I found the head wound quickly and enlisted Dee, who had followed me in, to put pressure on it with a towel. Winnie had lain down next to Yaz and was licking her hand.

"My shoulder," Yaz whimpered. Her left shoulder was misshapen and very obviously out of its socket.

I took her face in my hands and held her gaze.

"Do you trust me?" I asked her. She stared straight at me for a moment and the world melted away. The sound of the wind, the shouting around us, everything faded other than her breathing and mine. She nodded once and I rested my forehead against hers for a second before I pulled away, letting the world rush back in. Then I took her injured arm at the elbow with one hand, and her left hand with the other and rotated. She screamed once as it clunked back into place. Winnie started whimpering and barking at Yaz's side and, typical Yaz, through the pain and the stress she still reached out with her good hand to stroke Winnie's fur and reassure her.

"It's over now," I said softly, holding her arm across her chest and signalling for one of her friends to give me another towel which I made into a makeshift sling.

"Oh my God, Yaz!" Max's boom could be heard above all the noise around us as he forced his way through to his sister. "Is she okay? What are you doing treating my sister on the bloody beach, mate? You've nowt to see to her with here. She needs your fancy hospital, she does." Angry, worried Max was even more brusque and northern than normal.

I decided the quickest way to deal with him was to ignore him, so I took a moment to inspect her head wound behind the towel Dee was keeping pressed on it. There was still a slow trickle of blood and it looked like it would need a fair few stitches.

"Keep pressure on there," I told Dee. "I'm going to lift her." I lent down and scooped Yaz up off the sand to hold her up against me.

"If you want to make yourself useful, you can drive us to my *big fancy hospital* right now," I snapped at Max, who was standing in my way.

"What about the ambulance?" he snapped.

"This'll be quicker. We just need to get her there, Max."

Yaz's hand went out to Max's arm and he focused on her again.

"Listen to Heath, Maxie," she said. Her voice wavered for a moment, but then she cleared her throat.

Max glanced at her and nodded. "Alright, love. I know, I know. I just want you fixed up proper. When you hit that wall, I thought..." he swallowed, reached to Yaz and squeezed her good hand, then led the way to his car.

Chapter 32

Please, let me give you the sea

HEATH

"Well, of course she'll come home with us," Fern Hardcastle had decided and in her mind that was that. "She can't do anything for herself with her arm out of action. It makes sense for her to come home."

"Mam, no offence, but she won't want you fussing. She'll be reight with us, won't she, Mia?"

"I'd love to have you stay, honey," Mia said. "*You* looked after *me* not so long ago, remember?"

"She can stay with me," Dee put in. "I had a bad feeling about Bodhi. Always boasting about his mad skills on the water and how he only worked with Yaz so she could bring in the rich blokes when we all knew who the talented one was. I'm the one that should look after her. This is my fault."

"It's not your fault, Dee," said Yaz. "Don't say that. You did try to warn me, and I didn't want to listen. I'm the one that got taken in by him. I'm the idiot that set up a business with him." Her voice was flat and lifeless, and it was making my chest feel tight. Some of her spark had been knocked out of her. "Thanks everyone, but I'll be alright at home. I'm used to injuries. My shoulder has come out before, you know."

"*What?*" Fern shouted, and the room fell silent.

"It's not a big deal, Mum," Yaz said. "I did it about four years ago in a comp. Washing up was a bit of a bugger for a couple of weeks, but I managed."

"You dislocated your shoulder, and you didn't tell me?" There was real hurt in Fern's voice now. To my shock, I saw her eyes fill with tears. "My little girl was hurt, and I didn't even know about it?"

Yaz shrugged, then winced – shrugging not being the best idea with her shoulder. "I'm sorry Mum but–"

"That was when I was on *Dream Homes*, wasn't it?" Max said. "Four years ago – that was when all that shit was going on. Is that why you didn't say owt?"

"Max I–"

"She's just used to taking care of herself," I put in and everyone turned to me. "We've all treated Yaz like some flighty incapable child, when she's actually stronger and more resilient than the lot of us."

An awkward silence followed my words.

"*I* always knew you kicked arse, Auntie Midge," Teddy said, and Max pushed his shoulder. "What?" he said, shoving Max back. "I did, Dad. I knew all about her career and stuff. You lot never followed any of that shit. She's one of the most badass windsurfers around. And she really helped me with my exam anxiety last year."

"Not so badass now, squirt," Yaz said, giving him a small smile.

"What are you on about? Ten stitches and a dislocated shoulder is like... the height of badass."

"See, it's confirmed," Yaz said. "I'm a badass. And this badass can look after herself."

"If it was just a dislocated shoulder, Yaz, then maybe, but you've had a significant head injury, too. I'm sorry, but you can't go home alone," I said.

She sighed and rested her head back against the pillow again. "Right," she whispered. "Of course." Turning her head away from all of us to look out of the window, I saw her throat bob as she swallowed, and her eyes shine a little brighter with unshed tears.

"I'm sorry, love," Fern said, stroking her daughter's hair back from her forehead. "But I think Heath's right. It'll just be for a little while then we can– "

Yaz laughed then, but it was entirely without humour and it cut through me like a knife. "It's fine, Mum. I've got to get out of the flat now anyway. It's going on the market soon now Bryn's gone. His daughter's decided to sell up." Her voice cracked over Bryn's name.

"I'm sorry about that too, love."

"You and Dad were right after all," she went on, still in that hollow, emotionless voice. "I *have* buggered up my life. Business down the drain, losing my home. I'm right back at square one. I should have listened when you–"

"Don't you bloody dare!" I burst out and Yaz's mouth snapped shut, her eyes widening with surprise. It was the most animated I'd seen her for the last hour, thank God. "Don't you *dare* put down all you've achieved. You built up that business despite that utter prick working against you behind the scenes. Yaz, I'm sorry I ever contributed to making you feel you didn't deserve to be treated fairly. Nobody should ever have made you feel less than you are, and it kills me that I used to be the one to do it. But please, please know your value now. It's your talent and warmth that's made a success of all this. It's you who gives and gives to all us ungrateful sods. You who supports everyone, expecting nothing back. You will not give up on this business and we'll all be there to back you." There was a long pause as Yaz looked down at her hands on the bed, then her shoulders began to shake.

"I worked so h–h–hard," she said, her breath hitching on her sobs. Mia was moving toward her, but I just couldn't stay away. Not having her in my arms when she was this upset was intolerable. I pulled her gently to me as I sat on the bed. Her good hand clutched my shirt, and she sobbed into my chest.

"I know you did, darling," I murmured into her hair. "Everyone knows you did. And it wasn't for nothing. You won't lose the business. We won't let that happen."

"B–but–" she tried to say as she pulled back slightly.

"But nothing. There's no shame in taking some help from the people that love you, Yaz. I'm sorry if the way we've all treated you has made you feel that you have to go it alone. That's on us, and I promise we'll make it up to you. But you've got to let us help now."

"And what am I?" put in Dee. "Chopped liver? I can keep the well-being side running and there are loads of other instructors back from the season who can help while you're out of action. Okay, so you made a mistake with Bodhi the Dickhead, but the rest of the staff – me included – are pretty awesome."

"I'm sorry I didn't listen to you, Dee," Yaz said in a small voice. I hated hearing her voice like that.

Dee shrugged. "He was a convincing git. Chill, okay? I'm not going anywhere. And anyway, those stag-do dickheads paid you a fairly extreme amount of money – enough to buy in help for the next few months if you needed."

"Wh–"

"I asked Bodhi to leave after Heath carried you off... well, technically I kicked Bodhi in the balls and got some of the guys to drag him away, but same diff. Those London dickheads couldn't wait to pay after I suggested it might not look too good if it came out that they essentially stole your equipment and then necessitated you to risk your life saving their ungrateful arses. Plus, that idiot lost your kite in the end, anyway. This is the figure we agreed on – I gave them your business account details and then made them send me proof of transfer." She held out her phone to me with a photo of the transaction.

"Bloody hell, Dee," whispered Yaz, "That's insane. Thank you so much."

Dee shrugged. "That prick Bodhi's not the only one who can negotiate, you know." Yaz reached for Dee's hand and gave it a squeeze.

"I should have made you a partner and not Bodhi."

"Yaz, that's not why I–"

"I hope you'll consider it now?" Dee's eyes went wide and her mouth fell open.

"Of course I will," she sputtered. "But let's get you back to fighting fit before you make any big decisions."

Yaz's dad cleared his throat and shuffled around to the end of the bed. "Listen, love, I think now's a good time to let you know that your mum and I have decided we need to make things fair. We've worked out how much money we spent supporting your brother through his architecture degree, and we want you to have the same amount."

Yaz's gaze shot from her mum to her dad, her expression bewildered.

"What? But I thought that money was only for if I was in full-time education and that– "

"We were wrong," Fern said, cutting her off. Not a woman prone to outward displays of emotion, she straightened her blouse and cleared her throat before carrying on – but her eyes were a little too bright and her voice carried a very slight shake. "There's nowt wrong with the way you did things. Your Dad and I are stubborn old buggers and we're sorry, love."

Yaz blinked, and I nearly choked on the shocked breath I took in. I didn't think I'd ever heard Fern apologise to a living soul before. I wasn't even sure I would have said it was possible if I hadn't heard it with my own ears.

"Well, don't all stand around with your mouths open," she snapped, no shake in her voice now, just annoyance. "When I'm wrong, I admit it."

"Er... Gran," said Teddy hesitantly. "I don't think I've ever heard you say you're wrong before."

"Well, that's likely because I've not *been* wrong about owt before. Now then, young lady, I'll pack up your stuff and you can come stay wi' me and yer dad tonight."

"But Mum, I need to be at home at the moment. It's not like it's the first–"

"You need the sea," I said with such conviction that everyone looked at me, including Yaz. "You might not need *me*, but you need the sea, Please, baby," my voice dropped to a softer tone as I leaned into her like she had a gravity all of her own I could not resist. "I love you so much. Please, let me give you the sea. At least let me give you that. Just for a little while. I won't ask anything of you. I know I've screwed up any chance of–"

Her lips on mine cut me off, and the room melted away. By the time Yaz's dad cleared his throat and I snapped back to reality with a jerk, I'd pulled Yaz halfway into my lap and my hands were tangled in her hair. Yaz and I smiled at each other, but it only lasted a moment before I was yanked up onto my feet by a furious Max, who then punched me in the face.

"Max!" screamed Yaz as I staggered back, clutching my jaw.

"That's for snogging my little sister," Max said. "And also, for *not* snogging her for years, and treating her like crap."

269

"You're punching me for both snogging and not snogging your sister?"

He shrugged.

"You know, you didn't exactly treat Yaz with respect for a long while either, Max. Maybe you should punch yourself in the face."

"Ah, quit yer mitherin', pretty boy. You'd punch me yerself if you've owt backbone."

Mia stepped in between us, pushing Max back with one hand and me with the other. "There'll be none of that," she said. Her voice was tight and her face pale.

"Ah, shit, sorry, love," Max said. "I didn't mean to upset you."

"Yeah, sorry, Mia." Violence of any kind wasn't easy for Mia to be around. All the anger drained out of both of us.

"I'm fine. It's you lot that have lost the plot. You've both been total shits to Yaz, well done for finally admitting as much, but punching each other isn't going to solve anything."

I kept my mouth shut, but I didn't exactly agree with Mia there. I don't really think there was ever a way I could have snogged Max's sister and not been punched in the face. And anyway, it had cleared the air more effectively than any amount of discourse. Max was not a very verbal guy.

In all that went on, I hadn't noticed Yaz get out of the bed and make her way over to me until her small hand slipped into mine.

"Max, don't hit my boyfriend again, you numpty," she said. Her voice was back to calm, serene Yaz, emotionless despair now absent. I gave her hand a squeeze at the word boyfriend as hope shot through me for the first time in weeks. She looked up at me then and again the world faded away. "I'm rather in love with him, you see. And I like his face the way it is."

I could hear her dad in the background asking what the hell

was going on. Her mum still banging on about Yaz coming to stay with them, but it was like Yaz and I were in our own bubble.

"I'll let you give me the sea," she said, her voice the only one I could hear now. I smiled down at her and we started walking out of the cubicle with our family and friends trailing behind. "I only ever liked you for your house, anyway."

"Little shit," I muttered as I grabbed her discharge letter from a colleague, and we left the department.

Epilogue

Butterfly in a jar

YAZ

"Okay, I looked into it and there is some trial data that backs up your sea swimming therapy stuff," Heath admitted as we made our way down to the shore. During my recovery from the dislocated shoulder, I'd convinced him to come into the water with me before work every day, and now it was a habit. I maintained that a man couldn't live with a view like Heath's and not sea swim on a daily basis. We'd just had to get around Heath's slight aversion to cold and early mornings. I'd been waking up at dawn since my teens, so I barely noticed it. But for Heath, it took some adjusting.

"Ha, I told you!"

"I still don't understand how freezing my balls off every morning helps me live longer."

"Your balls are fine."

"You should hope so." He gave me a smug grin, and I rolled my eyes. "Jesus Christ," he snapped as his toes hit the water. "Okay – kiss me and I'll go in."

This was pretty much standard. He fussed like an old

woman about how cold the water was, demanded a kiss and then eventually made his way in and happily swam half a mile up the coast with me. Same routine for the last six months.

After I'd recuperated at Heath's house, he managed to convince me to move in, seeing as Bryn's daughter really did need me to vacate the flat. I wasn't sure if we should move so fast, but Heath was so adamant that he'd lost too much time with me already due to his being a 'stubborn blind prick of the highest magnitude'. He begged me to not make him wait, using Winnie as additional emotional blackmail – apparently I was an essential component of her recovery. Heath convinced that both man and dog had abandonment issues which I would be compounding if I refused to move in with them permanently.

I'd been back on the water and teaching now for the last few months. Dee had become my partner, and we were able to put much more emphasis on the kids' teaching programme than before. I'd hired another two instructors to help us out with the yoga, and the vetting process for employment at Ocean Blue, our new company name, had become a lot more rigorous since I discovered that Bodhi wasn't even Nigel Fuller's real name. I expect he'd just watched *Point Break* a few too many times and thought that the name 'Bodhi' would fit the persona he was projecting. I was using a proper accountant now as well – she was actually the same one Max used. That was another big change. I'd learnt that accepting help from my family wasn't the end of the world, and that I didn't have to sacrifice my pride in order to do so – although I'd yet to accept the money my parents insisted I was owed. I knew it upset them, but I was holding on to that small bit of resentment for their dismissive attitude over the years. It would take me a bit longer to shake that off, but I was getting there. Mum had started occasionally coming to beginner yoga sessions. She even accepted a special pot of essential oils I mixed up for her to help with constipation.

Once Heath and I got far enough out, he dived down under the water and I followed. He'd been trying to learn how to free dive over the last few weeks and could nearly hold his breath for as long as me. When we were both hovering above the ocean floor, he touched my arm and I turned to him. He was fumbling about with his pocket with one hand, while struggling to stay under the water with the other. I cocked my head to the side and floated next to him, my hands rhythmically pushing the water away so that I didn't float back up. Heath frowned and a stream of bubbles left his mouth. It looked like he was swearing to himself. I smiled and swam over to him, rested my hands on either side of his face, and kissed his mouth. He stopped yanking away at his pocket and pulled me towards him to kiss me back. We both floated up and broke the surface with our mouths still connected. When he pulled back, he was looking at me with the same awestruck expression I'd grown accustomed to. My arms were around his neck, his resting on my waist. I gave him another light kiss on the lips.

"Wanna skip the mile today and find another way to get those endorphins going for a bit?" I asked, giving him a wink and a wide smile.

"Yeah," he rumbled. "Let's go back–" then he closed his eyes and shook his head. "No, no!"

"Er... okay?" I said, thoroughly confused. "We don't have to–"

"Grr! No, I mean yes to that. Very much, yes. Just... crap, wait a minute."

He was back to fiddling with his pocket again. I raised both my eyebrows expectantly.

"Ah, fucking finally," he said, withdrawing a small box from his pocket just as a large wave crashed over our heads. When we both came up for air, spluttering with the water we weren't prepared to inhale, Heath fumbled with the box trying to open it and it fell into the water. With reflexes honed from years of practice, I flew down after it and grabbed it before the wave could carry it away.

"Here you go," I said, handing the small box to Heath, who was now looking thoroughly disgruntled.

"You do realise I'm known as a pretty smooth operator with everyone but you," he grumped. "This was supposed to be *perfect.*"

"What was? What's in the...?" My mouth fell open as I put it all together.

"It was supposed to be under the water. I would sign that I loved you, offer you the ring on the sea floor, and then we'd float up together in perfect synchrony. Then–"

"Heath," I cut him off. "Give me my ring."

He opened up the box. Inside was a perfect sapphire in a platinum setting, which looked like waves crashing around the stone. I snatched the ring out and put it on my finger before Heath could drop it again.

"Yes," I told him.

"I didn't ask you yet."

I raised my eyebrows, and he took a deep breath.

"Yazmin Hardcastle, I love you. I never want to be without you. You've brought me back to life. Please, would you do me the honour of becoming my wife?"

I kissed him again.

"I'm going to take that as a yes," he said, smiling against my mouth. "Now, about those endorphins you were talking about."

I smiled and pushed away from him abruptly, pausing only for a moment to admire my ring.

"Race you!" I called over my shoulder as I dove towards the shore.

HEATH

"Jesus Christ, you and my sister are completely fucking bonkers," Max grumbled as we strode across the sand, waving at the crowd of our friends and family spread out over the sand. "It's inhuman for me to be anywhere but in bed with my wife this early in the morning."

Winnie gave a bark from where she sat at my feet and I reached down to scoop her up so she could lick my jaw.

"You spoil that dog," Max said.

"You would totally pick up Roger if he wasn't a good ten stone and you know it." Roger nuzzled into Max's side and Max gave him a head scratch.

"Crazy hippy wedding with dogs," he muttered, still stroking his dog I might add.

I chuckled. "God, you are such a grumpy bastard, Max. You could give smiling a try today."

"It's too fucking early to smile. I've never smiled before midday in my life."

This I could believe.

"You'll smile now. For Yaz, you'll smile." My voice was firm. Max was going to smile at his sister when she arrived if I had anything to do with it. Today would be perfect for Yaz. Unconventional, a little wacky, but absolutely perfect.

It had taken a while to get her to admit *what* her perfect scenario for today would be. She was worried I'd want something formal and "dead posh" as she put it. The truth was, I simply wanted to make Yaz happy. In the end she confessed that she wanted to get married by the sea. Of course. And if we wanted to have this stretch of beach to ourselves, it had to happen just after sunrise, hence a grumpy Max and about a hundred bleary-eyed guests. Fern hadn't been on board at first, but both Yaz's parents were getting better at appreciating the amazing person Yaz was, and trying not to push their agendas onto her life. They'd even started helping out when Yaz ran the kids' clubs in the summer. Fern made a mean sandwich platter, and Aubrey enjoyed showing the kids how to rig up. Yaz had even convinced them both about the benefits of sea swimming. Aubrey was out there every time he visited now. Last night he quoted a whole load of that trial data about the benefits of sea swimming and explained how his daughter "Knows what she's on about with this stuff. Change the way you live – that's the key." It seemed that after years of scepticism, he was a full convert to lifestyle medicine.

"At least you don't have to wear a suit," I said, and Max's frown softened.

"I guess that's one good thing about having a batshit crazy sister."

"She's not..." I started to speak, but then caught sight of them walking up the beach, and my annoyance with Max, along with anything I was about to say, flew out of my mind.

~

YAZ

"Are you sure we shouldn't even wear shoes, love?" Mum looked down at her bare feet, then back up at me with a grimace.

"Come on, Fern," Verity said, linking her arms through Mum's and tugging her forward. "New experiences and all that."

"What must the vicar think? And just look at your father. It's practically indecent."

"Yaz taught the vicar to do a forward loop last week – he's just glad to be out of that stuffy old church."

I smiled. Bit of luck really that this particular branch of the Church of England was so keen on water sports.

"And Aubrey," Verity said turning to Dad, "you look in fine fettle this morning – splendid set of pins you have there."

Dad laughed. "Well, it might traumatise the congregation, but I am a stickler for the dress code."

"Your father's *legs* are *exposed*, Yazmin," Mum said in horror, making the sign of the cross over her chest. "And that shirt..."

"Everyone's wearing Hawaiian shirts, Mum. Just chill, okay?" I wrapped my arm around Mum as we were walking and gave her a kiss on her temple. She huffed, but it did coax a small smile out of her.

"You've been on about me "chilling" since you were ten years old, young lady. I think you might know by now – I'm not daft and I'm not chilled."

"Come on Mrs H," Dee said, twirling on the spot with her arms spread wide and her long hair flying out behind her. "Nothing like some sand between your toes first thing in the morning. This is hands-down the most comfortable I've ever been at one of these things."

Mia slipped her hand into mine, and I turned to look at her. Her other arm was secured under my niece's bottom, as Mia held little Sophie on her hip. "You look beautiful, Yaz," she said in her quiet voice, which just about carried to me above the wind. Sophie kicked her stubby legs and launched herself at me. I caught her in my arms and blew a raspberry into her soft neck, eliciting those gorgeous baby giggles I loved so much.

"Sophie!" Mia exclaimed, reaching for her. "Careful of your Auntie. You don't want to mess her up."

"It's fine, Mia," I said, giving Sophie's soft cheek a kiss before I let her go back to her mum. "There's not really any make-up to mess up. Maybe I should have let Verity–"

"No," she cut me off, her hand going to my arm to bring me to a stop. "You look beautiful *your way*. Perfect."

The other three had also stopped with us and we formed a small circle in the sand.

"She's right," Verity said, taking my other hand. "Your way is perfect." Verity had not made a secret of the fact that she was very happy to be gaining an official little sister. She'd thrown herself into wedding planning with a vengeance, but I was worried about her. There were dark circles under her eyes recently and, despite her genuine joy for me and Heath, she still seemed anxious for some reason. I could read people well and Verity was hiding something. But that was a talk for another day. For now, I simply smiled at her and squeezed her hand.

"All the make-up would have come off anyway once we were in the water, so it would have been a bit pointless."

Verity had brought a suitcase of products to the house that morning, but all I had allowed her to apply was a touch of waterproof mascara. Mia had pinned half my hair back and added the flowers that Dee had picked on her way over. My dress was white, but simple and light. The only jewellery I was wearing, apart from my engagement ring, was the shell neck-lace Heath gave me last month. He'd managed to sneak a cheeky diamond and a sapphire in there as well, passing them off as "cheap crystals with healing energy". I knew better after speaking to the jeweller, who'd been surprised that one of his most expensive commissions of the year had been something where he had to incorporate a couple of shells from Bournemouth beach with stones that cost thousands of pounds.

"What do you mean by 'in the water', love?" Mum asked, her tone a little panicked, as some of the colour drained from her face. Verity made an eek face behind Mum's back and I stifled a laugh.

It had taken a while to convince Mum that a church wedding and reception at a local hotel with canapés and posh drinks was off the menu. It was probably best that she found out the rest of the plan as we went.

I heard Mia giggle as we started moving forward again. Mia, Dee and Verity were all in the same dress as me but in blue, and Mia had threaded flowers through all of our hair. None of us was wearing shoes. But that wasn't out of place. The crowd of family and friends we were heading towards were all either barefoot or in flip-flops. There were a lot of boardies and Hawaiian shirts on display. Quite a few of the women (especially from my cohort) were in bikinis with cover-ups over. The vicar was striding towards us now and even he had paired his black shirt and dog collar with a pair of boardies. The man was a legend.

"Right," he said with a wide smile. "There's not exactly an aisle but if you're ready, then we can cut a path down through the crowd and—"

One minute the vicar had been in my line of sight, and I'd been concentrating on what he had to say, and the next Heath was there blocking him from view and the vicar's words trailed off.

"You're here," Heath said, his voice rough with emotion and his expression a little fierce. I smiled up at his handsome face and rested a hand on his chest.

"Of course, I'm here, you daft article. Where else would I be?"

He let out a breath, closed his eyes in what looked like relief for a moment, then his head came down and he kissed me. And not just a peck on the cheek. No, this was a full-on kiss, complete with him lifting me up off my feet and causing my small bouquet of daisies to fall to the floor while Winnie barked at our feet.

"Er... we're not quite at that part yet, chaps," the vicar's amused voice cut through the kiss haze and I pulled back. Heath lowered me to my feet but kept me within the circle of his arms. The crowd was all riveted to our premature display of affection and there was a growing amount of laughter, which then turned to applause as we tore our eyes away from each other to look at them.

"She's not yours quite yet, son," Dad said, his voice full of amusement at Heath's expense. "I haven't given her away."

Heath cleared his throat and an uncharacteristic blush hit his cheekbones. "Right. Yes, well. Jolly good. I'll just..." He trailed off and looked back down at me.

"You have to let me go now, handsome," I whispered. "But I'll see you in a sec. I'll be the one in the white dress by the sea. Right?"

"Right," he whispered back, a smile spreading over his face. "Okay."

"Come on, you chuffin weirdo," Max cut in, having followed Heath to me. His daughter launched herself from Mia's arms into his and he settled her onto his hip. "Get your paws off my sister until it's legal, you cheeky sod." He grabbed Heath's arm with his free hand, pulled him away from me, turned him in the other direction and marched him towards the shoreline through the crowd. "You look good, kid," he threw over his shoulder at me with a wink. Heath was still smiling as he allowed Max to drag him away. But once they got to the shoreline, his smile dimmed a little and I could see the tension back in his face. My friend Toby started playing his guitar. Dad took my arm. The crowd parted, and we started making our way through the sand.

~

HEATH

I'd felt better when she was in my arms, but the anxiety I'd been feeling came back as Max dragged me away. Marriage was just so conventional. It felt too restrictive for my Yaz – like I was tethering a wild creature, or putting a butterfly in a jar. But Yaz had said yes. I'd been so ecstatic after she agreed to marry me that my feet had barely touched the ground for weeks. Then she'd been worried that a beach wedding at the crack of dawn wasn't what *I* wanted. What I wanted was to marry Yazmin Hardcastle. If I'd had to do that suspended upside-down over a sea of man-eating crocodiles, or standing on hot coals, I would have. And anyway, this was the only way I could ever imagine Yaz getting married – next to the sea she loves with the people she loves.

So yes, up until yesterday I'd been floating on my own cloud of bliss. That was until I went to spend the night at Max's, so that Yaz and the wedding party could get ready at mine. I'd had one beer with Max, Teddy and Aubrey, when I'd started to doubt that Yaz would be there the next day. I think it was part of being let down so consistently as a child. I wasn't used to people following through. I convinced myself overnight that Yaz would remember what a prick I'd been in the past and not bother showing up. It wasn't until I'd seen her on the sand, so beautiful she almost looked like a mirage, that I could finally breathe again.

Shoving my way through the crowd to get to her, and then snogging her in front of all our family and friends before the ceremony had even started, wasn't ideal. But I just didn't have the self-control to stand there and wait for her to come to me. Waiting for her now as she walked up the improvised aisle on her father's arm, smiling straight at me, and looking so happy she was almost glowing, was a struggle – but I stayed where I was until she was at my side and I could grab her hand in mine and hold it tight.

"I *still* haven't given her away to you yet," Aubrey grumbled, and the crowd rippled with laughter again. I looked at him and tried to convey how much it meant to me that he trusted me with his daughter, that he'd treated me like a son when my own parents hadn't ever bothered.

"Thank you," I said. "I promise I'll look after her. I swear it."

"I know you will, Heath," he said, his voice gruff and his eyes looking bright with emotion. "Just like you've looked after your sister and my Max. You're a good lad and no mistake."

I don't think that any other compliment I'd ever received in my life would ever compare to Aubrey Hardcastle calling me a good lad before I married his daughter. Yaz squeezed my hand, and I looked down at her before pulling her closer to my side.

"I'm not going anywhere, you know," she whispered.

I gave a tight nod, but didn't loosen my grip on her hand.

It was only when we were saying those vows to each other out loud that I felt the tension I'd been carrying start to dissipate.

But, in truth, it was really only after the ceremony – once we had all run off into the sea – only when Yaz and I were holding hands under the water with her dress swirling around her legs and her amazing hair around her face, that I felt truly at peace. That was the picture we had blown up and put over our fireplace – the two of us under the waves, smiling at each other like lovesick idiots. Just looking at that picture is enough to centre me nowadays. To remind me how lucky I am.

YAZ

"I need to talk to you about something," I said to Heath as he walked through the door. He frowned as he approached me.

"It's nothing bad, I promise," I said, giving him a hug to reassure him. His arms came around me and he pulled me into his chest, before kissing me the way he always did when he'd been out of the house and arrived home to find me there – with relief, like he couldn't quite believe I was still here. It broke my heart a little for him each time, but I was hoping that his fear of abandonment would slowly fade over the years. Therapy was helping. Me telling his mother to fuck off and blocking her calls after I found out that she'd been intermittently contacting him for money had also helped.

This had only come to light when I'd answered Heath's phone one Sunday morning when he was out for a run. I'd recognised her voice immediately and she'd launched straight into her spiel about what *she* needed. I'd told her never to call my husband again, and then blocked her. When I gently confronted Heath, he looked like that little broken boy again. Said she'd threatened to go to Verity. That he was protecting his sister. Well, I'd put a stop to that bullshit. The bitch was now blocked from both of their phones.

"Let me say something first," Heath said once he released me and put the kettle on. "I know you've not been right the last few weeks–"

"Heath, I–"

"No, Yaz, don't deny it. I can see with my own eyes you've not been yourself. More tired, pale, you've lost some of your spark and it's my fault."

"Er... okay, well, it is kind of your fault, I guess. But not in the way you–"

"Well, I'm going to put it right."

My eyebrows went up, and I crossed my arms over my chest. "It's a bit late for that, handsome."

"I don't think so," he said as he pulled out a sheet of paper from his back pocket. "It can't be too late. Not for us. I won't allow it."

He handed me the paper, and I frowned down at it. It was a flight itinerary for two people to Brazil, leaving next month.

"I know you turned down Brazil, and I know you did it for me. But it's too much of a sacrifice to make. I've spoken to work and I'm going to take a sabbatical. Dee's able to manage the business while you're away, and it's the off season right now anyway. We can go out there for three months at least. And... and if you want to move out there, then I can do that too. I'll learn Portuguese. I'm sure they need doctors out there as well. I can–"

"Heath!" I cut him off and he frowned at my smiling face. "Oh my God, I love you, you crazy bastard." I launched myself at him and crushed him in my own fierce hug. His work meant everything to him. That he would let my windsurfing supersede his career was nothing short of incredible, and showed just how much he loved me. But the stupid man had got totally the wrong end of the stick. I pulled back a little and looked up at his face. "I can't go to Brazil. Soon I won't even be able to windsurf at all. At least, not for a while."

"What?" he said, confusion in his expression and his body tense with worry. "Why on earth?"

I rolled my eyes. "Bloody hell, for a doctor you don't exactly catch on that quick, do you? I'm having a baby, you idiot. *We're* having a baby."

He froze in my arms, his eyes flying wide in shock.

"H–h–how...?"

"Er... again with the whole doctor thing I would have thought I wouldn't have to explain but: when a mummy and a daddy love each other very much, they have a special cuddle, and the daddy gives the mummy his–"

"You're having my baby?" he whispered, his voice full of awe. A smile started to appear, but then his expression clouded. "What if I'm a rubbish father?" His voice was a little panicky now. "You saw how I grew up. I have no frame of reference for this stuff. What if—?"

"You won't be a rubbish father," I said, and he relaxed slightly at the firmness of my tone. "Are you forgetting that you're Sophie's favourite?"

His chest puffed up a little at this. "I am, aren't I?"

"You're the baby whisperer extraordinaire. Listen, the fact you're even worrying about being a good father is proof that you will be. And you won't be doing it alone anyway. We'll be a family – you, me, the baby and all those other crazy bastards that won't leave us alone." Mum, Dad, Max, Mia, Teddy, and Verity were all very much involved in our lives. Some might say *overly* involved, but it was something I knew would comfort Heath now.

"A family," he breathed, then his face lit with an expression that I can only describe as complete pure unadulterated joy.

"Yes, love," I said softly. "Of course. We're a family. *Your* family."

His eyes glassed over, but he pulled me into him before I could see any tears fall. "Thank you," he said into my hair, his voice rough with so much emotion it made my heart squeeze. "Thank you for being my family."

"Heath," I said, moving back slightly so I could see his face. "You know there's no getting rid of me, right? I'm not going anywhere, and neither is this baby. I love you. I will never leave you."

"You do love me, don't you?" he said, framing my face with his hands.

"Of course I do, you numpty."

He closed his eyes and leant his forehead against mine. I

could feel the muscles of his broad chest relax under my fingers as he let out a long, slow breath. He'd get used to this. Used to being loved unconditionally, to having stability. Eventually he'd settle into his new forever with me.

Because he is worthy of love and, so am I.

The End

Acknowledgments

I'll start by saying a massive thank you to my readers. I never dreamt that people would take the time to read the stories I have thought up in my freaky brain, and I am honoured beyond words. I am also eternally grateful to the reviewers and bloggers that have taken a chance on me – your feedback has made all the difference to the books, and is the reason I've been able to make writing not just a passion but a career.

To the Badgers! You guys are fabulous. Thanks for all the encouragement and inspiration. I couldn't do this without your expert advanced reader skillz. You are all wonderful humans.

Susie, Carly, Katie, Curly, Jess, Jane and Ruth – thank you all for your wonderful alpha reading. You're the best!

To Jo Edwards, my fantastic editor and dear friend – thank you, thank you and I'm so sorry about all the semicolons!

Thanks also to Steve Molloy for such a wonderful cover design.

Thanks to all my water sports friends down in Poole for your sage advice about all things sea-related, and for inspiring me with your kiting / windsurfing / sailing / winging prowess.

Last but not least, thanks to my very own romantic hero. He's been married to me for thirteen years now and he supports me unconditionally. I love you and the boys to the moon and back.

About the Author

Susie Tate is a contemporary romance author and doctor living in beautiful Dorset with her lovely husband, equally lovely (most of the time) three boys and properly lovely dog.

Please use any of the below to connect with Susie. She really appreciates any feedback on her writing and would love to hear from anyone who has taken the time to read her books.

Official website:
http://www.susietate.com/

Join Facebook reader group:
Susie's Book Badgers
-
Find Susie on TikTok:
Susie Tate Author

Facebook Page:
https://www.facebook.com/susietateauthor

Email Susie at:
susietate79@gmail.com

Follow her on Twitter: @susietate79

Made in the USA
Monee, IL
09 November 2024

69729104R10177